Dream a Little Dream

Also by Rosie Archer

The Girls from the Local
The Ferry Girls
The Narrowboat Girls

THE MUNITIONS GIRLS SERIES
The Munitions Girls
The Canary Girls
The Factory Girls
The Gunpowder and Glory Girls

THE BLUEBIRD GIRLS SERIES
The Bluebird Girls
We'll Meet Again
The Forces' Sweethearts
Victory for the Bluebird Girls

THE CRITERION GIRLS SERIES
The Picture House Girls
I'll Be Seeing You

THE TIMBER GIRLS SERIES
The Timber Girls

ROSIE ARCHER

Dream a Little Dream

QUERCUS

First published in Great Britain in 2023 by

QUERCUS

Quercus Editions Ltd
Carmelite House
50 Victoria Embankment
London EC4Y 0DZ

An Hachette UK company

A CIP catalogue record for this book is available
from the British Library

HB ISBN 9781 5294 1 931 3
EBOOK ISBN 978 1 5294 1 932 0

10 9 8 7 6 5 4 3 2 1

Typeset by CC Book Production
Printed and bound in Great Britain by Clays Ltd, Elcograf S.p.A.

Papers used by Quercus are from well-managed forests and other responsible sources.

For my mother.
Thank you for my absolutely amazing life.
I wish I'd known you.

Chapter One

Late summer 1942

Trixie Smith watched the blackout-reduced rear lights of the ancient lorry until its sight and sound were swallowed into the darkness of the stormy night. Now, standing outside the MacKay Estate in Talmine, and despite having her three best friends about her, a feeling of insecurity settled over her, like a shroud. Sutherland in Scotland must be the loneliest place on earth, she thought, definitely the least populated, and with nothing but mountains, lochs and heather for miles and miles.

There was no warmth in the explosive, blustering wind. The squalling rain was already beginning to drip down her neck and work its way into her clothes. The waterproofs provided by the Women's Timber Corps were as much use as blotting-paper in this lot, she decided.

Inside the lorry she'd been cold, but being outside in the elements was much worse. Was that the sea she could hear? Trixie listened hard. Or were the wind and rain playing havoc with her senses?

'Are we standing out here all night?' Trixie's befuddled brain was pierced by Henrietta's cut-glass voice. 'We're going to drown. That's if we don't freeze to death first.' Hen was trying to control her blonde plaits, which had become unpinned by the forceful wind that had whisked away her sou'wester. She usually wore her waist-length hair coiled about her head in imitation of the famous skating star Sonja Henie. Now it blew wetly around her face and shoulders, like a flapping net curtain.

Happily, she looked healthier than she had before they'd left Shandford Lodge this morning, when Hen had hurriedly pushed herself away from the breakfast table and run to the lavatory where she'd been sick. By the time Trixie had caught up with her she was moaning about the food.

'I should never have eaten those Spam fritters,' Hen said, taking the handkerchief Trixie passed her and dabbing her mouth with it.

'I had the same as you and I feel fine,' Trixie said.

Hen gave her a weak smile. 'We all know you've a cast-iron stomach,' she said.

Hen didn't usually have problems with food, Trixie thought. 'We're expected,' she said, quickly bringing her attention back to the massive wooden door that was keeping her, Jo, Vi and Hen from seeking shelter. Evidently the gate was the only entrance to the huge property that loomed ominously amid the tussocky heather and gorse-covered Scottish hillside.

Suitcases and bags collapsed wetly at her feet while Trixie searched for a knocker, a bell, anything that would allow them to alert those inside to their presence. But all her frozen fingers found was scrubby ivy ending in brittle twig-like branches, no doubt sheared off by the wind's ferocity.

Trixie wished she hadn't been so eager to have the lorry driver take his leave after bringing them the forty miles from Lairg station. Before they'd become too tired and cold to chat, she'd asked him if he was acquainted with Noah MacKay.

'Och, aye,' he'd answered dourly. 'He's well known. These trees all belong to him.' Through the darkness, Trixie had made out the forests nestling beneath the mountains. The trees seemed to go on for miles. Then the man had had a sneezing fit and, fearing she might take his attention from driving along the narrow road, Trixie hadn't questioned him further. She'd been only too happy to reach their destination.

'Don't you worry about us,' she'd said. 'You get off home to your warm fireside. Noah MacKay is expecting us.'

The elderly man had been spluttering, coughing and blowing his nose into his huge handkerchief as they'd trundled along in the blackness. His sickness had unnerved her. For any of them to fall ill on their very first job as fully fledged lumberjills would be a catastrophe.

The wind had whistled inside the ragged canvas-topped vehicle as it had swayed along, narrowly dodging sheep grazing and wandering the single-track road. It seemed to her that they had been journeying for ever since leaving Shandford Lodge, where the four of them had completed their training for the Forestry Commission.

Now, Trixie felt like bursting into tears. 'There's no damn bell or knocker,' she shouted.

'Don't be stupid. There's got to be a way in!' Vi's pragmatic but weary voice was little more than a whisper. She might be the youngest, thought Trixie, but she was always the first of them to state the obvious. Trixie knew Vi's childhood had been hard. She thought it gave the girl an awareness of life often lacking in the others.

Trixie stared at her friend's thin face framed by her sou'wester. Vi had cunningly used her mackintosh's belt to anchor the hat securely to her head.

4

'You'd have thought they'd have left some indication of how we should see our way in,' Vi said. 'It's as black as the ace of spades out here.'

'Perhaps they have no electricity in Sutherland,' Hen said. 'Not everywhere is as blessed as Gosport.'

Trixie realized she was probably right.

'Arggh!'

Jo's sudden scream sent alarm roiling around Trixie's brain. She cried out, 'What's the matter? What is it?'

Jo had been wandering along the wall but she'd now rushed back, her fingers grabbing Trixie's arm as though for safety. 'It's there, looking at me!' she shrieked. 'With huge goggle-eyes . . .'

Trixie stared to where Jo was pointing. In the gloom she could just make out a panicking animal, obviously scared by Jo's screaming. It skittered against its companion, snuffling and snorting.

'For Heaven's sake! Pull yourself together!' shouted no-nonsense Hen. 'They're sheep, sheltering by the wall! And you're scaring them!'

Trixie felt Jo relax as she peered at the thick-fleeced animals staring at her. They were definitely undecided whether to bolt or stay. One sheep let out a resigned bleat.

Loud clanging cut through the wind and rain. The sheep scattered.

'What's that?' Trixie swung round, her heart beating fast.

Vi's eyes were the size of dinner plates. 'I found this chain in the ivy and I pulled it!'

'Thank God you did,' said Hen, loudly, calmly. 'You've discovered the bell pull. Well done, Vi!' She pushed her wet hair away from her face.

Vi perked up. 'Shall I pull it again?'

'Best not,' Trixie said. 'It made enough noise to wake the dead. I hope whoever's going to answer hurries up!' Every second of waiting felt like an hour. She patted the top pocket of her jacket beneath her waterproof. The letter of introduction from the Forestry Commission was inside and Trixie hoped the rain hadn't made it unreadable.

Eventually she heard a small voice. 'I'm coming. I'm coming as quickly as I can!' She saw a brief, satisfied smile light Hen's face. Thank goodness. They were about to be rescued.

The huge heavy door began to open inwards.

Vi and Jo leaned forward in anticipation, smiles already creasing their lips.

Carrying a lantern in one hand, a hunched figure appeared wearing a collection of shawls. Trixie could now see it was a woman and a broad smile was etched across her wizened face. At the sight of them the woman's smile was replaced by an open-mouthed look of disbelief.

'We're from the Forestry Commission,' Trixie said. 'Noah MacKay requested tree-fellers and here we are.'

The woman seemed to be in a trance, until she blinked her button-bright eyes and said, with a frown, 'But you can't be!'

'Can't be what?' asked Trixie.

'You can't be from the Forestry—'

She was cut off. Hen had pushed herself in front of Trixie and demanded, in her cultured voice, 'This *is* the MacKay residence?'

The woman nodded.

'And you are?' Hen asked,

'Housekeeper to Noah MacKay, Morag MacBeath.'

'Very well, Morag MacBeath. We're cold and wet. I suggest you attend to your duties by showing us hospitality and allowing us immediate shelter. Then summon your master, and tell him of our arrival from the Forestry Commission. And is this the only way into the estate?'

Perhaps, thought Trixie, it was Hen's upper-class English accent or maybe the authority in her voice, which came from her public-school background, that did the trick: the housekeeper gathered herself together and moved aside to allow them to enter.

'My apologies,' she said. 'Welcome. There is another entrance at the back that's used by tradespeople but you'd not have known that. I have hot broth simmering on the fire and no doubt you could all do with a nice cup of tea.'

Trixie noted the musical Scottish Highland lilt in her voice.

Hen, suitcase in hand, bag and gas-mask case over her shoulder, swept through the gate, muttering her thanks.

Trixie breathed a sigh of relief. 'Tea would be wonderful,' she said, picking up her dripping luggage and following Hen. Sometimes, though she didn't like Hen's occasionally overbearing attitude, it worked wonders.

Morag MacBeath waited until they were all inside. then closed the gate. 'Follow me,' she said, walking ahead through the courtyard. 'Mind your feet! When it's wet the cobbles are like glass.' Ignoring the huge door at the front of the dark building, she stepped over slippery stones until she finally arrived at a back door, which had been left on the latch. A heavy blackout curtain stopped the light shining out.

Trixie gasped as, in the kitchen, the warmth from a fire burning in the huge hearth enveloped her. A ham and two pheasants hung from the ceiling. She could smell fresh baking from the large black-leaded oven that stood beside the fire. A pot of broth was bubbling above the glowing peat turves, and its meaty fragrance made her realize how hungry she was. Oil lamps provided the lighting.

'Take off your wet things and dry yourselves,' Morag said briskly, shutting the door. 'I see you all have your gas masks too, though I doubt you'll need them up here. Not enough people for the Germans to bother about.' After removing most of her dripping assortment of shawls and leaving them hanging over the fireguard, she passed the girls threadbare towels that had been drying there. Morag's long grey hair was pinned into a bun from which wet tendrils had escaped.

Trixie dropped her case, thankful to be out of the rain and wind. Looking at each of her bedraggled friends, she could see how weary they were. 'Is the weather always this awful?' she asked.

Morag fixed those button-like eyes on her. 'Och! No. Sometimes we have snow.'

It took Trixie a moment to grasp that the housekeeper was teasing her. She returned the older woman's smile.

'Shouldn't you announce to Noah MacKay that we've arrived?' Hen enquired.

Morag glared at her. 'Plenty of time for that,' she said curtly. 'You need warmth and sustenance first.'

With a folded rag she pulled down a large blackened kettle

hanging from a hook above the fire and carried it to the stone sink where she replenished it with water that gurgled noisily out of the tap. The water was brown.

'Good thing we know it's pure,' Trixie said, drying her face with the warm towel. The incessant rain and wind rattled the windows. She felt happier now, out of the elements.

Morag began, 'The water's perfectly safe to drink—'

'Just like at Shandford Lodge,' Hen interrupted. 'It's the iron and manganese present in the soil.'

Morag's eyes narrowed. Trixie could sense hostility between the two women, which was a pity.

Vi was struggling to untie the belt that fastened her dripping sou'wester. Jo moved her cold fingers away and completed the job for her. 'Probably safer than the reconstituted water coming from the taps in Gosport,' said Jo. 'Anyway, it makes a lovely cuppa, which is just what I could do with now.'

'Which you'll get directly. Hang your wet outer clothes over there.' Morag nodded towards a large wooden stand by the door. Several coats adorned it.

Trixie was towelling her bleached-blonde hair now, but she paused long enough to ask, 'Do we call you Morag or Mrs MacBeath? Is there a Mr MacBeath?'

'Aye, I've a husband and he's attending to night chores

elsewhere on the estate,' she said. 'Best call me Morag, for now,' she added, opening a waist-high door in an aged, paint-chipped wooden dresser and taking out deep pottery bowls, which she placed on the scrubbed table.

Trixie put her damp towel on the long, metal three-fold fireguard to dry off and smoothed her hair. She looked around the kitchen at the tiled floor and the worn but comfortable furniture. A print of the famous *Stag at Bay* painting, in a dusty carved wooden frame, hung above the fireplace. A brass box full of fire-ready peats stood next to the grate. She decided it was a welcoming place even if it was in need of a good clean and some attention to maintenance. The blackout curtain moved as the wind thundered against the ill-fitting window frame. The ceiling was darkened with years of smoke from the fire. She wondered if the upkeep of the house was down to Morag alone or if Noah MacKay employed additional help. The only other large Scottish house to which Trixie could compare this one was Shandford Lodge where the girls had completed their training. That place had smelt of polish, and although Trixie had hated the animal heads, with horns and antlers, that had dominated the hallways, she knew that money had been spent on its upkeep. But if the rest of this house, including their sleeping quarters, was as comfortable as the kitchen, she wouldn't care how rundown it was. The girls weren't helpless, were they? They could keep their own quarters tidy and possibly help Morag with a bit of cleaning. None of them expected to be waited on.

'That's not long been baked, has it?' Vi peered at the fresh tin loaf on a wooden breadboard sitting on the table and smiled contentedly.

Trixie hadn't seen such an appetizing loaf in ages. Bread wasn't rationed, like many commodities, but due to war shortages the ingredients weren't always completely faithful to the recipes. Trixie thought of the grey bread back home in Gosport's shops. Suddenly, with a light heart, she was humming her favourite song of the moment, 'Dream a Little Dream of Me'.

She'd heard the song on the wireless and thought of Cy, the American sailor she loved. She'd had no letter from him for ages, even though she wrote regularly to the only address she had for him. She felt happier persuading herself it was merely postal hold-ups for his lack of letters to her. Trixie pulled her thoughts forward to the present.

'No, the bread's not long from the oven,' Morag answered, stirring the broth. 'If you'd like to sit at the table, I'll serve you now,' she added. 'And I think the tea's stood long enough, don't you?' She glanced at the cosy covering the teapot. 'As soon as you've eaten your fill, I'll away to find Mr MacKay.'

Trixie looked at Hen, Vi and Jo sitting around the table. Hen's hair, still a little damp, framed her pretty face, hung over her shoulders and tumbled down her back, like a fairy-tale princess's.

Morag cut thick slices from the loaf and passed them to the girls. 'There's butter,' she said. Jo had already discovered the golden delicacy inside the white porcelain dish with its matching lid.

'The meat in this stew tastes heavenly, Morag,' said Vi. 'Women queue for hours outside butcher's shops in Gosport for bones and scraps for meals that before the war they'd have fed to the dogs.'

'Is that so? Glad you think the meat's tender, dear,' Morag said. 'We're fairly self-sufficient here and haven't really felt the full pinch of rationing. We help where we can.' She frowned, then confided, 'We do have what you English call a spiv, He's a southerner, like yourselves, in Spean Bridge, who can provide, for a price, what we can't get in the local shop. I think it's down to people's consciences whether they buy from him or not. But that's another story. With the sea and lochs on our doorstep, and rabbits and deer running wild, we manage, we trade, and we help our crofters. We've a gillie to manage our fair few acres, the poultry, cattle and sheep. That's rabbit stew you're eating. We don't, in this house, go short of most things,' She paused, then said with passion, 'Though many aren't so lucky . . .'

Trixie smiled at Jo, who grinned ruefully at her after hearing sheep mentioned. But why shouldn't Jo be scared to encounter sheep in the dark? Probably the first sheep she'd ever seen had been through the train windows as she'd travelled to Scotland. There weren't any sheep sheltering against walls in Gosport, were there?

Trixie could see Vi didn't know what a gillie was, and not being quite sure herself, she asked, 'Is a gillie like a gamekeeper?'

Morag smiled. 'Aye, that he is. Duncan served here before the present owner took over so there's nothing he doesn't know about the estate.'

Trixie decided she liked Morag. She hadn't been so sure when Morag had seemed so astonished at their arrival. She wondered about the confusion at the gate – and Morag had referred to the 'present owner'. It sounded as if Noah MacKay hadn't been the master here for long.

Trixie had been surprised at the way Hen had spoken to Morag earlier. True, it had persuaded Morag to let them in but Trixie didn't think Hen should have talked to her like that.

'Tell me about the forestry training you've had.' Morag seemed genuinely interested in their work at Brechin. She listened avidly, asking questions about the tasks they'd undertaken, eyes wide at their answers, then marvelling when Hen told her how, because she was quick at mathematics, she'd learned to measure trees and assess correctly how much per acre lumber was worth.

It was good that they weren't eating in silence, Trixie decided. Conversation seemed to dispel the girls' tiredness. Morag, too, was eager to chat and obviously enjoying their company.

'I hear the south of England has been severely bombed,' she said, changing the subject from forestry.

'I should say so,' said Vi.

Trixie glared at her, then saw that Vi had realized it wouldn't do to say too much. Only recently the girls had discovered that Jo had been keeping a terrible secret and it wouldn't be prudent to remind her of Gosport's bombing. On a recent trip back to the town without Jo, and finding themselves near Bedford Street, the girls had decided to visit her home and let her relatives know she was well and learning about all aspects of forestry.

Jo had never confided to any of the girls that she'd returned home from the picture-house to discover that her

Gosport home had taken a direct hit. Her child and her mother-in-law had been killed. Previously the War Office had written and told her that her husband was missing, believed dead. She had become a lumberjill to build a new life for herself.

Obviously, her feelings were raw and, being fragile, she'd kept all of this to herself. When Trixie had first known her, her moods had been mercurial. She seemed much more at ease with herself now. Slowly her new life was giving her confidence, but Trixie was well aware that Jo was easily hurt by thoughtless talk. She looked across the table at her, buttering a piece of bread. She appeared not to have been following their conversation and Trixie breathed a sigh of relief. Jo was sometimes quite an aloof and solitary person.

'Wick was bombed in 1940,' continued Morag. 'So far enemy attacks have been confined to the RAF airfields at Caithness, and Scapa Flow, where the submarines are,' she said. 'Here we have mountains and heather and I'm thankful that, so far, the Germans have left us alone.' She asked more about their training in Angus and about their lives in Hampshire, in England. She seemed interested in all of them.

The wind and rain still flung themselves against the old house. Trixie knew she shouldn't allow herself to become too complacent about Morag's friendliness because they had yet to meet their new employer, Noah MacKay. She patted her pocket to make sure the introduction letter from Shandford Lodge was still safe.

Morag, clearly seeing that the girls were replete, began removing the breadboard and bowls from the table. Trixie jumped up to help stack dishes on the wooden draining-board. 'That was a superb meal, Morag, thank you.' She glanced quickly at each of the girls in turn. 'We'll do the washing-up.'

'Hear, hear,' said Hen, rising to her feet. As she moved, her chair scraped across the tiled floor. She faced the older woman. 'Morag, I'm sorry I was sharp with you earlier. I don't really know what came over me. Let me get you a cuppa – you deserve a sit-down.'

'Och, no, it's not my way,' Morag said. 'But when the table's cleared I'll tell the master his foresters are here.' A frown crossed her face. Then she took a deep breath. 'I cannae go on without explaining why I was dumbfounded at seeing you outside the gate . . .' She seemed to tail off as though she was searching for the right words to finish the sentence. Another deep breath followed. 'I'll not allow you four girls to be as lambs to the slaughter.'

Trixie, confused, opened her mouth to speak but Morag

waved a hand to silence her. 'Noah MacKay needs help to bring this estate back to its former glory. He owns huge forests, wood that will certainly help the great lumber shortages in Britain . . .' She paused. 'The master is a good man, take my word for it, but he's not going to be best pleased to find four pretty girls sitting in his kitchen. He's expecting men.' She sighed. 'He's been expecting the Forestry Commission to send him strong, able men to do hard graft.' She took a breath. 'He believes his employees to be hard workers but they're not trained.'

Hen broke in, 'Are you implying that we don't know what we're supposed to be doing?'

Trixie felt hostility rise again between the two women. She knew that Hen would not be belittled or denigrated in any way. Her education had taught her to believe in herself, and why not?

Vi and Jo stared open-mouthed at Hen, who said, 'I think it's time you told your master we've arrived, Morag.'

Chapter Two

Trixie hoisted the heavy kettle over to the sink and filled it with water. It took her a while to make sure it hung correctly on its hook over the fire without tipping. She wondered how long it would be before the water became hot enough to use for washing-up. Hen, as usual, had been right: the place seemed bereft of electricity or gas. Oil lamps on sconces were dotted around the walls. Next to the fireplace, sharing the same chimney breast, the large oven gaped. It was there that cooking and baking were done.

The clatter of pots and pans, the wind and rain beating against the window broke the silence as each girl pondered what Morag had said.

Eventually Vi said, 'Morag's been gone some time.'

'She'll come back when she's ready,' said Jo.

Vi glared at Jo. 'She's hardly likely to return before she's ready, is she?'

'There's no point in us snapping at each other when we've no idea what's going on, is there?' Hen was adamant. 'There's a war on and somehow a mistake has occurred. Whether that mistake is Noah MacKay's or the Forestry Commission's it shouldn't really concern us.'

'It matters if we're to be chucked out into the rain.' Vi was angry.

'Perhaps Noah MacKay will read the letter of recommendation I've brought,' Trixie said, patting her top pocket.

She had no time to say more, for Morag came into the kitchen. Her face was inscrutable. 'The master will see you in the library,' she said, 'if you'd like to come with me.'

Within moments they were following the housekeeper down a dimly lit corridor that smelt strongly of damp. Even with the light from an oil lamp Trixie could see the patches of mould climbing the walls. The wooden flooring creaked with their combined weight. Small flakes of distemper fell from the high ceiling, reminding Trixie of dirty snow. She brushed them off her clothing.

Morag stopped outside a door, knocked softly, and a man's voice called, 'Come in.'

Morag ushered them into the room but refrained from joining them. She closed the door behind them.

Trixie saw the room was high-ceilinged, its walls covered with shelves full of books. She shuddered at the sad thought that many might be damp and unreadable, despite the fire now burning in the large grate. Heavy floor-length curtains shut out the dark and the weather. The man, dressed in brown corduroy trousers, a flannel shirt and a sleeveless pullover, made his way to a large wooden desk where he put his hand on the back of a sturdy chair to steady himself. Trixie expected him to sit down but he didn't. He was using the chair as a prop to enable himself to stand and speak to them. The few steps he had taken showed he favoured one leg over the other. Trixie noticed a walking cane hanging over the back of the chair.

For some reason she had expected Noah MacKay to be an elderly Scot with greying hair. Never in a million years could she have believed the tall, unsmiling double of Alan Ladd, possibly in his thirties, with a fall of dirty-blond hair lying across his forehead was the rightful owner of the forests they had come to cut down.

He gave them a cursory glance. 'I can't say welcome,' he said flatly. His well-modulated voice spoke Home Counties English. Another surprise for Trixie.

She tried to assemble her thoughts in some kind of order. She glanced at Vi's shocked face. Obviously she, too, had been anticipating someone different from the taciturn man standing in front of her. Jo was quite still, listening, as was Hen, who was watching him intently with no emotion showing, until she said, 'I don't believe you didn't expect us. Shandford Lodge would have informed you of our imminent arrival.'

Trixie could see he was taken aback by Hen's verbal attack and her educated voice.

'I requested forestry workers,' he snapped.

In a cold, flat voice, Hen said, 'You've been sent three experienced forestry workers and an accredited measurer.'

'I need men. I have vast forests of hundred-foot trees that can provide lumber for pit props, telegraph poles, shipbuilding and God knows what else! And about a dozen workers who don't know their arses from their elbows! My trees need to be felled and sent to sawmills other than the tin-pot local operation nearby. What I don't need is a bevy of Land Army girls cluttering up the place.'

He grabbed hold of the walking cane, jabbed it on the floor and stalked angrily, with heavy steps, towards the door. It opened immediately, to reveal Morag standing wide-eyed behind it. He said to her, 'I'll drive into Dornoch in the morning and sort this mess out. See that they have a bed tonight.' He inclined his head to the girls. Then he added, 'Tomorrow they leave.'

Hen moved forward quickly.'You ignoramus!' she cried. He turned. Anger flared across his face. She didn't give him time to speak. 'We most certainly are not Land Girls. And how dare you behave like this? We're from the Women's Timber Corps. Women are doing men's jobs while the men fight to save this country, and people like you do nothing but live in the stone age!' He stared at Hen. Her outburst had left him stunned.

Then he turned to Morag and said quietly, 'Show them to their room.'

He walked past Morag, out of the library into the barely lit corridor. His stick clacked on the stone tiles.

Hen was about to go after him but Trixie stepped smartly forward and held her back. 'Why make things worse, Hen?' she said.

'You could have shown him the letter from the Forestry Commission,' Hen barked.

'He was in no mood to look at it. His mind was already made up.'

Deflated, Hen said, 'I suppose you're right.'

Morag said, 'I've already prepared a room. It's not fancy,

but it's comfortable enough and the best I could do. If you hadn't already guessed, this place isn't oozing money through its walls to pamper guests.'

'Thanks, Morag. I'm sure it'll be fine. I'm so tired I could sleep on a clothes line, but I'd kill for another cup of tea first. I've been left with a nasty taste in my mouth . . .' Trixie said.

'Come back to the kitchen, then,' Morag said kindly. She stared at Hen. 'He's not a bad man, lass. Since he took over he's been trying to get this place back on its feet and there's precious little money coming in.'

'That's no reason for him to treat us as though we don't know how to do our jobs . . .' Hen tailed off.

Trixie could tell her temper had cooled a little and for that she was thankful. She admired Hen for standing up to Noah MacKay and later she'd tell her so. The man hadn't even had the decency to ask or wonder why the Forestry Commission had sent them to his estate.

The four girls worked in all weathers, brashing, stripping, felling trees, with manual saws and heavy axes, then loading heavy timber onto carts ready to be transported to sawmills. At Shandford Lodge they'd been taught well. They'd worked until every bone in their bodies ached. There wasn't one iota of felling lumber and its distribution they didn't know about.

And what of Hen? She was a first-class measurer, who could tell exactly how much good timber a forest contained, what it could be used for and the price it was likely to make. They might be women but they could work as well as, if not better than, men. Yet Noah MacKay hadn't given them a chance.

Following Morag and Hen back along the dingy corridor, Trixie saw anew how rundown the place was. The smell of damp soured the air. Particles of lime wash hung from the walls and Trixie was sure a couple of good door-slams would start a snowstorm of distemper.

And what was it Morag had said? 'Since he took over'. That suggested Noah MacKay definitely hadn't always been the rightful owner of this estate. What was the story there?

Trixie looked ahead of her at Hen and Morag walking side by side. Hen stumbled and Morag put out a hand to save her. Hen grinned and Morag smiled back at her. Trixie was glad things seemed to be thawing between them again. Behind her, dragging their heels, came Vi and Jo.

'Hurry up,' she called back to them. 'By the time you reach the kitchen your tea will be cold,' she joked.

They were all tired. Vi especially looked washed out. It had been a long day. A smile tipped the corners of Trixie's lips. Hen had certainly told Noah MacKay what she thought of him. Trixie knew she'd never have answered him back. Was it because Hen had gained her independence since becoming a lumberjill?

Hen had told them that she'd had to defer to her strict, overbearing father in everything until she had escaped her Alverstoke home to join the Women's Timber Corps. Apparently she'd been kept in cotton wool all her life, denied nothing except the company of men. Her father had even decided that Hen should marry a chinless wonder destined for the House of Commons so she would have a place in society.

No wonder Hen had escaped to live a life of her own. And in the time Trixie had known her she'd certainly kicked over the traces by going out with any man who asked her. And why not? She'd been like a child let loose in a sweetie shop.

It seemed to Trixie that Noah MacKay was another such man who compartmentalized women and liked to think they should be kept in what he supposed was 'their rightful place'.

Was he really a man who refused to see how the world had changed now women could vote? Women had joined the services, were driving buses and ambulances, toiling in factories, and had become forestry workers . . .

Trixie's thoughts were whirling. Noah MacKay obviously

didn't believe women were up to doing jobs they had been trained for.

But . . .

An idea was fermenting in her mind.

What if they could prove him wrong?

Chapter Three

Noah MacKay pulled up the blankets beneath his chin. The room was cold, an added deterrent to his falling asleep tonight, he thought, but not the main reason. He was seething with anger because that blonde vixen had dared to stand up to him.

She had challenged him. And what had she called him? An ignoramus?

He was doing his damnedest to get this estate up and running after the previous MacKay laird, the father he'd never met, had selfishly run it into the ground, with his gambling, whoring and drinking. He sighed. He hadn't known that Rufus MacKay had sired him until he had inherited this draughty pile and the land that went with it.

Noah needed money, not just for himself and this mausoleum, which fell further apart each day, but to help the crofters, who depended on him for their homes and livelihoods. He thought about the impoverished families on his land whose homes were in need of repair. He, as their landlord, was supposed to keep them in good order.

And why were his crofters so hard up?

For years, walls, roofs, byres and fences had fallen into decay and remained that way. Farm animals wandered, to be injured falling into ravines, swept away in burns or killed by wild animals or poachers. No crofter could be bothered to grow vegetables for food or market when cows and sheep trampled and ate anything green. And so it had been for many years while the previous laird had squandered money.

Rufus MacKay had a lot to answer for.

Noah had been shocked at how the estate had been allowed to disintegrate.

The one redeeming factor was the acres of trees that could be his and his crofters' salvation. If he could cut and sell the lumber for a decent enough price, it would go a long way to solving all his problems and would also help the war effort.

Lumber was badly needed. He'd heard the country was down to a remaining seven months' supply, and the enemy occupation of Norway and the blocking of sea routes were preventing ships from bringing in stocks. He had an abundance of timber. What he didn't possess was sufficient, knowledgeable manpower. Sutherland was a huge area but sparsely populated. Able-bodied men had joined up to fight, to make their country proud. Those remaining were the elderly or infirm, and boys too young to work. And what did he, a crippled ex-army officer, know about chopping down hundred-foot trees and selling them? Nothing. He needed help badly.

He thought about the nondescript band of men who already worked for him. They did their best, but he was sure they knew less about the job than he did.

He'd applied to the Forestry Commission for help.

In due course a letter had arrived telling him that the Newfoundland Overseas Forestry Unit at Golspie trained loggers from Canada and British Honduras in a new initiative, begun in 1941, to help manage Scotland's forests. Golspie was just sixty miles away. After visiting, he was promised help.

And what was the result? He'd been palmed off with three pretty girls and a blonde harridan, who had turned up like drowned rats saying they'd work for him.

It was beyond a joke, wasn't it, sending him girls?

Well, tomorrow he'd drive into Dornoch, have a word with someone in authority at the unit in Golspie and get this unholy mess sorted out.

Wherever had they said they'd come from? Shandford Lodge in Brechin? Well, he wasn't going to pay to send them back there on the train from Lairg. Whoever had orchestrated this mistake could rectify it. The sooner the girls, especially the blonde spitfire, were out of his sight, the happier he would be.

He could always take them with him to Dornoch and let the authorities send them back to Brechin from there. But that would mean he'd have to endure sixty miles of chattering women. No, he wasn't that hard-hearted. Let them stay here tomorrow, recover from their journey, and no doubt they'd be collected the following day. He could stay in Dornoch overnight, have the rare treat of a meal and a night at the Falls Inn. It'd been a while since he'd enjoyed a drink and a chat with locals in a bar. And the girls would be gone when he arrived home.

So, he'd rise early to check over the 1936 4/4 green Morgan roadster in the barn, one of only a few useful treasures Rufus MacKay had handed down to him that wasn't in pieces or mortgaged to the hilt. He'd motor on to the Falls Inn after he'd sorted out the mistake made by incompetents.

It would be pleasant driving down if the weather lightened. It changed daily up here in Sutherland, sometimes even hourly, he thought.

And while he was in the barn readying the roadster, he'd turn over the 1930s Volvo lorry's engine. It had been lying idle for a while, and he needed to be prepared for the men, when they arrived, to use it.

He let out a deep, soulful breath. The pain in his leg was bad tonight, no doubt exacerbated by his frustration, he thought. He felt around on the table next to his bed. No aspirin tablets. He must remember to ask Morag to get some. His fingers touched the paper packets of the Beechams powders. Damned leg. He twisted around so that he could sit up and light the candle, smiling wryly to himself. His room always looked better in the darkness. Daylight showed where the once fancy silk wall-hangings bulged due to damp attacking the plaster. It was best not to dwell on that now, he thought, and grimaced as another stabbing spasm attacked his knee. He undid the screw of paper containing the powder and tipped it into a glass. From a carafe he poured in water, stirred it thoroughly to mix and drank it. In a few moments hopefully the powder would afford him some relief.

He sighed again. This time he whispered aloud the words he'd previously only thought as he blew out the candle and settled back to try to sleep. 'Hasn't the bloody war already taken enough from me? God give me strength. I only want to do right for the people who depend on me.'

Funnily enough, his last thought before the pain subsided and he slept was how the sparks had danced in the blonde girl's eyes as she had told him exactly what she thought of him.

'I've made a mess of things, haven't I? I'm sorry for talking back to Noah MacKay.'

'Sometimes, Henrietta, a man needs to be put in his place,' said Morag. 'It seems to me the master has his wires crossed somehow. Being a man, he'll go ahead and do what he believes is right, even when it mightn't be.' She placed the oil lamp on a chest of drawers next to a carafe of water and lit a candle in a saucer, using Swan Vestas matches. She turned to Trixie. 'I repeat what I said earlier, Noah MacKay is a good man.' She sniffed. 'I hope you find this room comfortable. I was, as I said, expecting to cater for men. Still, it's only for one night, so please make the best of it.'

Trixie glanced around the poorly furnished room, at the sagging double iron beds, threadbare carpet and ragged rugs covering a bare wooden floor. Morag had caught her resigned look

'There's little furniture left in the place. Most of the good stuff was sold or seized to pay debts before Noah came up from England. The bedclothes are aired,' she added. Then she waved an arm towards a square porcelain sink with an oval mirror hung above, set in the corner. 'The water's a bit sluggish coming through because it has a long journey from the well.' She put her hand on Trixie's shoulder. 'I'll be sorry to see you all go. I've enjoyed your company.' Trixie looked into her face. Despite the baggy skin and wrinkles, Morag's blue eyes twinkled girlishly. 'I expect you've got your own towels. If you want anything, just tell me.'

It was on the tip of Trixie's tongue to ask if there was a piano in the house. When she sat in front of the black and white keys and played it made her feel good, so good that it didn't matter what was going on around her. The music gave her joy and brought her solace. While she'd been at Shandford Lodge she had played the piano nightly in the Yellow Duck, a public house. She'd grown fond of moustached Donnie, the big-bellied owner in his striped apron. When she found out she was being sent to the MacKay estate, he'd told her he had a relative living in Bettyhill, so at least there might be another friendly face nearby. Playing the piano in his bar had eased the pangs of homesickness she'd experienced.

Trixie had felt she could do more for her country than weigh potatoes in a greengrocer's so had joined up to be a lumberjill, not only to help win the war against Hitler: her widowed mother had met a lovely man who had moved into their house in Alma Street. Trixie, feeling like a gooseberry, had decided to give the lovebirds every chance at happiness by leaving home. Rose, her mother, and red-haired Des had invited all the girls to their pre-Christmas wedding this year. Trixie was ecstatic: her plan had worked.

But she missed playing the piano. After all she'd owned one, and before she'd left home had played at weekends in the Alma pub at the end of their street. She only had to hear a tune once and could play it, note perfect.

Looking around the sparsely furnished room, the black mould creeping up the walls, Trixie decided it was futile to ask Morag about a piano that couldn't possibly have survived the decay and damp of the house.

Another thought ran through her mind. 'Morag, where's the lavatory?'

'Ah, now, lassie, we're privileged to have two.' Her eyes twinkled. 'Maybe they're not as luxurious as some you've used. One is along the corridor from the bedroom. Dinnae think you can flush, flush and flush again – it willnae work. The other is downstairs along from the kitchen in a wee hut. The waste disappears down a hole in the ground. You cannae pull on a chain because there isn't one but I leave a bucket of water and a jug just inside the door so please use it to rinse down afterwards. It helps to keep the flies away.'

Trixie looked hard at Morag. The woman's honesty and common sense reminded her of her mother's practical way of looking at problems. Trixie had come quickly to like Morag very much. And she knew it was now or never if she was to voice the idea that had formed after Noah had spoken his mind in the library.

'What if we don't leave, Morag? How will that affect you?' She waited for her friends' reactions.

Vi, who was searching in her case for a nightdress and listening at the same time, looked up in surprise. Hen's mouth fell open. Jo, pouring from the carafe into a glass, allowed the water to overrun and it spilled onto the floorboards.

Morag was staring hard at Trixie. Slowly and thoughtfully, she answered: 'I cannae force you girlies to go. There's four of you and only one of me. And my husband, Angus, can barely manage his estate duties let alone throw you out.' A smile lifted the corners of her lips. 'I cannae see the authorities in Dornoch jumping to Noah MacKay's orders like Jack-in-the-boxes the moment he demands men instead of girls specially trained to do the work he's requested . . .'

'We wouldn't like you to get into trouble, though,' Hen said. 'What if he dismisses you for disobeying his wishes?'

Morag laughed, her shoulders rising and falling with the effort. 'He'll no do that. He knows fine well no one else would take on this draughty pile of stones,' she said. 'And I cannae remember the last time I was paid a wage.'

Trixie gazed at her friends. Hen was smiling. Trixie knew her well enough to assume she wouldn't like to leave the estate until she could prove to Noah MacKay that he was wrong and there was practically nothing a man could do that a woman couldn't do better. Jo was standing next to Hen with her hairbrush in her hand. She nodded at Trixie. 'Good idea. I don't think the Timber Corps have made a mistake.' Trixie was well aware she could depend on Jo's loyalty.

'I think we should show Noah MacKay just what Gosport girls are made of,' said Vi.

Trixie grinned at her. They understood each other perfectly. 'Good!' she said. 'Because I don't think there's been a mistake either. We've been sent here from Shandford Lodge because we're the best crew for this job. I'm certainly not going back to tell them we've been dismissed before we've even started. Do you all agree with me?'

'Of course! Hear, hear! Yes!' The voices rang out in

agreement. Morag's papery face was wreathed in a huge smile until she said, 'If you're resolved to stay, you'll need to know what's been happening on the MacKay Estate. But I think that's best left for tomorrow.'

Chapter Four

The chill in the room and the noise woke Trixie.

Her first thought was, as usual, of Cy. His photograph was tucked beneath her pillow and she kissed it each night before she slept. They'd met on the ferryboat the morning she'd left Gosport to catch the train at Portsmouth Harbour station to begin her lumberjill training in Scotland.

Sitting alone, she'd been surprised by the stream of fresh-faced American sailors descending into the fag-end-strewn cabin and talking in accents she'd only previously heard at the pictures. They were all wearing pea jackets over navy blue outfits, their white hats with turned-up brims sitting jauntily on their heads. Within moments Cy's eyes had met hers and, though she'd never really believed in love at first sight, her heart had told her to think again about love blossoming in the strangest places. Trixie did, however, believe in fate and knew immediately it was the start of something momentous. His friend Hobo had begun playing the harmonica and soon she was singing popular songs with them.

She smiled to herself. Cy Davis, the American sailor from New Orleans, returning to Portsmouth to rejoin his ship USS *Ready* after minor repairs, had stolen her heart.

They'd discovered more about each other sitting in the railway-station café while waiting for the London train. Like her, he loved music. She played the piano, and he played the bass saxophone.

They kissed and Trixie knew she'd fallen in love. That same love had grown with the many letters written and received while she trained at Shandford Lodge. He told her of his mother, his life in New Orleans. Trixie's photograph, he said, went everywhere with him tucked into his top pocket.

They made plans, many plans for the future, and then his letters stopped. The girls thought it was postal difficulties and Trixie had no recourse but to accept it. She knew Cy loved her. Some day his letters would catch up with her. She continued writing to him, without fail. Fate, Cy explained, had brought them together. Fate wouldn't allow them to part.

She realized she was alone in the iron double bed that, last night, had contained her and Hen. Snoring vibrations came from the other double bed pushed against the wall on the far side of the large bedroom. Jo was a mound beneath the candlewick bedspread, her red hair just visible above the white sheet. Vi's face was pressed down into the pillow; she had one arm slung across Jo's inert body and the other high above her head.

But there it was again, the noise that had woken Trixie. Hen? It sounded as if someone was being sick outside. She slid from under the covers, grabbed her dressing-gown against the early-morning chill and went in search of her friend. The cobwebbed landing made her shudder and the uncarpeted wooden stairs were cold against her bare feet. The kitchen still held the warmth and homely smell of the previous evening's meal as Trixie pulled open the outside door that had been left ajar.

Hen was bent over at the waist, one hand holding her long hair away from her face, the other pressed against the stone wall for support while she spewed onto the ground. Speckles of vomit had fallen onto her fluffy pink slippers. She raised her head and stared at Trixie.

'Oh, love.' Trixie stepped towards her white-faced friend, her fingers immediately picking away the strands of hair near Hen's mouth and tucking them behind her ear. 'What's caused this?' Sharp stones dug into her bare feet.

Before Hen had time to answer she'd bent forward and vomited again. Trixie felt in her dressing-gown pocket and nudged a handkerchief towards her. Hen took it gratefully, lifting her head, taking a deep breath and straightening up.

'Sorry, I didn't mean to wake you.' She wiped her mouth. 'It came over me quite suddenly. I made it down here just in time. I think I'm feeling better now. Have I woken everybody?'

Trixie noted the colour coming back into Hen's cheeks and shook her head. 'I don't think so. Doesn't matter if you have.' She slipped off her dressing-gown and draped it across her friend's shoulders. Trixie's long flannelette night-gown was probably warmer than Hen's flimsy silk one. Her gaze didn't waver as she stared at Hen. 'Why come down here in the cold when there's a sink in the bedroom?'

'I really would have woken everyone then, wouldn't I? Besides, we all have to wash and clean our teeth in it.'

Trixie understood and sympathized. Then she said quietly, 'Yesterday when you felt bad you blamed the food. But this isn't anything to do with what you ate last night, is it?'

For a moment neither spoke. A wealth of understanding seemed to pass between them.

'No,' Hen said. 'I don't think it is.'

Again, there was silence.

'Oh, Hen,' whispered Trixie, putting an arm around her friend's shoulders. She pulled her away from the mess, fast soaking into the peaty earth, and led her to a decrepit dry-stone wall close by.

Her first thought after she'd understood the probable significance of Hen's sickness had been to get them both back into the relative warmth of the kitchen to talk, but from behind the hillside a faint glow of emerging sun told her it was more than possible Morag was now up and about. They needed to be alone, and the wall would have to suffice.

Trying to ignore the damp and the lichen-covered stones poking through her nightdress, Trixie asked, 'How many monthlies have you missed?'

'Only one,' whispered Hen. 'But usually I'm so regular.' She shook her head so her long hair settled back around her face and shoulders.

Trixie frowned. 'You know you could be pregnant?'

A long sigh came from Hen. Then she nodded.

Hen leaned forward and threw her arms around Trixie. Between the other girl's sobs Trixie heard, 'It's wonderful being told I'm wanted, that I'm beautiful. I like being held, being loved . . .' Another sob shook her body.

'Didn't you get them to take precautions?' Trixie had

43

never made love with a man but she'd talked to friends. She knew there were sheath things men wore. Hen was older than her: surely she had to know how important it was to be careful. Hen pulled back. She seemed confused and shook her head.

'But it only needs one time . . .' Trixie's words petered out. Holding Hen's quivering frame, she realized there was nothing she could say that would alter what was happening now, or had occurred in the past.

Away from the suffocating restrictions of her home life in Alverstoke, Gosport, where her father had dominated her existence, Hen had given in to her impulses and accepted every crumb of affection she could, from any man she'd fancied, who'd told her he cared about her. She'd wasted no time about it, Trixie decided, if this was pregnancy sickness.

'Oh, Hen,' she repeated, thinking that Hen's personality was a puzzle, an enigma. The powers-that-be at Shandford Lodge had chosen Hen to become a measurer because of her skill with numbers, her excellent education at an all-girls school in Winchester, and her intelligence. But for one so clever, she wasn't too worldly wise, Trixie thought. She was a complicated being beneath all her blonde beauty. Last night she'd railed against the injustice of Noah MacKay's implication that, because they were women, they were vastly inferior to men, yet she practically grovelled for affection from the male sex. It made no sense to Trixie. But, whatever happened, Hen would need her, Jo and Vi now more than ever. And Trixie had no doubt that the four of them would stick together through everything.

'Don't say anything, please,' Hen begged. 'Not to anyone.'

'I won't,' promised Trixie. 'Truth has a way of showing itself, though.'

It was almost as if Hen wasn't listening to her now, for she said quickly, 'Apart from this sickness I feel really well, so maybe there's nothing to worry about. My period could be late for any number of reasons, couldn't it?' She didn't wait for an answer. 'Nothing will stop me doing my job with the rest of you girls.' Her eyes narrowed but not before Trixie had seen the glitter of tears. 'I mean that! Nothing! We have to show Noah MacKay exactly what we're worth and that he can't dismiss us out of hand.'

'And how do we begin?' Trixie asked, happy that Hen seemed back to herself, in fighting mood, the vomiting, if not forgotten, now ignored.

'We have to visit his forests. As soon as possible.' Her eyes shone. 'He's not going to be around today. We need transport of some kind. I must assess exactly how much good lumber the MacKay Estate has for immediate felling.

Discover access points, roads, rail lines, then debit those usage costs from the sale figures for the timber. I can do most of the latter on paper and over the telephone.' Her eyes grew misty as her thoughts took over. 'I'll have to discover if his trees are of a similar genus. Tree species are important commercially. If Noah MacKay sees I can get him a better price for his lumber, far and above whatever he's making now, we'll be on our way to proving we know our jobs.'

Trixie broke in, 'That's a lot of stuff I don't understand. You're the measurer, Hen. You're the one to turn Noah MacKay's business around to his advantage. From what Morag's said, the man has little idea of how to do it for himself.' She paused. 'The next stage will be up to us, me, Vi and Jo, won't it? It'll not be easy trying to persuade his present employees, men, how to improve on what they're doing.'

'Don't put obstacles in the way before we start, Trix. The most important thing is to get Noah MacKay on our side and that'll depend on me finding the right contacts and prices. I've been thinking about it and I have a few ideas. From the state of this place, and what Morag's already let slip about his finances, the master needs money, and you know what they say?' Hen's eyes glittered.

Trixie shook her head. 'What do they say?'

Hen grinned at her. 'Money talks.'

Trixie laughed. Then she became serious. 'I don't know how we're going to do anything with Noah MacKay breathing down our necks . . .'

'Which is why we need to start right now. He's planning on going into Dornoch to "right the wrong" today so we haven't a moment to lose.'

The rest of Hen's words disappeared as a gruff, time-worn voice shouted, 'Not only will you two freeze your arses off out there, your tea will get cold!'

A wizened man, who looked as if a breath of wind might blow him away, stood in the kitchen doorway. He reminded Trixie of a very skinny garden gnome.

'Angus?' both girls asked at once.

'Aye,' he answered. He promptly stepped back inside, out of sight. They laughed. So that was Morag's husband.

Trixie saw the sky had lightened since they'd been sitting on the wall, talking and planning. The sun was shining, but she decided the heat of summer had long gone, up there on the west coast. The light wind was ruffling the grass, and the air smelt fresh and clean after the storm. She could hear waves rolling across stones. The sea was nearby, she thought. Perhaps later she'd be able to explore Talmine. Away in the distance, towering, were the magnificent mountains, Ben

Loyal and Ben Hope. She remembered their names from looking at the map. Last night the wind, rain and darkness had blotted out the entire landscape but the mountains rising from the remote area of moorland wilderness looked, in this morning's early light, serene, beautiful, and incredibly lonely.

Trixie realized how cold she was, and shivered. 'Come on,' she said. 'Now you're feeling better, we should go in.'

'I'm sorry I'm such a nuisance,' Hen said. She made to remove Trixie's dressing-gown. 'You must be freezing,' she said. 'Take this back.'

Trixie halted her as she began untying the belt. 'Stop that!' she exclaimed. 'If you're intending to go into the kitchen in your silky frillies you'll give Morag's old man a heart attack! No doubt she's got a roaring fire on the go that'll warm us.' Her bare feet were frozen. She hobbled past Hen but her friend grabbed her hand, pulling her back.

'Promise me you won't say a word?' Her forehead was creased with worry.

'I'm your best friend! I already promised, didn't I?' said Trixie, grinning at her.

Hen smiled back, slipped her arm through Trixie's and they began to walk towards the big old house.

Chapter Five

'Sit down! You can't leave my kitchen without a decent breakfast inside you.'

Morag pulled out a chair near the fire, which scraped across the tiles. Trixie sat beside Vi, who was hungrily wolfing down the creamiest porridge Trixie had seen in ages. Hen was leaning back on her chair, chewing buttered toast, with a contented look on her face. She'd made a remarkable recovery from the white-faced girl who'd been spewing up earlier, thought Trixie. Jo was spreading creamy butter thickly onto a piece of crusty bread. She gave Trixie a beaming smile. 'This butter tastes lovely. Morag has a girl, Mairi, who comes in to help with the dairy. It's made from cow's milk. The cream is separated and put in a kirn,' she spelled it out, 'not "churn" as we would say. Then the handle is turned until the paddle whips the cream into butter.

Sometimes a little salt improves its flavour.' Jo beamed at Morag, who had presumably explained this to her.

'Don't forget to tell her about the salt,' Morag said, refilling the teapot.

'Oh, yes. You have to throw salt on the fire before you start or the butter won't come. And Mairi sings Gaelic folk songs all the time for good luck.' Her information shared, Jo took a huge bite of her bread. Trixie wondered if she was still asleep and all this was a dream.

'Oh,' she replied. 'Whatever would everyone do if there was no salt?'

Hen glared at her.

Vi put her hand on Trixie's arm. 'Don't let Morag persuade you to eat the porridge with salt. She'll tell you it's the way Scots prefer it.' Vi pulled a face. 'Urgh! That's awful,' she said. 'Say you want sugar and cream.' She grinned. 'It's heavenly.'

'I heard that,' Morag said. 'Water, oats and salt is the porridge I was brought up on. You southerners are soft.' She went on mumbling but nevertheless she spooned and scooped sugar and cream onto the porridge, then passed a bowl to Trixie.

Trixie was discovering that Morag liked to chat. But more than that she liked to ask questions. Without knowing it,

Trixie found not only she but Hen, Jo and Vi were confiding all sorts of things to the housekeeper.

'Thank you,' Trixie said. Morag treated her to a smile. Trixie began eating. The taste was, as Vi had promised, heavenly. The few meals she'd eaten so far, in that decrepit house, were far superior to the food people in Gosport were forced to eat.

Trixie realized it was imperative that Hen, indeed all of them, moved quickly to prove they were invaluable: if Noah dismissed them, their wages from the Home Timber Production Services would cease.

Trixie was wearing her working clothes of a green jersey, dungarees, open-necked shirt and boots. Vi, Jo and Hen were similarly attired in their Timber Corps dungarees. Morag, in an ankle-length dun dress that clung to her scrawny body, looked almost witch-like. She was busy at the turf fire that warmed the kitchen. Trixie felt as though she was acting in a film and things were moving too fast for her to understand. Hen's possible pregnancy, Noah MacKay's unwillingness to allow them to stay and Jo relating Scottish myths as though it was any normal morning around a breakfast table. A mug of strong tea was set in front of her.

'Thank you, Morag,' she said gratefully. 'Hen and I met your husband earlier this morning.'

Morag replied, 'He said you'd waited in your nightwear for the sun to rise. I never thought the pair of you were types to do that!'

Trixie could feel Hen's eyes on her. Morag, without doubt, suspected more than she was letting on but, for the time being, was prepared to keep Hen's sickness a secret.

'I made you tea but couldn't wait on you coming in, earlier,' Morag said.

'Thank you,' replied Trixie. 'We found it.'

'Angus and I always have tasks to complete before the master rises,' Morag added. 'Today he's away to Golspie in his motor and likely to be gone a couple of days.'

'Good,' Vi and Jo said simultaneously.

'We can make a start, then,' said Hen.

A huge carved half log of wood served as a mantelpiece above the fireplace. A slate clock ticked loudly. Letters had been pushed behind it, so many envelopes that, despite its heaviness, the clock sat on a slant. Trixie consoled herself that there might not be any electricity connected to the place but at least the postman called.

It seemed incredible to her that she and Hen had decided to override Noah MacKay's decision for them all to leave.

He'd be even less happy when he discovered they'd

resolved to try to run his business for him. Much could go wrong. On the other hand, there was more to gain if their plan worked: money for him, and service to King and country to help win the war.

But would the master see it like that? It was appropriate for Hen to make enquiries to firms on his behalf. Hadn't the Forestry Commission appointed her, at his request, as a measurer? As such she was within her rights to assess his forests. Hen had explained to Trixie much that she'd learned about her work. She could approach sawmills and plan transport. She could inspect his team of workers to oversee not only their safety but the misuse of forestland for the future. What Hen could not do was start anything that required his signature or consent, if he was unwilling to comply. That would be breaking the law.

Time was of the essence.

He'd already shown his displeasure at their presence on his estate, but until such time as the Forestry Commission removed them, they would stay and begin doing the work they had been hired for. Thank goodness Morag seemed to be on their side.

Trixie glanced up at the letters and wondered when she would hear from Cy.

'You haven't touched your tea,' Morag observed.

'Sorry. I was thinking.' She saw Morag had produced a large piece of paper that she laid on the table after brushing away breadcrumbs.

'If you've had enough, girls, I'd like you to look at this.'

'What is it?' Vi asked.

'It's a map I've drawn of the area to show you where the MacKay forests lie.'

Chapter Six

'He owns all that land?' Hen, staring at the paper, couldn't keep the amazement out of her voice. 'There's acres and acres!'

Morag was trying to keep the pencil sketch flat on the breakfast table. Vi stood the pepper pot at one end and the sugar bowl on the other to steady the large sheet.

'Aye, it looks grand, doesn't it? Of course, it's nowhere near the size of the forests the Duke of Sutherland owns, but that's to be expected. You passed the duke's castle on the way here, Dunrobin, at Golspie . . .' Morag put a hand to her head as though chiding herself for forgetting. 'Of course, you'd not have seen anything arriving in the dark as you did.'

Trixie, peering at the pencil lines, said, 'Looks a fair distance from here.' She touched the large cross that was supposed to represent Talmine and the MacKay Estate house. Directly behind the mark Morag had written 'Talmine Beach'. Beyond that she'd drawn fierce waves and pencilled in 'Atlantic Ocean'. Today, Trixie knew somehow, she'd try to make time to take a walk along the beach.

'You'll need transport. The lorry is full of fuel, with a spare full can in the cab,' Morag said, turning and taking an envelope from behind the clock on the mantelpiece. Passing it to Trixie, she said, 'Coupons, for the garage man at Bettyhill.' She took a breath. 'That's the nearest place to buy fuel. They've got the electric there. Tell him to charge it to Noah MacKay. He'll recognize the vehicle so he'll do as he's told.' Trixie was frowning. Morag gave her a narrow-eyed look. 'What's the matter with you?'

'We need to know this map is valid. Hen can't be measuring up the Duke of Whatsit's trees, can she?'

Morag glared at her. 'I copied it from the original Land Registry deeds Noah inherited from his father, passed on to him from the advocate. I can't very well give you the original papers, can I? I'm not supposed to know where they are!' There was a silence. 'I wouldn't do this if I didn't trust you.'

'We won't betray that trust,' Trixie assured her.

Morag's face softened. 'No, I don't think you will,' she said.

Trixie's eyes were downcast. 'But there's something else, Morag. I – I can't drive,' she said.

Morag's face turned ashen.

'Neither can I,' said Jo.

Vi was shamefaced. 'Nor me!'

'Then it's a good job I can, isn't it?' Hen was smiling.

'You never told us . . .' Inwardly Trixie gave a sigh of relief.

'Well, we're still finding out things about each other, aren't we?' Hen pointed out.

'I seem to remember that at Shandford Lodge when we first arrived we were asked who could drive. Several girls raised their hands and you weren't one of them,' Jo said.

'Of course not,' Hen said indignantly. 'If I had, I'd have been included in the group of women expected to drive heavy vehicles. I wanted to use my brain and be out in the forests, not forever breathing petrol or diesel fumes, towing logs or helping teach other volunteers how to drive.'

'Who taught you?' Trixie wondered. 'Your father?'

'God, no!' Hen shook her head. 'According to him, driving's unladylike! Geoffrey Wolstenholme.'

'The chinless wonder your dad wants you to marry?' broke in Vi.

'The very same,' Hen said, 'He has a racing car, a Talbot. He'd take me to race meetings in Weybridge – that's Surrey,' she added. 'He never won a race but occasionally, away from the crowds, he'd let me get behind the wheel. It started from there. Soon I'd be driving his MG TA when we went out together. My father would have died had he known.' Her eyes sparkled, remembering. 'That was the only decent thing about going out with Geoffrey. Certainly not his appalling bad breath. His kisses were wet and slippery and he'd try to force his slobbery tongue into my mouth! Ugh!' She made a noise like being sick. They all laughed.

Even Morag giggled. Then she stood up, folded the map and gave it to Trixie.

'Supposing we get lost?'

'Trixie, you cannae get lost. There's not enough roads to go astray on, if you follow that map,' Morag said, turning away from the table and going to a cupboard on the far side of the kitchen. Opening its door – the hinge looked about to fail – she took out a large, heavy-looking brown carrier bag with string handles, brought it back and handed it to Jo. 'I cannae have you going hungry. You'll be out most of the day, I expect, so I've made up four pieces for you.'

Morag must have seen the frown that passed between Trixie and Jo for she gave a short laugh. 'I knew you girls would want to help, so I made what you English call sand-wiches.' She smiled. 'There's nae cafés up here in the wilds.'

Jo began opening the brown bag whereupon Morag smacked at her fingers lightly. 'You'll find out soon enough when you're hungry what I've packed up for you. I'd better show you where the lorry is, hadn't I? Otherwise you'll still be sitting around this table when the master comes home.'

Trixie was already on her feet and searching for her wet-weather clothing on the wooden stand near the door. She glanced at the early-morning sun beaming through the window. Morag noticed. 'The weather changes so quickly here,' she said. 'Dress warmly. Cannae have any of you catching chills. I'll wait while you collect anything you need from upstairs.

'I'd hoped this morning to tell you a little more about Noah MacKay but it's best you get going. We can talk later. Just remember, you have my word that at heart he's a grand man.' She shuddered and added, 'Don't let the sun fool you. It'll be cold right enough and, before you know it, raining again.'

The barn was at the side of the house. They followed Morag through a long, damp passage with closed doors at either side, then to a door that led to an outside courtyard, and the girls were staring at a large flinty building with a steep slate roof. Trixie saw they were close to the gate in the wall that had seemed impenetrable last night. Was it really just last night?

Her attention was taken by a huge pile of peats in the opposite corner. 'That's an awful lot of stuff for the fire, Morag,' she said. She walked across and picked up a piece. It was uniform in size to the others, dry and hard as coal yet lighter in weight.

Morag was at her side. 'We've the right as crofters to peat diggings on the Moine.' She waved a bony hand upwards to illustrate that it was high up and far off.. 'Mountain peatland lying between Loch Eriboll and the Kyle of Tongue.' A smile lit her lips. 'It's inhabited only by wild creatures and birds. The Duke of Sutherland had a road built across it.'

Trixie stared at her. 'Peat diggings?'

'We dig in April. Peat is decayed matter. Reeds, heather, moss, even trees. The freshly dug wet turves are allowed partly to dry. Later we go back up and turn the turves, making them into piles, so the wind and sun can dry them thoroughly. In August we haul them home.' She paused. 'Today, stacked outside the crofts, you'll see enough peat dug to last the household through the winter.'

'So it's free fuel?' Hen asked.

'Not exactly free when it's backbreaking work digging in

60

a muddy trench,' said Morag, sharply. 'I've done my share of digging and turning, then bringing home the peats with a horse pulling a cart. She waved her hand towards the impressive pile. 'But now I cannae do it, the master and some of his crofters built that stack.'

'So,' Hen asked, 'Noah's not afraid to get his hands dirty?'

'Not at all,' answered Morag.

Vi, obviously fed up of all the talk about peats, said, 'At least the barn looks watertight. It's in better condition than the house.'

'Rufus had it built. Obviously, it's not as old as the main house. The sharp roof repels the snow – we get plenty of that,' Morag added. 'Rufus took care of the vehicles and tools he bought for his own use. I'll say that for him. If he had to spend cash, he made sure he got his money's worth.' She pushed against the stout wooden doors that were almost the width of the building. When one opened the girls trailed her inside.

'What a difference!' exclaimed Hen.

Trixie knew exactly what she meant: the air inside the barn smelt dry and dusty.

'I've often thought this would be a better to place to live than the house,' said Morag. 'No damp in here.'

Hen was looking over the Volvo truck. From the smile

that appeared, Trixie thought it met with her approval. Vi was exploring the back of the barn where she'd discovered sheet-covered boxes. 'There's books here!' she yelled. 'Dry ones without creepy-crawlies decorating the pages.' Vi paused in lifting some out. 'There's an Agatha Christie I haven't read.'

Jo was examining a wall covered with hooks and nails from which hung all manner of tools. 'I've found the wood-cutting stuff,' she called. 'The axes and saws are in better condition and much sharper than the ones we used at Shandford Lodge.'

'That'd be down to Mr Noah,' Morag chimed in. 'He made ready the equipment for the new foresters.'

'What are all these bottles of stuff?' Vi was holding a bottle filled with pale coloured liquid.

'Ginger beer,' Morag said. 'That batch is nae ready to drink yet. I keep it in here because it's cool. Some I move on to the spiv in Spean Bridge. I keep the ginger beer plant in the kitchen,' she said. 'It's made from sugar, ginger, yeast, water and lemons. All you do to keep it alive is add more sugar and ginger.'

Jo approached with a couple of axes and several billhooks in her arms.

'Lemons? I haven't seen a lemon for ages,' Hen said.

'The spiv can get hold of anything, for a price,' Morag said darkly.

'Better start loading the lorry, then,' said Trixie, looking at Jo.

'The keys are inside,' marvelled Hen.

'Well, who's going to break in here and steal anything?' Morag laughed. 'Och, it's in the cities that people would steal a person's eyes, then come back later for the lashes, but not round here. It's only the master's and my shame at the state of the place that makes him lock the main gate.' Trixie could see the logic in that.

Hen threw her wet-weather gear onto the stone floor and hoisted herself into the driver's seat in the large cab. She sat staring at the controls.

'What d'you think, Hen?' Trixie asked, after she'd gathered up Hen's clothing. Already anticipating her friend's answer, she slipped the bags and rainwear beneath the vehicle's tarpaulin covering.

'I think I can handle this,' Hen shouted. Trixie noted the determination on her friend's face. The lorry purred into life. Hen grinned triumphantly.

Simultaneous cheers went up from Vi and Jo.

Trixie walked back to where Morag was standing. 'Thank you,' she said. 'I'm really happy that you believe in us.'

Morag smiled at her, then delved into her apron pocket drawing out a big metal key. 'Take this,' she said. 'It opens the main gate. I'm no walking out here in all weathers every time you come in or out.'

'Thank you again,' Trixie replied.

Morag was still talking. 'You'll be making me happy if you can lighten Noah's load.' A blush started above the shawl at Morag's neck and spread over her face. 'I wouldnae say this if I didnae mean it but in the time Noah's been living here he's tried so hard to pull things together—'

Vi gave an excited squeal. 'Piano! It's a piano!'

Trixie swung towards the back of the barn where Vi had pulled a sheet away from a large object, exposing an upright piano. Already she had pushed up its lid and was touching the notes. Trixie ran to join her. But before she had reached Vi, her initial excitement had dimmed for she could tell the notes were badly out of tune. The sounds coming from the keys were strangled. She turned to Morag and tried hard to disguise the pain in her voice. 'Oh, what a pity!'

'Do you play?' Morag asked.

'Play?' interrupted Jo. 'She's a genius! She only has to hear a tune and she can play it back note perfect.'

'Well, well, well!' said Megan. 'It was Rufus who played. That's his piano.'

Trixie ran her fingers lightly over the keys. She felt saddened that the glorious heart of the piano, its notes, had been allowed to deteriorate.

Hen, who had turned off the lorry's engine and climbed down from the cab, came to investigate. She put an arm around Trixie's shoulders. 'Is there nothing you can do to get it working? A bit of music around this place would cheer things up.'

Trixie shook her head. 'It needs someone to tune it and I know nothing about that,' she said. She put down the lid. A wave of sadness washed over her. She felt her eyes smart with tears but instead of giving in to her feelings she said brightly, 'We should leave. We've got a lot to do today.'

Morag nodded and looked thoughtfully at Trixie, then went to open wide the barn door so Hen had room to manoeuvre the vehicle out into the yard.

Hen was now back in the driving seat, the engine running, with all three girls squeezed into the cab beside her. Hen called to Morag, who was walking towards the main gate to see them off, 'I'll do as much as I can while we're out but there's a great deal of work on paper to be done. I've a notebook with me to jot things down. But I'll need to telephone around when we return. I hope that'll be all right?'

Morag was pulling open the heavy door. She screwed up

her face thoughtfully. 'The post office in Bettyhill has the nearest telephone, Hen. We have no electric. We have no telephone.'

Trixie looked at Hen, who was staring steadfastly at the door swinging open in front of her, and concentrating hard on driving the lorry through without mishap.

'Oh, dear,' Trixie said. 'None of this is going to be as easy as we all first thought, is it?'

Chapter Seven

Hen drove the lorry, at first hesitantly, then confidently, around the huge expanse of water separating Talmine from Tongue. Trixie was examining the map Morag had provided and noted it was written as the Kyle of Tongue. Very few croft houses nestled beneath the hills but Trixie smiled, remembering Morag's words, at seeing the crofters' distinctively shaped peat piles heaped alongside their dwellings.

'It's beautiful to look at,' said Trixie, nodding towards the mountainous scenery overlooking the lush trees and grassland. 'But it could do with a bridge across, to make this part of the journey easier. How far have we travelled?'

Trixie knew Hen could gauge distances better than she. The huge expanse of water glittered in the cold sunlight.

'Twelve miles or so,' Hen replied. A hairpin had worked itself loose from one of the plaits coiled across her head.

Deftly she released a hand from the steering-wheel and pushed it back into place.

'You're doing well,' Trixie said. She could see Hen was vigilant in driving on what was little more than a single-track road with sheep skittering about or chewing grass. Huge-horned red-coated shaggy cattle gathered together, masticating, like little old ladies chattering in a Gosport shop queue.

'I just love those cattle with their long fringes. I suppose they can see all right through all that hair covering their foreheads?'

Trixie guessed Jo didn't expect an answer. She loved all creatures, big and small.

'There's some sort of ruined castle high up there – don't you look!' Trixie panicked that her observation had made Hen's concentration wander from the road in front of her.

Hen laughed. 'It's all right. I'm not going to hit anything!'

'I wonder what it is. It looks very small and old,' Jo said. 'Sort of like it's guarding the land below.'

'Ghostly,' said Vi, in a flat voice. Trixie had long decided Vi preferred towns to the countryside.

'Actually, it's called Caisteal Bharraich, if that's the right way to pronounce it,' said Hen. 'Or Castle Varrich in English.

It's supposed to represent the seat of the clan MacKay of Sutherland.'

Vi sniffed. 'How d'you know that, clever clogs?'

'Because she went to posher schools than us,' laughed Jo.

'No! When the Women's Timber Corps told us where we were being sent, I looked the area up,' answered Hen.

Before she could say anything else, Vi gave a shout: 'Look over there!' She waved frantically towards some trees. Trixie stared at Hen in case Vi had put her off her driving, but her eyes and concentration were still on the road. 'Whatever is that huge bird?'

'It's an eagle,' Jo informed them, staring at its gigantic wingspan as it dived earthwards towards rabbits scattering in all directions into the undergrowth. 'You don't see many of them in Gosport.'

Trixie remembered one night in the woodland around Shandford Lodge while Jo informed her of all the wildlife to be found in their hometown. 'They nest on mountain ranges, out of the way of predators,' Jo added.

'Do you want me to stop so you can have a look?' asked Hen. She flashed a quick smile at Trixie to show she was willing to park if the girls wanted.

'I think not, Hen,' Trixie answered. 'This might be our first day looking at things in the daylight but I reckon it's more important to get on with the work we've set out to do. You need to get a good idea of Noah MacKay's forests, and do your sums. Of course, it would have helped if he hadn't been so prejudiced about us being women. He could simply have given us the information you need.'

'And maybe not,' said Hen. 'The impression I received from Morag suggests to me that he's unsure of his legacy, if that's what it is, of the actual size of his estate, and what's entailed in looking after it properly.'

Trixie stared at her.

Jo and Vi were listening intently. Hen was obviously waiting for Trixie to answer, so she did. 'Is that possible?'

'Depending on the circumstances, yes,' Hen said.

'Morag said she'd explain later. We'll find out more then,' said Trixie. 'But now we have too little time to finish what we've begun so . . .'

'I agree,' Hen concurred. 'If we drive first to the furthest area of the MacKay Estate, though I suppose it really makes no difference where we begin, I'll start making estimations on the value of his trees. I'll find out if there's insect infestation or disease. I'd also like to visit where his men are working to ask questions without them thinking I'm being too nosy. But not until later in the day, in case we bump into him checking up on their work.'

'That would certainly put the cat among the pigeons,' said Jo.

Hen's voice grew thoughtful, as if she was thinking aloud of the work she needed to accomplish. 'I'll have to cover all points, not just the price he can expect for selling, but transport costs. Whether there's a railway nearby or the lumber has to go by road. I need to find out if he's selling all parts of the trees, the brash to go for paper or fencing, tops for firewood, as well as the trunks to be used commercially . . .'

'Whoa!' said Trixie. 'You're making my head spin! So, after we've travelled around, measuring acreage and volume of saleable trees, you'll need to use a phone?'

Hen shook her head. 'Not quite. I'll need a modicum of peace and quiet—'

'Why don't you just say you'll want us to clear off and leave you alone to work out sums?' Vi broke in. 'Oww!' Jo had dug an elbow into her ribs, hard.

'After I've worked out the sums . . .' Hen grinned at Vi, who was rubbing her side '. . . we'll go to Bettyhill and ask to use the telephone at the post office and also to fill up with fuel at the garage.'

Trixie nodded. The plan was time-consuming but seemed logical, and it wasn't raining, so that was a plus, she thought.

'Here's the crunch, though,' Hen said. 'I'd really like to get back to Talmine before the light goes. The lorry's equipped for use in the blackout with its shaded lights but I'm not so sure about driving in the pitch dark.'

'Fair enough,' said Trixie. 'Are you in agreement with everything, Jo? Vi?'

'Of course,' they chorused.

Once more Trixie marvelled that Hen could show such determination to commit to her job when, earlier that morning, she had been practically in tears at the possibility she might be pregnant. She decided Hen was a great deal stronger than she looked. A small voice broke into her thoughts.

'We'll need money to pay for the telephone calls. I have some but not a great deal.' Vi was voicing her thoughts. 'I sent most of my wages down to Gosport for my mum to be looked after.'

'How is she?' Trixie felt bad. She'd not thought about Vi's mother. Moving to Sutherland had consumed her energy. Alice was dying of consumption. A good friend and neighbour, Irene, came in every day to look after her. They were dependent on Vi's money, which she sent by post to Irene's house in case Alice's ex-boyfriend, Alec, took the money for his own nefarious purposes.

'Is Alec still lodging with her?'

Trixie shuddered. He was a bookie's runner working for the London gangster Billy Hill. He'd broken into Vi's bedroom when Trixie had spent the night at Vi's house in the run-down area of Gosport, near the gasworks. Neither of them had been hurt. Trixie had marvelled that Vi had managed to escape his clutches for so long. When Trixie had first met Vi, it had troubled her to see the girl covered with bruises that she'd tried valiantly to hide. The bruises had remained long after Vi had begun her training at Shandford Lodge. Alec had tried time and again to rape her. Her mother had begged her to leave home. Vi had lied about her age, telling the authorities she was older than she was so she could join the lumberjills.

'No, he's not. Irene said he's left Gosport. I can't say I'm sorry,' Vi muttered.

'That's a blessing,' agreed Jo. 'I wonder where he's gone.'

'Don't know, don't care,' said Vi. 'And I don't want to talk about him any more.'

'Don't blame you, Vi,' said Hen. 'Anyway, don't worry about money. I have some. Plenty for phone calls and whatever else we might need.' She paused. 'Incidentally, I'm paying for the fuel we use today. There's no way I'm allowing that tedious man to suggest we used his transport without asking, then made him pay for fuel.'

'Ooh! Hark at the little rich girl from Alverstoke! Gosport's poshest area!' cried Trixie. She said it without malice, knowing Hen would laugh with Vi and Jo.

Hen's laugh was cut short. 'Damn!' she exclaimed, braking and pulling the lorry to a standstill in a passing-place just in front of the forked road ahead. 'So far we've not passed or been overtaken by another vehicle and now I've no idea which way to drive because all the signposts have been removed. Pass us that map, Trix. God, I could do with a cuppa.'

'So could I,' agreed Trixie, handing her Morag's carefully drawn map. 'Shall I get out the bag from the back? I saw two flasks in there when Morag gave it to me.'

'Tea break it is, then,' said Hen. She blew air from her lips. Without glancing at the map, she put it on the seat.

As Trixie moved to open the cab door, Hen said quietly, 'I'm really sorry the piano isn't fit to play. We could do with some of your lovely tunes. It's so quiet in the house without a wireless.'

'I know,' answered Trixie. 'From what I saw of it, the piano looked in fairly good condition, certainly not damp. I expect it just needs tuning.' She turned to Jo and Vi. 'If you want tea, you'll have to get out of the lorry to drink it. I don't want us to make a mess in a vehicle that doesn't belong to us.'

She got no further. Jo, alternately studying the map and staring out through the windscreen, said, 'Look down the left-hand fork in the road. See those trees? They belong to Noah.'

Trixie, tugging the bag containing food and flasks from beneath the tarpaulin, peered along the road. Hen had climbed out of the driver's side. She was holding her hand in front of her eyes to shade them from the sun's brightness. 'Those trees, as you call them, Jo, my love, are Scot's Pine, *Pinus sylvestris*, to give them their proper name. I hope you're right about them being MacKay forest because there's road access and, more importantly, hundreds of them. I can't wait to get closer.' Her excitement was almost palpable.

'Let's have our tea, first!' moaned Vi. 'I'm gasping!' She was already unscrewing a large, dented vacuum flask.

Hen was talking again: 'Not only will they make telegraph poles, but there's no wastage from pine trees. The tree can be tapped for resin to make turpentine. Rope can be made from the inner bark, dye from the cones, which can also be used as kindling for fires, and tar can be extracted from the roots.'

'Take this, Teacher,' said Vi, handing Hen a tin mug. Hen sipped the contents gratefully. Then she walked up the road a little way and stood gazing into the distance. When she walked back to Trixie, Vi and Jo, who were lounging by the lorry chatting, she said, 'There's a lot of trees. And if Morag's map is correct, there's a hell of a lot more further on.'

Chapter Eight

'So far today's been hellish, surveying and measuring all these trees. I won't have any legs left after all the walking I've done.' Vi waved at the boots she'd kicked off her tired feet, popped the last bit of oatcake into her mouth and began chewing. When she'd swallowed it, she added, 'I could eat a hundred of those. It seems ages ago since I came downstairs this morning and Morag was cooking oatcakes over the fire on a flat tray thing.'

'A griddle,' said Hen.

Vi wiped her mouth with the back of her hand. 'I don't know how she manages to come up with delicious meals when she has only the bare essentials to cook on. Wasn't it lovely of her to pack us sandwiches?'

'Pieces!' intoned Trixie and Hen. Jo laughed into her mug of tea and started coughing. Vi slapped her on her back. The mug dropped from Jo's hand and the tea spilled on the grass.

'Are you all right?' Hen asked worriedly – Jo was red in the face and spluttering. Quickly she passed over her handkerchief and Jo put it to her mouth, stemming the choking sounds. She managed to nod. Vi picked up the empty mug and transferred half of her tea into it for Jo to sip.

'Sorry. I didn't mean to hurt you by slapping so hard,' Vi said.

Jo, watery-eyed, said, 'You didn't, not really, and you're not the only one with aching legs. My feet are killing me.'

'We're all tired.' Hen paused. 'It would have helped if Morag had known exactly how much agricultural forest the master owns. Luckily, most of his land we've seen has road access, so travelling in the lorry has helped. I'm sorry I had to walk you the length and breadth of the forests we've stopped at earlier today. It was necessary to use the conversion factor, multiplying feet to square feet, then dividing by 43,560, which is square feet in an acre, to decide acreage. I do need facts and figures before talking to possible buyers, the Forestry Commission, and sawmills . . .'

'Have you got enough information?' Trixie asked. She thought of Hen wandering through the pines, squinting up into the light above the tall trees.

'Look at these.' Hen had rubbed pine needles between her fingers, examined bark and peered along branches.

'Whatever are you doing?' Trixie asked. Hen hadn't replied straight away. It was as though the drama she was performing contained just two players, the living tree and herself.

'Checking the growth quality,' she'd replied. Then, pulling a stick from the front pocket of her dungarees where her pencil, tape and notebook were secreted, she began measuring. 'I need the tree's height,' she added. Holding that stick vertically at arm's length, Hen walked about until she had lined it up exactly where she wanted it: the lower end was aligned with the base of a tree, the other perfectly in line with the tree's top branches. 'This gives me the Scots Pine's height.' Hen wrote in her notebook. 'Now I need the girth.' Using a tape at her breast height, she measured around the trunk. 'I can tell the volume by just looking at the trees.' Trixie admired Hen's aptitude for mathematics, which she herself lacked.

'Yes, for the moment,' Hen said now, in answer to Trixie's question about information. She began gathering up the mugs, paper bags and flasks from the grassy knoll by the side of the road, where earlier they'd decided to sit and eat. 'I know everyone's tired,' she said, 'but we have to remember why we're doing this. Noah MacKay thinks we women are worthless—'

'Just a minute,' broke in Vi. 'So far, you're showing him you're the one with brains. We're damned good foresters but we haven't put any of our equipment near a tree.'

'We can't do everything at once, can we?' said Jo, ever the pacifier.

'I'm glad you understand that,' said Hen, 'because I've gathered, with your help, enough information to be left alone to work out some sums.' She swept her arm dramatically across her face, like a heroine in a melodrama. 'As I said before, I need a modicum of peace and quiet!'

Vi stared at her, then laughed. Trixie and Jo joined in.

'You daft bloody ha'p'orth,' Vi said, and still laughing, taking the bag full of empty bits and pieces from Hen, tucked it beneath the covering on the lorry.

Jo wiped laughter tears from her eyes with Hen's handkerchief, then shoved it into the pocket of her dungarees.

'I suppose it's time for us to visit the site where Noah's men are working, then,' she said.

'Yes,' Hen said. 'It's a fair distance from here. When we get there, if you don't mind, I'll take a wander on my own. You three know exactly what should be going on in a clearing where trees are being felled, so . . .'

'We're to ask questions, in a nice friendly manner, look around, see what's what, tell the men who we are . . .' Trixie began.

'They'll probably guess anyway,' added Jo. 'Noah may have told them to expect extra help.'

'If he hasn't been there today, they might also expect us to be men . . .' Vi said.

'It'll be a surprise for them as well, then, won't it,' Trixie said, 'when we turn up?'

'We could beg for a cuppa,' said Vi. 'Sit and chat and find out loads of stuff, like who's buying the lumber, how it arrives at the sawmill, which sawmill . . .' She was getting excited now.

Hen added, 'Whether the logs are sold by the load or if there's a contract is important. The former is called "pay as cut". It allows the buyer to pay by the log load, not a good idea. If the owner isn't on site, the load could be very much in excess of what it should be.'

'Isn't it all a bit personal for three strange women to ask workers how their boss sells his timber when they've never met them before?' Trixie asked. She knew that, with Hen's looks and her attitude to men, most of the opposite sex would fall over themselves to tell her anything she asked.

But did the three of them, herself, Jo and Vi, have enough 'womanly wiles' to persuade the men to open up and tell them what they needed to know?

'I'm doing my job. Now it's your turn to assess whether Noah MacKay is possibly, knowingly or unknowingly, being swindled by his workers. You're all well aware each tree is worth its weight in gold, and is needed to help win this damned war.' Hen, who now had the map in her hand, looked at them all in turn. 'I say we go now. Morag's marked the area where the lumber's being cut by his men. It's a fair journey from here.'

Hen didn't wait for their replies but opened the door, put the map on the seat beside her, and hoisted herself into the driver's seat. She started the engine and Trixie climbed in beside her, leaving Vi and Jo to squabble about who would sit next to the window.

'We've driven some miles today but I never knew Sutherland was so under-populated,' said Trixie. 'It's breathtakingly beautiful, with its lochs, streams and mountains.'

'And never-ending heather,' said Vi. She sighed. 'There's very few houses. I wouldn't like to live here permanently,' she said. 'The place scares me.'

'I think it's wonderful,' Hen put in. 'The air's so fresh.'

'But we've seen hardly any people,' Vi persisted. 'How

does anyone enjoy themselves? Where's the picture-house? Where are all the shops?'

'There are probably more people in the bigger places, like Bettyhill,' Trixie suggested. 'If it has a post office and a garage, there's probably a school, a pub, all sorts going on . . .'

'We've only just arrived, don't forget,' said Hen. 'We haven't had a chance to look around.'

'I want to walk on the beach near the house,' said Trixie. 'I've heard the sea but I haven't seen it yet. I want to paddle.'

'The light will almost have gone by the time we get back,' said Jo, 'but there's another day tomorrow. You can paddle then.'

'Talmine looked such a deserted place when we drove through,' Vi said, 'just a few houses. But I saw a church. If there's not much to do we can always go along to the graveyard and spend time reading the headstones . . . Ouch! What did you elbow me for?'

'Because you're being disrespectful,' said Jo.

'Sorry,' Vi said, rubbing her ribs, 'if that's what you think. But why have gravestones with stuff written on them if they're not supposed to be looked at? Actually, Morag was telling me about some get-togethers they have, Kay something . . .'

'Ceilidhs,' said Hen, 'pronounced kaylees.'

'Smarty-pants!' laughed Vi. 'I know – you looked it up! Morag said people sing, tell stories and dance. Of course there's plenty to eat.'

'And drink?' Trixie asked.

'Morag said only tea and squash,' Vi said.

'Oh?' Trixie queried.

'She said the men would leave bottles of whisky outside the hall in the heather and every so often nip outside to have a drink . . .' Vi said.

'What about the women?' Trixie asked. 'Do they hide alcoholic drinks?'

Hen shook her head. 'It's all right for men to drink but, just like it was in England before the war and still is in some places, up here women going into pubs and doing what men do is frowned on. Ceilidhs are traditional Scottish social family gatherings. Sometimes the women have sherry but not usually at ceilidhs because quite often the church minister is there and no one wants to get on the wrong side of him, do they? An unsavoury reputation stays with a woman. Anyway, we're here to work, not gallivant about.'

'Oh, Hen.' Trixie's eyes were on her friend, who was watching the road ahead. 'We'll work, and hard. But we need . . .' She saw then how white Hen's face had become, drained of its usual healthy glow. 'Are you all right?'

'No, I don't think so,' Hen muttered. She swallowed. 'I'm just going to pull over in that passing place . . .'

'What's the matter?' Vi asked.

Hen braked and the lorry stopped. With her hand to her mouth Hen was hastily out of the driver's door, bending over by a furze bush and being sick onto the grass before anyone could answer Vi.

Trixie scrambled out of the vehicle and, hovering at Hen's side, pulled a handkerchief from the pocket of her dungarees and pressed it into her friend's hand.

'What's wrong?' asked Vi. She and Jo were now beside them, worry etched on their faces as Hen threw up again.

Trixie frowned at them and shook her head, an unspoken request that they ask no more questions. 'All right now?' she murmured to Hen. Using the handkerchief to wipe her mouth, Hen nodded. Trixie was relieved to see colour flooding back into her cheeks.

Hen took a deep breath. She walked back to the lorry and leaned against it. She faced her three friends. 'I could tell a lie and say Morag's "pieces" upset me but it wouldn't be right.' Trixie saw the glint of tears sparkle in Hen's eyes. Another deep sigh seemed to shake her whole body. 'Please don't talk about this in the house. Noah MacKay thinks little enough of me as it is and I'd like to keep this secret as long as I can. I think I'm pregnant.'

Chapter Nine

The lorry was eating up the fifty or so miles of lonely road to Helmsdale where Noah MacKay's men were chopping down trees. In Gosport, Trixie thought, you could barely see to the next corner because so much was going on. Here, virgin heather-covered landscape stretched beneath the mountains as far as the eye could see. The girls travelled in silence, each consumed by her thoughts.

Hen's outburst had stunned Jo and Vi, but Trixie guessed she wasn't ready yet to discuss how she felt about the baby. She would talk to them, of course she would, but not now: the timing wasn't right.

Trixie continued staring through the windscreen at the green countryside, lochans glinting in the sunlight, topped by the never-ending pale sky. Way ahead on the snaking road a small bus was travelling towards them. She could just make out its cheerful red colour and contrasting yellow roof.

'It's the post bus,' said Hen, anticipating Trixie's unspoken question. 'Apparently it doesn't only carry letters and parcels, but milk, food and people as well.' She chanced a quick look and a smile at her friend. 'There might be a letter from Cy forwarded to you from Shandford Lodge.'

'Oh, I do hope so,' Trixie said. 'I haven't heard from him for so long. I'd like to know he's safe.'

'Perhaps his ship hasn't docked anywhere mail can be collected. There's a war on, don't forget.'

Hen was trying to reassure her, and Trixie felt her anxiety lift a little. When eventually the small red bus paused in a passing place so their lorry could drive by, the driver tooted his horn and two elderly passengers waved. The thought that a letter from the young man she loved might be waiting when they returned to the Mackay Estate cheered her.

Helmsdale was a tiny, pretty place and it didn't take long, with the aid of Morag's map, to drive to the expanse of woodland where Noah's men were working. Hen paused the motor on the track outside the forest clearing.

'Must be break-time,' said Jo.

Three elderly men were sitting on logs around a fire. A billy-can was perched on the burning embers, steam tumbling angrily from its spout and lid and hissing into the flames. A couple of grubby towels lay on the pine needles, rags used to protect against the burning and scalding of hands, thought Trixie. A cardboard box contained an opened packet of tea-leaves and a crusted sugar bag that looked almost empty.

A young man was filling another billy-can with water from a nearby fast-running stream. Around him tin mugs and crockery lay on the wet stones. Trixie was drawn to his bright red hair, brighter even than her mum's fiancé Des's hair. And this lad, who was slim, reminded her, as Des did, of a Swan Vestas match.

'I'm dropping you off,' said Hen, breaking into Trixie's train of thought. She was speaking softly so the men, who were now staring at the parked lorry, wouldn't overhear her. 'I'll add up a few figures, so I'll know what I'm talking about on the telephone when we arrive at Bettyhill. But I'll not be gone long. Find out as much as you can about the day-to-day running of Noah MacKay's business. Prior knowledge of possible problems gives us an advantage.'

Trixie, Jo and Vi climbed down and watched the vehicle turn. With a wave and a smile from Hen, the lorry disappeared and they walked into the clearing.

'We've visitors, Andy,' an elderly man in an old army greatcoat yelled at the lad now rinsing crockery, whose back was turned to them. 'Andy!' The man's voice was a roar. The lad turned. 'Better rinse out a few more mugs.' The man gave a laugh that was more like a rumble of thunder. Trixie saw Andy frown but his face lit up in a good-natured smile as his eyes fell on them.

'Go and help him carry the crockery, Vi,' Trixie said. 'If they're providing us with tea, the least we can do is assist.' Vi glared at Trixie, but she ambled down to Andy.

The man in the greatcoat rose to his feet from the log he was sitting on and walked towards Trixie. He held out his hand in greeting so she could shake it. He was smiling. 'I know who you three lasses are. The boss had been expecting you.' His laugh showed strong yellow teeth. For a moment Trixie wondered if she'd noted a hint of sarcasm in his voice.

Trixie took his hand, which was warm but rough, and shook it.

Jo surprised Trixie by stepping forward for her own welcome handshake. 'Expecting us, or big, brawny men?'

The man let another laugh rumble out of himself. 'I like a girl with a sense of humour,' he said. 'We knew last night the boss wouldn't be best pleased with lasses turning up. My name's Callum, and that's Duncan.' He pointed to another man, slight and balding, rolling himself a cigarette. Duncan grinned. 'Lachie's there nursing a wee dram.' Lachie looked as if he'd already had more than a little one. He tried to rise from the log to greet them, but stumbled and sat down again, then looked indifferently at Trixie.

'We've finished for the day so a drop of the water of life, *uisge beatha*, is in order,' Lachie said. 'Will you take a little sip in your tea?' He produced a battered hip flask from his pocket.

Trixie shook her head so her blonde hair floated around her face. 'We don't drink.' She could smell the alcohol on him. Whisky made her feel sick. It was not so long ago that, at a dance in the Yellow Duck public house, Trixie had unwittingly drunk orangeade laced with whisky that Ben Tate, a Canadian airman, had bought for her. Vi's quick actions, in the garden, with a hefty wallop on the man's head from a metal watering can had prevented him raping her. The nightmares remained, though.

Trixie was well aware that if they agreed to join the men in their sips of whisky they would risk losing all credibility as hard workers and their reputations would be in tatters. She was relieved to see Lachie replace his flask in his pocket.

'We've come to meet you,' she said, 'before we begin working together.'

'Oh, aye,' said Duncan. 'We heard from the lorry driver who'd brought you from Lairg station that you'd arrived.'

Trixie laughed, as Jo whispered to her, 'And I thought Gosport had nosy neighbours!'

'Well, it's nice to meet you, Duncan. Hen, our driver, will be back later.' She thought she'd better mention Hen as, no doubt, he was aware there were four of them. 'My name's Trixie. This is Jo, and Vi is getting acquainted with Andy.' She nodded towards the couple at the stream where a great deal of giggling and loud laughter was already going on.

Duncan called, in a deafening voice, 'Young Andy, this billy's going to boil dry if you don't make the tea.' The billy-can was still spluttering. Trixie guessed Duncan wouldn't demean himself by removing it from the heat. She decided it was not prudent for her to interfere and caught Jo's eye, happy that Jo also understood the situation perfectly. Duncan didn't like Andy and Vi larking about.

She looked around the site. A huge pile of lumber was stacked, ready to be moved on, either by road or possibly by road and train.

Jo had walked over to the logs. She smiled at Trixie, who could see from where she stood that the wood wasn't brashed properly. Twigs and branches were jutting out untidily from the trunks. At Shandford Lodge they'd have been reprimanded for stacking lumber that hadn't been cleanly dressed as ready to leave the site.

Vi and Andy had returned, Vi with her arms full of washed but dripping mugs. Trixie smiled at her. It was good to see Vi at ease in the company of someone her own age, especially a man. Vi was mistrustful of men, which was natural enough after her experiences with Alec.

Andy knelt near the fire and, using one of the old towels, carefully lifted the billy from the fire and set it on the pine needles. He began spooning loose tea inside the raised lid. Trixie licked her lips. The tea would be strong. If there was one thing she disliked it was weak, dishwater tea. He set aside the first can, picked up the second, the one he'd brought back from the stream, and moved it onto the fire.

'You've no charcoal burner?' Jo was scanning the clearing.

Andy didn't reply. A grunt that could have meant anything emerged from Lachie. Duncan took a drag on his almost non-existent skinny fag and shook his head disinterestedly.

'We cannae be doing with crawling around picking up bits of wood for that, can we?' said Callum. 'Our old bones don't agree with too much bending. We'd have to take time off with aching backs and that wouldn't do at all, would it, lassie?'

Trixie had been quite taken by the charcoal burners in the forests at Shandford Lodge. To her, burning wood for charcoal was essential. Not only had she loved the heat from the kilns on a cold day but also hunting for alder branches, which made the best charcoal and could be ground down finely for gunpowder. It seemed silly to her not to take advantage of everything the forest had to offer for free, especially when they were trying to win a war, and the more money that could be made from the logs and trees was a blessing, surely. She knew Hen felt the same about charcoal kilns.

'Perhaps not,' said Trixie. She smiled broadly in an effort to show she agreed with Callum. 'But I was under the impression Noah MacKay had more men . . .'

'The day before yesterday,' said Duncan, the thin cigarette now stuck to his bottom lip, 'we loaded lumber to go to the sawmill at Inverness. Now several of the men are away to their beds with injured backs.'

Trixie nodded. She understood how stressful carrying heavy lumber was but she also thought there was a chance the men might be taking advantage of Noah MacKay.

'Is that tea ready yet?' Jo asked Andy, who had his back to her and didn't answer.

'Andy!' Callum's loud voice could silence birdsong, thought Trixie. 'Is the tea mashed, yet?'

Andy shook his head and smiled at Vi, who was setting out mugs and cups on the pine needles.

'Andy has hearing problems,' Vi said.

'Aye, his dad was a bit handy with his fists when Andy was a young 'un,' supplied Callum. Trixie realized the men used Andy as a convenience to do chores they couldn't be bothered with. Not that he seemed to mind. He did their bidding cheerfully enough.

'There's no need to shout,' Vi said. She was talking primarily to Jo and Trixie, but loudly enough for the men to hear.

The way they used his hearing defect to belittle him had touched a nerve with her, thought Trixie. Vi stopped Andy wrapping the drift of towel around his fingers to prevent his hand becoming scalded when he started pouring the tea. He looked questioningly into her face. She said, in a soft, clear voice, 'Andy told me he applied to join the army but they rejected him because of his hearing.'

Andy nodded. 'Doesnae matter,' he said, 'not now,' and gave a white-toothed smile. 'I like it fine here in the woods.' Trixie heard him but knew that at one time it had mattered to him very much. So many young people wanted to serve their country. To discover this was impossible was a terrible blow.

Gently, Andy touched Vi's hand. She turned so they were face to face again.

'Thank you,' he said. Trixie swallowed, holding back a tear. The lad was thanking Vi for bringing his deafness to their attention.

Vi guffawed. 'You're the best lip-reader I've ever known. You don't miss a trick.'

He threw at her the towel he was holding. It missed and fell to the grass. Trixie marvelled that Vi, usually so ill at ease with men, especially those she'd just met, accepted his cheeky manner. 'Where's your dad now?' Jo asked. She'd taken over the tea-pouring, had counted heads and made sure that Vi had set out the requisite number of mugs and cups. She was careful, Trixie noted, to make sure Andy knew she was talking to him.

Andy shrugged. 'Long gone. I look after my ma now.' He picked up two mugs and passed one each to Duncan and Callum. Neither said a word as they reached for their tea. A sudden snore came from Lachie. Clearly he wouldn't be wanting any, thought Trixie.

The sunlight danced through the pine needles on the trees. Their branches waved in the slight breeze. The weather was turning cold fast, thought Trixie. And up here in Sutherland she imagined the winters could be cruel, with snow that drifted high and cut off townships for days. But, for now, it was soothing to listen to the birdsong and to smell the pine wood, which somehow always reminded her of Christmas.

A gentle but high-pitched horse's neigh saved Trixie from nodding off. She yawned. It seemed a lot had happened since she'd comforted Hen during her bout of sickness that morning. She glanced around her to see Andy was on his feet and walking lightly down towards the stream where a brown horse was grazing near an elderly wooden cart. Trixie watched the lad bend to pick up the nosebag from the grass and slip it in place over the horse's head. He was talking to the animal and petting it. Trixie smiled as the horse nudged him. Andy's actions, his obvious affection for the animal, immediately reminded her of Alf, her mentor at Shandford Lodge, who had painstakingly taught her what she needed to know of forestry. Trixie had had great affection for Alf and his Lulabelle. She watched as Andy moved about picking up heavy axes and saws from where they'd been thrown to the ground. He took the tools to the cart and stowed them inside for when the men were ready to leave. He was a good-looking lad, Trixie thought, and kind.

She raised herself from the log she was sitting on and walked down to the stream taking several dirty mugs with her. When she reached Andy, she looked into his face and said, 'Thank you for making Vi laugh. It was good to hear her happy.' She knelt on the bank, and swished the remains of the tea from the mugs.

'I've never met anyone like her before,' he said.

She smiled and nodded but didn't speak.

'They're not such bad fellows,' he said. 'The men. I'm young and strong. I can take it . . .'

'All three of them are lazy,' she said.

'There's work left in them, though. And, regardless of their age, there aren't so many men around who would rather labour in the forests than join the forces and fight. And many older men don't want to work at all.'

Trixie nodded. 'You think the team needs shaking up?'

'It needs more hands-on-axes and someone here all the time to keep an eye on things. Mr MacKay is a good man but he's new to this. He wants to do what he believes is best and that's to sell the trees but not the land. He's looking ahead, past the war, to the future for others after him to enjoy. It means replanting—'

Trixie broke in: 'Surely if he sells the land along with his trees the new owner or owners would do that.'

He shook his head and raised a hand to push back his gloriously coloured hair. 'War or no war, money is king. You really think a new owner of the land will care what happens to it when they're dead and gone? Noah MacKay is looking ahead to his children, his children's children. That's why, even for an Englishman, he's better thought of than his father ever was.'

'You think so?'

He treated her to a wide grin. 'Aye, I do. And it'll be a good job when you all start working here.'

His voice was lost in the raucous noise of a lorry's horn beeping.

Chapter Ten

Noah MacKay bent down and pulled a dry apple log from the pile on the hearth and pressed it onto the dying embers of the fire. It flared briefly, then settled to a steady, sweet-smelling burn. He rubbed thoughtfully at his knee. All the walking he had done today was telling on him. But he was alive, wasn't he? Unlike some of the poor blighters left behind on that beach in France.

He picked up his pint, swallowed a mouthful, then sat back in the armchair, his drink in his hand. It was good to be sitting here in the bar at the Falls Inn. For a short while he could pretend he didn't have a care in the world.

A couple of elderly men were playing dominoes at a table near the window and three others were propping up the bar with pints and whiskies at their elbows while they discussed the business of the day. A fug of familiar-smelling tobacco smoke floated over the locals and travellers. A good atmosphere and a comforting, congenial scene. Upstairs a snug bedroom was waiting for him, with no damp patches on the walls or ill-fitting window frames.

Why, then, did he wish he had driven straight back to Talmine after visiting the Newfoundland Overseas Forestry Unit? Was it arrogance and pride that had stopped him, or was he afraid of looking a fool? Maybe it was simply because he was a man and didn't know how to apologize.

Of course he hated to be proved wrong. It was a bitter pill to swallow. But why had he allowed himself to carry on driving up to the Falls Inn, thinking he could postpone redressing the situation with those women until tomorrow when he returned to his estate?

He'd thought it would be so simple, but now the guilt was eating him up.

Would they still be at his house? He'd told them to leave. Would they have decided to make their own way back to Brechin? He remembered Officer Skellig's words, aided by mugs of tea. 'I'm surprised at your attitude. Those women have been fully trained. There's precious little they don't know about forestry. Male labour isn't possible to come by. We're at war, for God's sake! Men are needed to fight. I can put in a requisition form for prisoners of war to work for you, but you'll still need proper instructors to teach them.'

The officer had paused, then went on, 'And you've been sent good, dependable instructors and workers. Did you read the letter of recommendation sent with them?'

Noah had to admit he hadn't.

He'd drunk more tea and sat in the draughty hut and listened as the officer had said, 'Are you aware of how the Women's Timber Corps was formed?'

Noah knew he was about to be enlightened so he helped himself to another cup of tea and settled back.

'Lady Denman set up headquarters in 1939 at her home in Sussex. Twelve hundred women from the Land Army were recruited into the Women's Timber Corps to learn forestry work because the country's timber reserves were at an all-time low and likely to last just seven months. The Women's Timber Corps and the Land Army are now two separate entities, such is the success of the lumberjills. Enemy occupation in Norway and the blocking of sea routes means lumber can't be safely brought in from abroad. These women have stamina and strength. They'll not only wield axes and transport lorry-loads of logs to railway stations but supervise workers felling and the distribution of lumber to sawmills.'

A long pause followed. Noah, chastened that he had had no idea of the women's worth, apologized and prepared to leave.

As he had driven onwards to the Falls Inn he despaired at his ignorance in ever imagining he could make a success of running the estate and helping the war effort by selling his timber.

He took another swallow of ale. He had thought he was a reasonably intelligent man after his years of costly education and his distinguished army career. His family history had always been a bit of a mystery and his inheritance had come as a shock. The truth had emerged only recently, when a solicitor's letter had reached him in the hospital in Essex where he was recuperating from wounds received while he was rescued at Dunkirk. He thought about his grandparents living in Southsea, England, whom he'd loved but had never been close to, probably because from the age of seven he had spent his time at boarding school. His mother had died in childbirth and he'd accepted that her parents simply wanted what they'd thought was best for him. As a schoolboy he'd never thought to question how they'd been able to afford the exorbitant fees while living so modestly themselves. At first, he wrote often, eager for news of them, and pretended to be unconcerned by tardy replies. During the holidays, he'd remained at school, as did boys whose parents resided abroad. He'd often wondered why he had been given the benefit of a good education when interest and love were lacking. As he became older and his questions remained unanswered, the gulf between him and his grandparents grew until their deaths severed all ties.

The army beckoned when the war began and, as officer material, he thought he had discovered his niche. He was conscientious and well-liked by all ranks, which surprised him because he thought of himself as a studious, quiet man. He wasn't ashamed of his physique or looks and he had had his fair share of women. He'd finally fallen for the spoiled sister of an old schoolfriend. He'd not grown up among women and disregarded her selfish ways as 'feminine'. He'd smiled at Helen's tendency to prioritize her own desires above all others because her dark beauty captivated him. He'd received a letter from her while in hospital ending their affair as she had met someone else, with a title. All he'd felt was relief, tinged with sadness that women were essentially weak and could not be trusted.

He'd met the solicitor in the grounds of the hospital.

Simon Entwistle shook his hand. They'd sat together on a wooden seat in the weak sunshine.

'There's little money in your inheritance, I'm afraid. It's

taken a while to find you. This was sent on to us from your father's advocate.'

The tall, thin young man reminded Noah of a runner bean in his dark green suit. He handed him an envelope containing the deeds to his land, with a house, in the north of Scotland. Noah's true gain, however, was the story of his procreation. 'I'd rather hear it from you, and read about it later,' he said, and handed back the document that contained information he'd wondered about all his life.

'Rufus MacKay met your mother, Doris, in Edinburgh, at the opening of the North British Railway Hotel in 1902. He was with a group of male friends. She was working there as a chambermaid.' There was a daguerreotype of a very young girl in a high-necked dress, sitting on a chair. Her hair was coiled high on her head. She looked ridiculously young in the portrait that had obviously been taken professionally.

Noah had looked at her image and tears had risen. This was his mother? He'd swallowed the tears. It wasn't done for a man to cry.

'She became pregnant. There was no question of him marrying her as she wasn't of his class, and she was sent home to England,' Entwistle continued. 'Your father, however, had a certain . . . attachment to the girl. Unbeknown to his family he kept in touch with her and was inconsolable when she died giving birth to you. Rufus had a reputation as a rake, a womanizer. He lavished gifts on people and incurred ridiculous debts. It was never common knowledge that he paid for your education. He never married. He had no more children. He died penniless and in debt. All he had left, his land, he willed to you.'

Noah had hobbled with the aid of his stick to the end of the hospital drive and said goodbye to Simon Entwistle. Afterwards, he sat for a long while, alone, in his room, thinking. His first thought after the initial shock had passed was to sell the land. He had no dependants. He was a free agent. Then he thought of Rufus, his father, who had obviously wanted him to have what was rightly his.

And in that moment he knew when he left the hospital, medically discharged from the forces with an honorable discharge from the army, he would go to Scotland and take up his inheritance. He knew nothing of Sutherland, of wilderness, of forests, of acres of land to be looked after, but he was determined to learn.

'Marie,' he called to the woman behind the bar. 'I shan't need my room tonight, after all.'

Noah MacKay drank the last of his pint and set the glass on the table at his side. Using his stick to haul himself from the chair, he began his journey back to Talmine.

Chapter Eleven

Morag poured the thick black tea from the enamel pot and Trixie licked her lips in anticipation.

'Well, how did the day go?' The housekeeper pushed the mug towards her, but Trixie was scanning the mantelpiece. Hadn't she seen the post bus travelling towards Talmine? Oh, how she longed for a letter from Cy. She'd vowed she'd not stop writing, no matter how long it was before an envelope from him came winging back to her.

'Hen knows more about that than we do,' Trixie replied. 'But it's all good news. If only she can convince Noah MacKay to go along with her ideas.'

Vi was sitting on the floor tugging off her heavy boots. She paused, grinned at Morag and gestured at a large, covered bowl standing on the floor in the corner near the fire. 'What's that?'

'My ginger-beer plant,' Morag said. 'It's water, ginger, sugar, yeast and lemon. There are other variations but that's my recipe.'

'But you've loads of bottles in the big barn,' Vi said.

'That's because I keep feeding the plant, adding ginger and sugar.'

'Can I taste some?' Vi asked,

'Not until it's ready, which will be soon,' Morag said.

'I met a really nice feller today,' Vi said, brushing strands of hair out of her eyes. 'I think we'll work well together. I feel at ease with him. He's cheerful, good-hearted.' She got up, came over to the table and sat down on a high-backed chair. 'This mine?' She motioned to a mug of tea, and Morag nodded.

'And where's the wee girlie?' Morag set the heavy teapot on the hearth to keep warm. The kitchen smelt of fresh baking, and a large black metal pot of something savoury and meaty was bubbling over the fire.

'Hen's upstairs having a wash and freshening up,' Trixie said. 'She's been driving nearly all day and using loads of brain power to work things out. She said she wanted to check that her figures were correct.'

'And Jo?' Morag asked, as she picked up a long-handled spoon and stirred the food in the pot. Removing the spoon, she blew on the morsel it contained and tasted it. After a moment, she nodded, then swung the pot on its chain away from the fire's direct heat.

'Jo's gone for a walk.'

Morag looked up with a frown. 'She'll get bitten to death by the midges.'

'Oh, don't worry about her,' Trixie said. 'She needs time on her own, especially when she starts remembering the family she lost. We're quite used to her disappearing for a while. It does her good. She says it recharges her battery.'

'But it's black as pitch out there,' Morag remonstrated.

'She'll be all right,' said Vi. Then, 'I said I met a really nice—'

'That'd be Andy, red-haired, one of Noah's lads.'

'How d'you know that?' Vi put down her tea and stared at Morag in amazement.

Morag laughed. 'Haven't you been to visit the men today? There's no many young fellers left up here who haven't joined the services and he's the nicest I can think of.'

Trixie smiled, as Vi sighed and mumbled, 'Everyone knows everything in Talmine!'

'Aye! And what they don't know, they make up,' said Morag. Then she reached above the fireplace and took an envelope from the pile of correspondence behind the clock, 'And I know the postie's brought you a letter!'

Trixie's heart leaped.

'No, Trixie, love, not you. Lady Vi here!'

Trixie's heart plummeted as Morag handed the letter to Vi.

Vi took it from her, murmuring thanks but staring at the envelope as though it might contain a bomb. 'It's Irene's writing. It's been sent on from Shandford Lodge.'

'We passed on this address to our families, didn't we? Go on, open it,' urged Trixie. She and Morag watched as Vi tore at the envelope. Trixie said to Morag, 'Vi regularly sends money to her mum, care of the neighbour who looks after her, but no news is good news and it's not often Irene needs to reply.'

Morag nodded. She was given to chatting away about what went on in the house and with the neighbours in Talmine. Although the girls had known Morag only a short time, she'd already managed to wheedle out lots about them and was familiar with Vi's homelife.

'Oh.' Vi put the letter on the table. Her face now matched the white cloth for colour. 'Mum's taken a turn for the worse. She's in hospital, the War Memorial, in Gosport.' Her eyes filled with tears and she threw herself into Trixie's arms, sobbing as if her heart would break. After a while she lifted her head and, in a whisper, her face streaked with tears, she added, 'Irene says I should go home. As soon as possible.'

'You must!' Morag was emphatic. 'You'll never forgive yourself if you don't.'

'How can I? We don't know what's happening here. Last night Noah MacKay told us to leave.'

Morag leaned over and took hold of Vi, pulling her away from Trixie and enfolding her in the many shawls she wore. 'There, there,' she murmured, as if she was talking to a child. 'You'll only ever have one mother and you should make the most of her while you can. My ma told me many times, joking, that I'd miss her when she was gone. I used to laugh at her, but she was right. I'm an old woman and should know the ways of the world but there's many a time I wish my mother was still with me.'

Vi began, 'But—'

'But nothing! Tomorrow morning Hen can drive you to the station at Lairg and you can board a train to Inverness, then down south to London and homewards. I'll give you the fare if you havenae got it.' She paused and looked at Trixie. 'I have a little bit put by. I keep offering my few savings to Noah but he willnae take them. Aye, and you'd better travel with her, Trixie. She cannae go anywhere alone in the state she's in.' She pushed Vi away to arm's length, but holding her hands, she said, 'I won't take no for an answer.'

'But what about the master?' Vi's wet eyes were now red-rimmed.

'What about the master?' parroted Morag. Her eyes narrowed. 'You leave him to me.'

Just then the door to the kitchen opened, and Hen came in. She looked pinkly scrubbed, her long hair hanging damply about her shoulders and back like spun silk. A cream silk nightdress could be seen peeking above the marabou-feather-trimmed satin dressing-gown that nipped in at her small waist. Her feet were shod in matching satin slippers with heels. In one hand she held the notebook she had carried around with her all day.

'You look like a film star!' exclaimed Morag. 'Come and sit by the fire before you catch your death of cold!'

Her eyes on her notebook and the fountain pen in her hand, Hen said, 'Thank you. I brought these pretty clothes from home. I never wore them at Shandford Lodge because the girls all had pyjamas and long warm ... What's the matter?'

'I hope you'll cover yourself up before my Angus gets home! He's never seen the like of them fancy things and I don't want him getting ideas. The master neither, I should think. And you'll not dry them bits and pieces on my line for all to see. Talmine's a God-fearing place . . .'

Trixie realized Hen, despite Morag's rant, had noticed the strange atmosphere in the room.

Morag said quietly, 'The lass's mother is very, very ill. She's to go back to Gosport as soon as possible and I've suggested you'll drive Vi and Trixie to Lairg in time for the train very early tomorrow.'

'Of course, I will,' Hen said, putting the notebook on the table and moving towards Vi, sadness etched on her face 'Oh, I am sorry.' She took one of Vi's hands in hers, and said, 'Now, I want no arguments. We've had travel warrants to move about the country up until now, but you'll need money and I can see to that.'

Vi wiped a tear from her cheek. She gave Hen a watery smile. 'You're very kind, thank you. I'll pay you back, I promise. Morag's offered—'

'And you'll take that too,' said Morag. 'You never know what the pair of you might need.'

'But I—'

'But nothing, Trixie,' Morag interrupted. 'Why don't the pair of you go to your room and ready yourselves for the journey? Come back down dressed warmly in your pyjamas,' at 'warmly' she threw Hen a sly look, 'and bring something down to cover that one up. She'll be getting the place a bad name. Then we'll eat.'

That made sense to Trixie. But she looked at Hen, who shook her head, as if to convey that the worst had already happened to her. Trixie gave her a sympathetic smile.

'In the meantime, Hen can tell me about today's accomplishments,' added Morag.

'Is everything to your satisfaction, sir?'

Noah smiled at the elderly man behind the desk. The Falls Inn had the highest reputation and Noah knew it was unusual for a guest to book in for a night then leave before the evening had passed.

'Of course, James,' he cleared his throat, 'but I'm needed back at the estate.' The tall, angular man nodded knowingly. It wasn't his place to pry unless customer gratification was involved.

While awaiting the bill for the excellent meal he'd eaten and the drinks he'd consumed, Noah allowed his eyes to wander around the vestibule. The usual antler collection and mounted animal heads adorned the walls, casting shadows on the highly polished dark oak furniture. A pile of magazines lay on a table, next to a comfortable chair. He was drawn to the object next to the magazines. It was a large, highly polished box-like receiver in a mahogany cabinet. A handwritten notice stated it was for sale.

'What's this, James?'

James slid his spectacles back up his large nose and began a solemn speech that probably included all he knew on the subject. 'A Selecta portable wireless, sir. It has four valves, an accumulator and a spare. It needs earthing and an aerial but imagine listening to music from as far away as Berlin, Vienna, Paris, Madrid, and all at the turn of a switch.'

'Quite so,' said Noah. 'Does it work?' He had heard of these machines.

'Sir!' James exclaimed. as if the idea that the Falls Inn would offer something faulty for sale was highly offensive. 'Why—'

'A guest found he was inconveniently embarrassed when paying his bill and asked if we would consider taking it in part-payment.'

An idea was fermenting in Noah's brain. 'Show me how it works. I might be interested.'

'Certainly, sir.' Within moments James had fiddled with knobs and a crackly, rendition of 'Dream a Little Dream of Me' was playing.

Noah recognized the tune. One of the girls had been humming it back at the house.

'That's Ernie Burchill singing, sir,' added James, swinging open the back of the set. 'The machine is not set up properly here.' He coughed, then pointed to a small meter inside it. 'That shows how much charge is remaining, sir. But, of course, with the spare battery, especially if you leave one at the nearest garage to be recharged, you'll never be without music.'

Noah drummed his fingers on the glossy wooden table. 'Carry it outside to my car and add it to my bill, James.'

It had been a long while since he had bought anything but necessities for the house. He never spent frivolously, and the lump sum of his army discharge pay had dwindled alarmingly in paying estate bills. However, he didn't like to hurt people and he'd been incredibly rude to the four girls who'd come to work for him. His house was silent. The wireless would help dispel the quiet.

Now all he had to do was hope he wasn't too late, that the blonde vixen and her cohorts hadn't yet left the estate.

Chapter Twelve

'Your Angus might be ancient but he's as strong as an ox,' said Noah, watching from behind the kitchen door's blackout curtain as the old man waved, then walked across the courtyard to continue with his nightly duties before retiring. 'I'd never have managed to carry that in on my own with this daft leg.' He tapped his knee with his cane.

With satisfaction he gazed at the portable wireless set. Morag peered at the contraption perched on top of the sideboard. He knew she wouldn't ask what it was until she was consumed with curiosity. He decided he wouldn't tell her, unless she did.

He shrugged himself out of his coat, and Morag took it from him, then hung it on the stand in the corner. He glanced around for some small token belonging to the girls that would reassure him they were still under his roof. He could see nothing except a notebook on the table.

Morag, as if reading his mind, said, 'I told them to stay.'

'Put yourself in my shoes, now, have you?' Was it really only last night that he had told them to leave?

She smiled at him. 'Aye. Sometimes it's necessary,' she said.

'And how am I to pay their wages? They won't work for nothing.' The words he spoke were meant only to tease her. She knew as well as he did that their wages would come from the government.

She gave a long-drawn-out sigh of resignation, picked up the notebook and handed it to him. 'Sit down by the fire and read through this while I make you a cup of tea. I'd have had something ready for you to eat but I didnae expect you back till morning. Have you had anything?'

He nodded, walked awkwardly towards the armchair by the fire and eased himself into it, the notebook in his hand.

The contents of the pages were a revelation. He had assumed the four girls, in his absence, would make plans to leave the estate. Instead they had used the opportunity to investigate acres of his land, including the site where his men were working. A detailed account of their findings was noted. Logical improvements were suggested. They had correctly judged he wished only to sell trees. More favourable rates were quoted from sources he had not considered, and the writer had considered extra labour, where to obtain it, thus increasing output. Step by step the owner of the notebook had explained whom she had contacted and the results of all actions. The writing was clear, concise. All figures tallied.

'That young woman, with the long hair, Henrietta, knows her stuff,' Morag announced. 'Drink your tea before it gets cold.'

Noah looked up from the notebook. 'And you were privy to all this?'

'Yes. The girls were sent to help. You waved them away. I thought to let them attempt to do what they were trained for.'

'You took a great deal on yourself, Morag.'

She looked at the clock on the mantelpiece. 'Not much has changed since you left this morning, except you now have written evidence of the money you could expect for your lumber instead of the pittance you're presently receiving.'

He struggled to stand, the notebook slipping to the floor, then stamped towards the back door, fumbling in the folds of the blackout curtain to open it. When he stepped out into the black of the night, it was to feel the cold spray of fresh rain on his skin.

Talking to Officer Skellig had shown Noah how useful the girls could be. But to arrive home and discover just how intelligent they were in matters over which his control was practically negligible had surprised him. And Morag, his staunch supporter, the auld besom he had come to care for deeply, had colluded with them.

He ran his hand over his wet hair, sweeping away the rain that had settled there. He knew it was because she cared about him and about the estate.

As he re-entered the kitchen, leaning on his stick, Morag handed him a worn warm towel.

He smiled at her. 'Clever women are just like clever men,' he said, 'and I should be grateful for them, shouldn't I?' He lowered himself back into the chair and began towelling his hair.

'I think so,' Morag said, removing one of her shawls and draping it across his shoulders. Already in the warmth of the room his shirt was steaming.

'Are they in bed? I'd like to talk to the measurer.'

Morag nodded. 'But you'd do well to wait until Hen gets back in the morning from seeing Trixie and Vi onto the early train at Lairg.'

'They're not leaving?' There was disappointment in his voice.

He'd made peace with himself and his thoughts and now couldn't bear to think that two of the girls weren't going to stay.

'Vi's mother has been taken poorly. She's in hospital. They'll be back directly,' Morag replied, busy now with the brown teapot.

'Oh dear. Is it serious?' He felt relief that their leaving had nothing to do with him.

'I think so. Vi's going to need Trixie with her.'

Noah frowned. 'Quite so. She should have a friend beside her in those circumstances.' He looked at the notebook, which was back on the table. 'She, the measurer, is exceptionally accomplished.'

'Aye, she knows how many pennies make a shilling, Hen does.' Morag paused. 'She's aware her research can only go so far without your agreement.'

So the measurer was the blonde vixen? He might have guessed.

'There's a meeting with the Forestry Commission arranged for a couple of days' time. A representative wants to look at the trees. Do you think she'll accompany me?' he asked.

'Why ask me when it's Hen you should be talking to?'

He sighed again. 'I'd like her to be there. She should be there.'

Morag poured fresh tea into a metal mug. 'You'll work together then, all of you?' She allowed the heavy metal teapot to bump onto the wooden table as she put it down.

'I'd be a fool not to, wouldn't I?'

'Your words, not mine,' Morag said.

He opened the notebook once more and flicked through as though he was looking for something. 'I like how she's arranged that the lumber could go by road to Lairg station, then by rail straight into a Brechin sawmill. Somehow, she's organized an excellent price with the owner, Lachlan MacLeod . . .'

'She mentioned him. Said they'd met when the girls were at Shandford Lodge. You should have seen Jo blush when Hen announced that Lachlan asked after her! Maybe there was a romance, I don't know . . .' She tailed off as though she was remembering what had occurred earlier, but then said harshly, 'The lassies drove into Bettyhill to make phone calls. Hen's the driver.'

Noah stared at her.

'And insisted on paying for those calls themselves and the fuel they used today.'

'They needn't have done that.' He felt embarrassed.

'As they were doing this without your permission, they didn't want you to be out of pocket if you disagreed with the final findings.'

More shame heaped itself on him at his childishness. 'I really don't know what to say, except I'm glad they didn't leave.'

'Drink your tea, Noah. I don't want to throw away another potful.'

Noah closed the notebook and picked up his mug. He quite liked it when Morag treated him like the son she'd never had. He would have loved to have a mother like her.

Morag stood in front of him, picked up the damp towel he'd used on his hair and face, and spread it over the fireguard to dry.

'You ken your father's piano in the barn?' Her feet in their slippers were planted in front of him.

'Piano?' Was a piano hidden among the objects left in the barn?

'Aye. That young Trixie plays the piano. Only she can't play that one because it needs tuning. I've asked Rory McCullum to come and look at it.'

'Something else you've arranged without my knowing?' he said, his smile a mile wide.

'Well, you know now,' she replied, returning his smile. 'And I cannae hold back my curiosity any longer . . .' She was peering at the square mahogany box on the sideboard. 'What is that thing?'

'I knew you'd give in and ask eventually. It's a portable wireless set, Morag. It has four valves, an accumulator and a spare battery that I'll leave at the garage in Bettyhill to be fully charged when it's needed. We'll have music for the girls, and you, Morag, from Vienna, Paris, London, all at the turn of a switch . . .'

Noah held his breath. Dismembered bodies, separated arms and feet, some still in boots, the smell and the flies. He was slithering below the dunes and sands above the flat beach at Dunkirk, dragging his commanding officer, Grant Mainwaring. Wet seaweed glistened, thrown up by breaking waves. Noah was too tired to be afraid, hunger and thirst spurring his instinct for survival. Voices . . . He could hear voices above the roll of the sea. He willed his body to complete stillness. His companion emitted a strangled cry. Noah despised himself for doing it because the man was dying but he had no option but to clamp a hand across his mouth. That the gut-wrenching sound could alert the noisy Germans just beyond a wall of sand and struggling vegeta- tion was unthinkable. He could smell the brewing bitterness of ertsatz coffee. It was 1940, the first week of June. Hitler had, incomprehensibly, briefly ceased killing off the British Expeditionary Force, and Allies trying to escape onto the small boats, ships and carriers had all but disappeared now. The skies were miraculously free of duelling Hurricanes and Messerschmitts, which rained down maiming bullets before spiralling out of control.

In the distance Noah could hear shouting and guttural commands. More enemy soldiers. He couldn't make out how many there were. Mainwaring, still breathing, had quietened. Noah lifted his head, trying to ignore the sand and salt stinging his eyes. Way beyond, the shouting grew louder. A soldier, still alive, he thought, was being clubbed, probably with rifle butts and bayonets.

The ship, a motor torpedo boat, small, maybe a thirty-footer, hovered in the water, waiting for him.

Further along the beach German troops were moving between abandoned tanks and equipment. Voices called excitedly at useful finds, at personal effects abandoned in their owners' haste to escape Dunkirk's shores.

It was imperative to board the MTB. Broken bodies littered the beach. Noah slid across them, dragging his officer, as if the dead beneath him were no more than fly-blown, rancid cushions and bolsters covering a sandy bed.

The water was warm, red-tinged. The rope ladder dropped from the ship's side. Noah's body shielded Mannering's as he pushed, heaved, him upwards.

It was no more than a sting but the bullet had found its mark. When Noah looked down, his leg was shattered below the knee. He was amazed at the brightness of his blood.

'C'mon, mate, we've got you. You're all right now.'

Mainwaring was hauled aboard.

Then a hand, an arm came forward to pull Noah to safety and, for a split second, as he grabbed the top guardrail he looked up into the smiling eyes of his unknown rescuer.

A German bullet ripped into the man's flesh. Before the surprise had had time to imprint itself on his face, the man jerked back, his warm blood splattering onto Noah.

Despite the chill in his bedroom, Noah's skin was slick with hot sweat. He reached across and picked up the mug of cold water, his hand shaking as he gulped it down.

He didn't want to remember Dunkirk, but how could he ever forget?

Would the nightmares ever leave him?

Chapter Thirteen

'Mr MacKay!'

Noah was opening the barn door when Trixie spotted
him through the window. The darkness and chill of the
early morning enveloped her as she hurried towards him.
He looked surprised to see her, she thought. No one else
had stirred yet in the house, except Morag and her husband,
who were talking quietly in the kitchen.

Noah acknowledged her with an unexpected smile. The
wind nudged coldly against her face making her shiver.

'I wanted to apologize for needing to leave here today, to
go back to Gosport with Vi. Her mother's in hospital . . .'
She knew she was gabbling. Why had she felt the sudden
need to say sorry when he'd already made it clear he didn't
want them there?

'Slow down,' he said quietly. 'I've read Henrietta's expansive notes and Morag's explained everything.' He retrieved his stick, which he had propped against the side of the building, then turned back to her. 'You're . . .' He paused.

'Trixie.' She realized he had yet to distinguish the four of them by their names. He had, however, remembered who Hen was.

'Do you have everything you both need?' His question was unexpected.

Trixie thought of the plan made for Hen to ferry herself and Vi to Lairg station, the money Morag and Hen had pressed upon them for train fares. 'I'm sure we have,' she said.

'And how is Vi?'

His consideration surprised Trixie.

'She'll be better when she's seen and talked to her mum,' she said.

'Quite so. If Vi knows she's being well cared-for in hospital and soon to return home, she'll feel happier about staying in Scotland.'

Trixie had to force her head to stop spinning. Was he accepting that they would work for him? Yesterday Noah MacKay had wanted the four of them off his property. Today he had mellowed. This was surely due to the comprehensive forestry information and advice Hen had written in her notebook and which he said he had read. Clever Hen.

Trixie swallowed. She knew she should follow up on this conversation but her confidence had left her. She wished Hen was there. Hen would have known how to say the right things to him. He must have sensed her confusion for he added, 'Do what you have to do in Gosport and come safely back.' He turned to the barn door and Trixie knew it was her cue to leave. She shivered – she had been foolish to leave the house without her coat.

'Bye,' she muttered.

She had taken but a few steps back towards the house when she heard him say, 'Trixie, it's easy to be wise after the event. I'm sorry, too.'

'We're going to have to run!' Vi screamed at Trixie, as they hurried for the Portsmouth train. Shoulder-bags and gas-mask cases banged against their overcoats as they scooted around servicemen on the platform, chatting and smoking cigarettes, while mothers tried to keep unruly children from misbehaving. From overhead a disembodied voice spoke indistinctly. Bowler-hatted men in suits with sharp umbrellas and briefcases stepped in front of the two girls as passengers vied for carriages on the southbound train. The guard was already slamming doors when Vi jumped aboard dragging Trixie after her.

'Phew! I didn't think we'd make it.' Trixie dusted down her Women's Timber Corps overcoat before falling into an empty seat and letting her brown carrier bag fall at her feet. Morag had provided a 'wee piece' and some apples for the journey but the girls had already eaten their sandwiches.

'You won't feel the benefit of that coat if you don't take it off now,' warned Vi.

'I will, in a minute,' said Trixie. 'You've done nothing but moan at me since we left Scotland.' She looked at Vi's swollen eyes and relented as her friend folded her own heavy overcoat, stretched up and put it in the overhead rack. 'Sorry,' Trixie said. 'I keep forgetting how awful this must be for you, going home to visit your mum in hospital.'

Ignoring the other passengers now crowding into the carriage, Trixie stood up and removed her coat. Vi took it from her as a girl with long plaits bounced onto the train's window seat opposite. A harassed woman followed, carrying a baby and a shopping bag. 'Loads of spare seats in this one, Mum. There's only two Land Army girls in 'ere.'

'We're not Land Army, we're Timber Corps.' Vi settled herself beside Trixie. At her feet her carrier bag contained toothbrush, nightdress and sundry items for an overnight stay.

'Same difference,' the tired-looking mother said, sitting down next to the girl and carefully rearranging her sleeping baby's shawl.

'Actually, no,' said Vi, in quite a haughty voice. 'Land Army girls work on farms and in fields. We chop down trees and the lumber helps . . .'

Trixie shook her head at Vi, whose nerves today were like blue touchpapers: she was liable to explode at any moment. As if her mother being in hospital wasn't stressful enough, she was terrified that Alec might be in Gosport.

'I'm glad we decided to wear our uniforms,' Trixie said, trying to smooth over the uncomfortable atmosphere. 'I'm proud of what we do.'

Vi looked down at her green jumper, dungarees and highly polished black lace-up shoes. Her green beret, with the Timber Corps badge of a fir tree, was clipped securely to her glossy dark hair with grips. She smiled, and Trixie smiled back, glad the tension of the previous moments had passed. The woman opposite must have sensed the mood in the carriage lifting for she bent towards the large handbag open at her feet on the floor of the compartment and pulled out a crumpled bag.

'Fudge, anyone?' she asked. "I made it myself using carrots and orange juice. It's a bit sharp but tastes all right!"

Soon the carriage was filled with the smell of oranges and, through the windows, Trixie regarded the destruction wrought by Hitler's bombers. She thought back to Hen driving her and Vi to the station when she'd told them about her earlier short meeting with Noah MacKay.

'Your detailed notes have given him something to think about, Hen,' Trixie had said.

'Do you think that's why he got that super wireless set for us?' Vi had asked.

'He must have bought it before he came home and read the results of our day's survey of his forests,' Hen said. 'I think someone or something else persuaded him to give us a chance to show him what we can achieve.'

'You don't like being praised for your cleverness, do you?' Vi said.

Trixie knew she didn't mean it unkindly. Hen was beautiful and intelligent but insecure about both attributes.

'I'm simply saying Trixie's idea about not leaving and showing Noah MacKay we can work better than some men still has to be proved.'

'But he's thawing,' said Trixie.

'Yes indeed,' Hen had answered.

As the train wound its way south towards Portsmouth, Trixie saw broken houses shored up by wooden planks and scaffolding, gaps in streets where buildings had been blown asunder. Endless queues of women waited outside bleak shops. Everywhere seemed bleached of colour, a uniform grey of dust and grime.

Trixie suddenly wanted to cry. Not only for herself, because she'd not heard from Cy, or because Vi's mother was in hospital, but for the unfairness of war. For everyone who had to carry on, regardless of what was happening all around them.

'Cheer up!' said Vi, who seemed to have tuned into her thoughts. 'It could be worse.'

'I don't see how,' Trixie said. And laughed at the absurdity of it all. Of war, of life, of death, and Vi laughed along with her and uttered a strangled 'Thank you,' as the bag of fudge went round once more.

'Are you sure your mum won't mind me sleeping at your place?' Vi asked Trixie, when their laughter had abated.

'You know she thinks the world of you,' Trixie answered. 'She wouldn't like to think of us alone in your mum's house.' She was looking out of the window and familiar landmarks told her that they would soon reach their destination of Portsmouth Harbour station. Soon they'd be sailing across the stretch of water to Gosport, perhaps sitting on the ferry-boat where she had met Cy. She'd have to keep a tight rein on her emotions. After all, there could be any number of reasons why she was not receiving letters from him. Faulty mail deliveries had to be the answer, surely.

'Doesn't Gosport look sad?' she said, her nose pressed up against the bus's window. They'd left the Provincial Bus station, skirting debris of the previous night's air raid that hadn't yet been cleared away. There was no green grass or heather here, she thought, or canopies of bright green pine trees smelling like Christmas. Instead thick dust covered everything in sight until it was pierced by gaps where shops had once stood. Rubble was piled there now. Trixie turned to Vi sitting next to her.

'The jeweller's gone,' she said. 'That was Higgs, the shop where Des bought my mum's engagement ring.'

'Just as well he got it before it was bombed, then.'

It wasn't like Vi to be so negative, Trixie thought, though not surprising when her mother was so ill.

The bus trundled past a butcher's shop where women in headscarves chatted while waiting in a queue that snaked along the pavement. Trixie eased her gas-mask case, which had been digging into her hip, onto her lap. 'Shall we get off at the next stop and walk down Molesworth Road towards Alver Bridge?'

Vi's mother lived three doors away from the Robin Hood public house, near Workhouse Lake, overshadowed by the gasometer. It was an extremely poor area where people spoke with fists rather than words.

Vi nodded. Trixie knew that if it hadn't been for her mother, Alice, Vi wouldn't have wanted to return to Gosport, certainly not to the hovel where she'd been brought up and where her mother's boyfriend, Alec, had broken into her bedroom while she was sleeping. It had been Alice's idea that she become a lumberjill and live away from home. Alec, with his Brylcreemed hair and chiselled jaw, quite a ladies' man, was a bookie's runner for Billy Hill, the London gangster, and took care of black-market business in Gosport for him.

When they reached Alver Bridge, Trixie paused to watch the swans swimming among the broken bedsteads and rusty bicycle frames in the muddy water of the creek. With her arm tucked into Vi's, she could feel her friend shivering, despite the heavy coat she wore. 'I know you didn't want to come back to your house but we need to find out which ward your mum's in and Irene can tell us that.'

'I suppose so,' Vi agreed. Skirting the dogs' mess that

dotted the broken paving stones, they carried on until they reached the door of Vi's mum's house.

Nothing had changed since the last time Trixie had stood outside the paint-blistered front door. Vi fumbled in her shoulder bag for the key. Unlike where Trixie's mum lived in Alma Street, keys were never left on pieces of string down this road. Trixie knew that would be an invitation to burglars. The broken letterbox was still packed with cardboard to keep out the draught. Vi inserted her key into the lock.

'It won't move,' she said. She wiggled the key. 'The door won't open.'

Trixie looked down at her feet where an empty crisps bag had lodged itself behind a dirty milk bottle.

'Is it the right key?' She received a withering glance from Vi, who removed her key and re-inserted it in the lock.

'The door must be bolted on the inside,' Vi said. 'I'd better ask Irene what's going on.' She slipped the key back into her pocket and grabbed Trixie's arm, pulling her away from the overgrown garden out through the broken gate and towards the tidier house next door.

After Vi banged loudly on the knocker, the net curtain moved and Irene peered out. Seeing Vi and Trixie, she mouthed, 'Just a minute,' and attempted a smile. Within moments she'd opened her front door. Her hair was tied up in a turban but it didn't disguise that her face was blotchy with tears.

'Irene, I can't get inside the house.'

Irene threw herself into Vi's arms, then stepped back. 'Oh, my love, my love,' she said. 'You're too late. I'm so sorry. She's gone. I walked up to the telephone box on the corner several days ago to phone the War Memorial Hospital to find out what kind of night she'd had and they told me she'd gone in the early hours.'

Vi stood quite still, gazing at Irene as if she hadn't understood a word of what she'd said. 'But I've come to see . . .'

Irene grabbed her and pulled her indoors. Trixie followed as Irene pushed open the door to the living room and sat Vi down at the table. The small room was crowded with furniture: a large table and four chairs in the middle and a sideboard pushed against the wall, two armchairs at either side of the fireplace. A framed print of *The Laughing Cavalier* faced *Bubbles* on the opposite wall. A small fire in the grate warmed the room. The smell of polish dominated.

'A cup of tea,' Irene said. 'Trixie, put the kettle on.' She waved a hand towards the scullery.

Vi shook her head. 'No, no tea,' she said. 'Tell me what ward Mum's on. I must go to her . . .'

'You're not listening to me, lovey. I said your mum's gone. She died. I wrote to you immediately,' Irene said.

All at once Vi's face creased, like a crumpled piece of paper, and she began to cry. Trixie slipped an arm around her shoulders. There didn't seem any point in her saying anything to try to make things better because there was nothing she could say or do that would take away Vi's pain. She moved around to the side of the chair and Vi held on to her, sobbing noisily.

Irene left them and Trixie cuddled Vi close while her tears flowed. From the scullery she heard the pop of the gas as Irene lit the flame on the stove beneath the kettle.

Vi's body heaved and shook.

Trixie had met Alice only once, when she'd spent the night at their home. Vi's mum had been unable to climb the stairs because the consumption made it difficult for her to breathe and to walk about. She'd practically lived downstairs. Irene had gone in every day to wash her and make meals, and every evening, she put Alice to bed in the front room. Trixie and Alice had immediately liked each other. Remembering brought tears to Trixie's eyes but she knew she had to be strong because Vi needed her. She was still holding her friend when Irene brought in a tray complete with teapot, milk, and cups and saucers stacked neatly.

'I only got your letter saying she was in hospital yesterday.' Vi wiped a hand across her wet eyes.

'Bloody post!' exclaimed Irene. 'I wrote as soon as they took her into the War Memorial. Everything happened quickly after that.' She paused. 'I've written another letter, told you all about it.' Vi was staring at Irene as if she'd been suddenly struck dumb. Trixie could see fresh tears welling in her eyes as she shook her head, trying to make sense of the older woman's words.

She waited for Vi to say something else about her mum but Vi sniffed, then asked, 'How come I couldn't open the front door? I used my key but the lock wouldn't turn.'

'I've locked up your house as securely as I can. That Alec has been nosing around. I guessed there'd be personal things in there that your mum wanted you to have. Once he finds out she's gone . . .' Irene hesitated, as if it was very difficult for her to speak. 'Once he discovers the place is empty, he'll go through it like a dose of salts, selling the furniture, taking whatever he fancies.'

'That's good thinking on your part,' said Trixie. 'But didn't someone say he'd left Gosport?' Vi was breathing quickly. Trixie knew she was still very frightened of the awful man.

Vi used the back of her hand to wipe her eyes, then said bitterly, 'He's like a cockroach, difficult to get rid of.'

For a moment there was silence, then Vi said thoughtfully, 'Irene, I've never really thanked you for all you've done for me and Mum. I do appreciate it.'

'I know that,' Irene said. She began pouring tea. 'Your mum had a small insurance policy to pay for her burial. She gave it to me some time ago for safekeeping . . .' She trailed off then continued, 'She always anticipated more trouble from that Alec. I've got some of her other important papers, birth certificates and her marriage lines, put away. She said you wouldn't want to keep stuff like that in your suitcase, not when your job could take you travelling all over the country. There's no money, I'm afraid. But you know that, don't you?'

Vi gave a tight smile of acknowledgement. 'Funeral? I haven't thought about a funeral.'

'Of course not, why would you? At the hospital I asked for her death certificate, love.' Irene took a handkerchief from her pocket and blew her nose. As soon as she'd tucked it inside her sleeve, her eyes became moist again. 'The funeral had to be arranged as soon as possible, what with the bombing being heavy in this area.'

Vi looked stricken.

'It's tomorrow, love. I told you in my latest letter.'

Irene was apologetic, even though Trixie knew she

Rosie Archer

certainly wasn't to blame for irregular postal deliveries to Scotland.

Vi looked at Trixie. 'Do you think Mr MacKay will mind if we stay in Gosport a bit longer?'

'Even if he does, I'm sure Morag will sort him out.' Trixie turned to Irene. 'She's our boss's housekeeper,' she said. 'She's quite old. She's very fond of him but I sometimes wonder who rules the roost, him or her.'

Irene smiled. 'I had to make all the arrangements, love,' she said. 'I know she wanted to be buried at Ann's Hill cemetery.'

Vi's eyes refilled with tears. 'You did all that for her, for me?'

'Of course. Look, love, me and your mum went to infants' school together. There wasn't much we didn't know about each other. The service is at St Mary's, Alverstoke, at two o'clock.'

Vi smiled, her eyes wet. 'Thank you. Now I know why you were her best friend.'

Irene looked embarrassed. 'Have you both got some-where to sleep tonight?' She turned from Vi to Trixie.

'We're going to my mum's in Alma Street,' Trixie told her.

Irene nodded. 'Well, before you go up to the War Memorial Hospital to see your mum – she's still there because the local funeral parlours are fit to bursting with bodies – would you like me to come into your house with you? We can get in at the back. If there's stuff you want, framed photos, keepsakes, you can leave them here with me. I'll look after everything.' She paused. 'Your house, being rented . . .' she took a sip of her tea '. . . well, the landlord'll want it back, won't he? So many people have been bombed out and have nowhere to live.'

Vi's face fell and her eyes darkened. 'Such a lot to do and in only a little time,' she said. Then, 'I don't want to go inside that house ever again. There are too many bad memories for me. I only want a couple of photographs. Both are in the front room. One's of my dad and me, I'm on his shoulders. And facing it, so Mum could see it from where she lay on the sofa, is her and Dad's wedding picture.'

Irene nodded. 'I understand. Leave it to me, love.'

Chapter Fourteen

'You didn't let me know you were coming home, Trixie. Frightened the life out of me, appearing in the kitchen large as life when I'd only just seen Des off to work on his night shift.' Rose Smith smoothed back her hair and stabbed a grip into it to stop it falling in front of her right ear again. 'Of course I'm pleased to see you, both of you,' she added, looking at the bunk beds and the outline of Vi beneath blankets on the top one. 'I only wish it was under better circumstances.'

'So do we, Mum. There wasn't time. And it would have been much nicer to spend the night in my old room instead of in the garden. But go on, tell me why you want to postpone marrying Des.'

'It makes perfect sense for us to wait until the spring before we have the wedding.'

Trixie stared at her mother in her flowered cotton wrap-around pinafore as she took in her words. 'You do still care about each other?'

She would have liked to ask if her mother and Des were still in love but it didn't seem quite right to enquire about her mother's love life. Especially as they were sitting in the Anderson air-raid shelter at the bottom of the garden while German bombs fell over Alma Street and the rest of the south of England. Of course they were in love, she mentally chided herself. You only had to watch them interact to see how much they cared about each other.

'Of course!' Rose sighed. 'But it's difficult to think about a wedding and all it entails when everything is in such short supply, especially just before Christmas. That can be an awful expense.'

Trixie felt a stab of guilt pierce her heart. There didn't seem to be a shortage of food on the MacKay Estate. Probably because Morag wrung chickens' necks and told them Duncan the gillie had recently shot a lame deer and set traps for rabbits.

Planes were roaring overhead. Even though she was under cover Trixie automatically ducked as she heard the scream of a falling bomb. The tension in her stomach knotted as she waited for the missile to land. The blast of high explosive ripped through buildings somewhere close outside and the shelter seemed to tilt and move with the force from it.

Rose grabbed the metal frame of the bottom bunk as though holding on to it would stop it toppling and cause the sleeping Vi to tumble to the earthen floor of the shelter.

The sudden silence that followed was almost deafening.

'That was close,' said Rose. 'I hope it's not our house.' Trixie saw her mother's face was white with worry. The smell of burning mixed with cordite was seeping into the small shelter.

'I hope it's no one's house, but I fear it is,' said Trixie.

Vi sleepily peeped from beneath a blanket. 'What's that?' Her voice was heavy, her face still puffy from the tears she'd shed earlier. Rose stood, sweeping up her knitting that had slid to the ground and placed it on her bed. She stretched up, put her face close to Vi's on the top bunk and said softly, 'It's gone now, Vi, love. You're safe, go back to sleep.' Surprisingly, thought Trixie, Vi did exactly as she was told.

The noise started again. Bombs were falling but now they seemed further away. Trixie knew the Germans were aiming for Portsmouth Dockyard, the armament depots and the airfields at Lee-on-the-Solent. Gosport simply got in the way of the enemy's bombing.

Rose used a match to light the Primus stove after shaking the kettle to gauge its water level. She smiled at Trixie. 'We'll have a mug of tea.' She felt around in a brown carrier bag with string handles and took out a green and black Peek Freans biscuit tin with deer and trees on the sides. It made Trixie think suddenly of Sutherland and how peaceful it was there. 'I've got some bread pudding in here. It's fresh – I made it yesterday,' Rose said. Then, while she waited for the kettle to boil, she sat down on her bunk again and began talking as if the bomb falling so close had never happened at all.

'I've set my heart on a honeymoon, a few days in Bognor Regis, and I want a proper sit-down meal after the wedding for the guests. I want a cake so Des and I can cut it together, and send everyone home with a little piece to put beneath their pillows and make a wish on.' Rose paused. 'I suppose you know that bakers are making cardboard cakes for weddings and christenings, with chalk icing? The damn Ministry of Food has forbidden sugar to be put on the outside of a cake! Can you imagine that?'

Trixie couldn't think of anything more awful. Except perhaps sitting in the waiting room at the hospital earlier today, worrying about Vi while she spent time alone with her dead mother in a tiny room off the ward. Vi needed time to say goodbye, of course she did, but Trixie was relieved when she emerged and asked if they could go home to Trixie's mum's house, where Rose had taken charge and settled Vi in bed with a hot-water bottle for comfort. And there Vi had stayed, sleeping, until Moaning Minnie was wailing, warning people to go to the shelters as enemy aircraft were approaching.

Now Vi huddled into the blankets on the top bunk. Every so often she snuffled and made an involuntary hiccuping sound because today she had shed so many tears.

Inside the corrugated-iron shelter, which was approximately six feet by four, half buried inside the ground and with more earth covering it, it was as cosy as Rose could make it. There was a camp bed, which Trixie now sat on, bunks and the Primus stove. Des had put it all together next to the lavatory at the bottom of the garden. It had cost seven pounds. Many people qualified for free shelters if their wages were less than five pounds a week, but with Des working nights as a porter at the hospital and Rose a cleaner there, their combined take-home pay just topped that.

'How's Hen and Jo?' Rose asked. She put down her knitting and looked at her daughter.

'They're both fine,' Trixie answered. Well, Jo was. She didn't want to talk about Hen pulling the lorry to a standstill while she heaved the early breakfast Morag had made them eat into the clumps of heather at the side of the road as they'd driven to Lairg station today. She'd promised Hen she'd keep the secret about the baby and she didn't intend to break her word.

'What's Morag like?'

Trixie smiled. 'Like a mother hen and not only to us. To Noah MacKay as well.'

'Do you get on with Mr MacKay?'

'So far we've not had much to do with him, Mum. He's an Englishman and a bit posh, rather like Hen. He expected the Forestry Commission to send him four men and when we arrived it upset his plans . . .' She went on tell Rose all that had happened, interspersed with a few giggles about being locked outside in the rain on their first night and how the sheltering sheep had scared Jo.

After she'd made a pot of tea, Rose went on with her knitting. She was using four steel needles to make socks for Des. Trixie could tell her mother enjoyed being with her again, just chatting, like old times. 'Mr MacKay's room is way down the landing, Mum, but I heard him cry out in his sleep, last night. He walks with a stick. I think he was injured early on in the war. He's certainly not old – he reminds me of Alan Ladd, the film star,' she said.

Rose frowned.

'Don't you remember? We went to the Criterion picture-house to see *Meet the Missus* about a year ago. Alan Ladd played John Williams, the daughter's boyfriend, and you thought he was really good-looking.'

Rose smiled, 'Oh, yes, I remember now. He was the lawyer.' A dreamy look came into her eyes. 'Blond hair?'

'That's him,' said Trixie. 'Noah MacKay's got blond hair as well.'

'Well, good-looking Alan Ladd might be but I wouldn't swap my Des for him.'

Trixie laughed, 'I should hope not,' she said.

'And how's Cy getting on?' her mother asked.

Trixie sighed. 'I still haven't had another letter,' she said. 'I won't give up writing to him . . .'

Rose laid her knitting on the blanket covering the bottom bunk and leaned across to put her arms around Trixie. 'Good girl,' she said. Trixie could smell her mother's favourite rose perfume. 'You mustn't give up hope. There's probably some simple reason why you're not receiving letters from him at present. You might even get a huge pile all at once. There's all kinds of reasons why the post—'

'Do you really think so, Mum?' Trixie interrupted. After all, hadn't Vi's letter from Irene been delayed? Already she'd put Cy's photograph that she carried everywhere with her, and one letter, beneath her pillow. She so wanted to believe her mum.

Later, when only one candle remained, lighting the inside of the shelter, and Rose was snoring gently on the bottom bunk, Trixie took an envelope from beneath her pillow on the camp bed.

She knew that above Gosport the searchlights would be criss-crossing the night sky, searching for German planes. Buildings would be ablaze and smoke would be swirling like fog. Already she could hear the clanging of fire engines. Their hoses would be snaking across pavements and roads while brave men tried tirelessly to quench flames and save lives.

The paper in her hand crackled softly as she reread some of the sentences from Cy's letter,

My Darling

Never doubt my love for you, Trixie. I love you so much it hurts.

We came together, you and I, through forces beyond our control and I know you are the girl I've waited my whole life to meet. When

I saw you sitting alone in the cabin on that ferryboat something clicked inside my heart, and like it happens in films or in books,

Rosie Archer

I fell in love with you, hook, line and sinker.

I've written to my ma about you and she's longing to meet the girl I've chosen to spend the rest of my life with. I've written several letters to you, hoping you'll get at least one of them. I can't tell you where I'm going or why, that's not allowed. I can tell you I share a bunk room with other guys, among them Hobo, who plays the harmonica all the time.

I have a request to make. Could you send me a photograph to pin above my bunk so I can see you when I close my eyes and when I wake up?

Yours Cy xxxxxxxxxxxxxxxxxxxxxxxxxxxxxxxxxxxxxxxxxxxxxxx
I will love you forever.

Trixie, holding the letter, fell asleep.

Chapter Fifteen

Trixie heard the soaring organ music coming from the church as she and Vi passed through the lichgate. She wondered how many coffins had waited there before being carried into the centuries-old church. Vi found her hand and squeezed it. Trixie returned the gesture.

'Ready?' Trixie asked, as they paused at the open doorway of Alverstoke's St Mary's Church. Vi nodded, then took a deep breath as they entered.

Irene, as if sensing Vi's nervousness, and wearing a hat that looked a little like an upside-down veiled mushroom, glanced round and saw them at the back of the church. Eyes swivelled in the direction of Irene's broad smile as she beckoned them towards her, where she had reserved their rightful spaces in the front pew.

Walking down the aisle, glancing at the backs of the

heads of people present, Trixie felt Vi's hand tighten and her fingernails dig into her flesh so deeply that she tried to pull away.

'Ow!' Trixie breathed in deeply.

'It's Alec! I'm sure it's him!' whispered Vi, as they neared Irene.

Vi sat down and Trixie rubbed some feeling back into her hand, saying soothingly, 'He wouldn't dare come, not today.' She chanced a quick look behind her at the sea of faces. Vi was mistaken, wasn't she? Surely her nerves were playing tricks on her. Nevertheless, she could feel her shaking with fear.

Trixie heard Irene say softly to Vi, 'You look so lovely in your uniform, dearie. Cuddle in next to me if you want to, when they bring in your mum. She was always so proud of you.'

When the service was over, Vi stood in the weak sunshine beside Irene on the gravel path between the aged gravestones.

'I didn't know my mum had so many friends,' Vi whispered. Mourners crowded around, shaking her hand and whispering endearing comments, telling her how her mother's life had enriched theirs.

'Your mum was a popular girlie,' admitted Irene. 'It was only when she became ill and that devil took up with her that her friends dropped away. He made them feel so uncomfortable when they visited that they just stopped coming. I put a funeral notice in the *Evening News*,' she added, glancing back at the church door. 'There's the vicar. I just need to thank him.' And she was gone, pushing through the crowd.

'So sorry,' said a small woman, giving Vi a shy smile. 'I was at school with Alice. She was a good friend, used to let me copy her homework.'

Vi smiled at her and whispered, 'Thank you for coming,' as the woman sniffed into her handkerchief and moved on. Trixie could see her friend was practically at breaking point. She was so proud of the dignified way Vi was handling her sorrow, while commiserating with people she'd never met as they offered their condolences and hugged her. At last, the crowd of people around Vi and Trixie thinned out to single numbers.

Trixie heard Vi's sharp intake of breath and felt her stiffen. A sudden sense of dread engulfed Trixie as she smelt the muskiness of his unforgettable cologne almost at the same time as the well-dressed man in the dark suit enveloped Vi in his arms. She heard Alec say smoothly, 'Scotland's a grand place, isn't it, Vi? Sutherland's so beautiful, I've

who drives birds out of the heather so they'll fly over people with shotguns.'

'That's horrible,' said Vi.

'Maybe,' answered Morag, 'but rich people pay a lot of money to shoot the birds. It's not how working people live, except to pander to the rich for wages. Those pursuits aren't for the likes of us.'

'I don't think Noah's father sounds a nice person,' said Trixie. She helped herself to another piece of shortbread.

'Well, I used to think that,' said Morag. 'He was always trying to chase dreams he didnae quite catch. It wasn't until after he was dead I found out he'd fallen in love with a wee servant girl working at the North British Railway Hotel, when it opened in Edinburgh. 1902 that would have been. She fell with a bairn. He couldnae marry a chambermaid, could he? Not the done thing to wed beneath him. She was sent back, in disgrace, to England. Doris, the wee lassie, died giving birth to Noah.'

'So Noah never knew his mother?'

Morag shook her head at Hen's question. 'All he has is a photograph. He keeps it in his room. She was a pretty little thing, masses of piled-up hair. Just a wee bairn herself, really.' Morag's eyes misted.

'And his father? Does Noah look like him?'

175

'Almost a mirror image, Jo. Blond, good-looking . . .'

'How did Noah survive?' Hen asked.

'He was left with his grandparents down south. They didnae really want him. When he was old enough he was sent to boarding school. Rufus didnae see his son but he paid to have him well educated.'

'A good education doesn't take the place of love,' Hen remarked.

'No, and you'd know all about that, lassie,' said Morag.

For a moment there was only the crackling of the fire and the ticking of the clock on the mantelpiece to be heard. Then Morag continued, 'Rufus had nae more children. He didnae marry. I believe he had truly loved Doris . . .'

'Such a waste of lives,' said Trixie.

'Aye,' said Morag. 'Noah was in hospital when the solicitor tracked him down to tell him of his inheritance, here in Scotland. He's practically bankrupted himself trying to get this place on its feet again.'

'Does Noah have money, then?' The words slipped from Jo's mouth.

'Not now. He had some when he was discharged from the army. He was in hospital for a long time. His leg wouldnae heal properly. Dunkirk, that was,' Morag said.

'He has nightmares,' said Trixie. 'I've heard him, poor man.'

'He was an officer,' said Morag. 'Stayed on the beach checking for men who were still alive after the awfu' carnage. He dragged a superior officer to safety, saved his life, he did. The things Noah's seen and experienced willnae leave his head. He's a good man. That's why selling the timber on his land for the highest price is so important to him. He needs to repair his crofters' homes. He wants to make this estate something to be proud of once more. I think he wants to right his father's wrongs.'

A heavy gust of wind sent something metallic skittering along the gravel outside.

Morag rose from her chair. 'I think the washing needs to be brought in, if it's still there.'

Chapter Seventeen

'I've been meaning to walk on this beach since the night we arrived and I first heard the sea,' said Trixie. 'It's even more beautiful than I expected.'

Hen linked arms with her. 'If only it wasn't so windy.'

'I don't mind the wind,' Trixie answered. 'See how the late-afternoon sun's rays touch the sand making it glitter like silver?' She gazed at the half-moon shape of the beach leading towards the long stone pier where spumes of angry sea crashed into the rocks, then shot high into the air to fall back into the water in a froth of white waves.

It was a lonely beach. Hen walked ahead while Trixie stopped to peer into a rock pool. She recognized winkles clinging to stones, like garden snails. Seaweed, green and brown, shiny and slippery. Small fly-like creatures that darted to and fro over the pool's sheltered stillness. A tiny crab, as small as her little fingernail, scuttled from the sand to beneath a wet rock. It was like a miniature world in the shallow water, she thought.

She and Hen were the only people on the beach despite the magnificent beauty around them. Vi and Jo had preferred to help Morag in the kitchen with the preparation of the evening meal. All this perfection and only them sharing it, she thought. Yet it was impossible to imagine families having summer picnics with young children, laughing, screaming, playing and building sandcastles here. Not like Stokes Bay in Gosport where, at the merest hint of brightness, people came out to sunbathe on the stones. Children learned to swim among the seaweed. Granddads sat on the sand in socks, with large handkerchiefs knotted at the corners to protect their heads from the sun, while grandmothers, with their knitting, occupied deckchairs, with flasks of tea at their feet. That wasn't a lonely beach. Even in the depths of winter it was a haven for walkers with their dogs, lovers, bait-diggers intent on fishing, and anyone looking for peace from the overcrowded streets of Gosport. When Trixie caught up with Hen, they gazed out at the sea, which seemed endless, grey and angry.

'See that big bird? What is it?'

Hen followed Trixie's pointing finger to the end of the

pier where, perched on a spar, a lone bird opened its wings and flapped them furiously before settling back to its watch over the water.

Hen said, 'That's a cormorant, or maybe a shag, same family. I can't see from here if it's got a head tuft.'

'But it's as big as a goose!'

'They dive very deep for food and eat anything from octopus to shellfish. Some people say they smell bad.'

Trixie was still watching the bird. 'Well, eating stuff like that, no wonder. There's so much wildlife up here I never knew existed.' She smiled at Hen. 'Don't tell me, you were taught about birds at school.'

'Of course,' said Hen. 'Didn't your teachers give you books on ornithology?'

'Whatever for?' Trixie asked, 'Sparrows, pigeons and sea-gulls, that's Gosport's birdlife.' She laughed. 'Oh, Hen, I do love you,' she said. 'Anything I ask, you always know the answer.'

'I didn't do so well when Morag was asking me questions, though, did I? I feel foolish now for crying like that, especially when I've brought everything on myself.'

'You can stop with the self-pity,' Trixie said quickly. 'You've got a damned good friend in Morag.' She thought for a moment. 'And Noah MacKay is turning out to be a decent bloke, after all.'

'You think I don't know that?'

The wind had pinked Hen's cheeks and pulled strands of her blonde hair from the plaits pinned across her head. Looking at her, Trixie was suddenly reminded of cherubs in old paintings. 'You'll keep the baby?'

Hen stared at her through narrowed eyes. 'Somehow, yes. I'm not even going to think about giving up him or her. You see, Trixie, I've never had anything, or anybody, of my own until now.' Hen placed her hands protectively over her stomach.

Tears sprang to Trixie's eyes but she blinked them away and the wind dried them, as she said, 'You're not alone.' She put her arms around Hen.

After a while Hen moved away. 'What do you really feel about Noah MacKay, Trixie?'

Trixie took her time in answering. Out here, away from the safety of the kitchen and the estate, she had time to think. High above the heathery hills, the sheep sheltering from the wind beside stone walls, the cloud-topped peaks of Ben Loyal and Ben Hope looked down over Talmine and the isolated croft houses.

Trixie breathed deeply of the fresh, salt-laden atmosphere.

Everything smelt so new and clean, she thought, as if nobody had ever used the air or sea before. The sea was right in the heart of Gosport, at the ferry, she mused, but the water smelt of oil from the boats and stuff left to rot in the mud. Also, there was spillage from factories that teetered on the edges of Gosport's creeks, which were usually decorated with sunken boats, unwanted household objects and broken bicycles. So many pubs lined Gosport's high street that the stink of ale never went away. Dirty old town. Bomb-damaged, broken Gosport, smelling of burned buildings and cordite. Two places, Gosport and Talmine, one at each end of the British Isles but so vastly different. Yet Trixie knew Talmine could never occupy the space in her heart that was Gosport's.

Noah MacKay? A man fighting demons in his head, scarred not only by the terrors he'd witnessed at Dunkirk but left with a shattered leg as a memento of saving another man's life.

Trixie had been hurt by Noah's narrow, biased view that, as women, they didn't know how to do the work they'd been trained for. It was definitely a man's world, in which women had to defer to husbands, to fathers, before they could make decisions. Slowly it was changing, especially now women could vote. It was silly for her to stay angry with the man who had purchased a wireless set so they could enjoy music in the house. A small beginning, maybe. But Noah had tried to make amends, which showed he had a good heart. And wasn't that what Morag was trying to impress upon them? A man who had saved another man's life and was determined to redress his father's misdeeds couldn't be all bad, could he?

Trixie looked at Hen. 'I think Noah's a decent bloke at heart. He must be, or Morag wouldn't care so much about him. And to save another man's life . . .' Her voice tailed off. Then she said firmly, 'I want to stay here and work with him. I've every faith in you and your calculations for the estate and I'm positive the Forestry Commission will too, so I'm going to help get this country back on its feet by chopping down plenty of lumber. That's why I joined the Timber Corps. Hitler can go to Hell!'

'I'm with you all the way,' Hen said, a big smile decorating her face. 'I think this is a wonderful place to be. I love the mountains, the sea, the space to think and be. And when Noah MacKay returns home later today, we'll find out exactly what his plans for us are. I know I'm pregnant but I'm feeling so well now. Did you notice I wasn't sick this morning? I long to be out in the forests, working again. These past few days of not doing manual labour have made me realize just how much I miss working.'

'Noah MacKay must like us, Hen. He's bought us a wireless set, hasn't he?'

'Ha! If he thinks he's bought me off with a peace-offering . . .' Hen retorted.

Trixie saw they had completed an almost circular walk of the beach and the hillside above it and were looking at the high walls surrounding the MacKay Estate. Inside the open gateway stood the green Morgan roadster. Trixie had a sudden memory of herself, Hen, Vi and Jo, wet and cold, on a filthy night, outside that gate and anxious to enter. Such a lot had happened since then.

'The laird's back,' Trixie said.

'The ignoramus!' said Hen. But she said it with a smile.

'C'mon, you don't really mean that.'

'I did when I first said it.'

Noah MacKay sat at the kitchen table, his cane hooked over the back of his chair. He was eating a Fly Cemetery and appeared to be thoroughly enjoying it. Several currants had fallen, unnoticed, to his shirt front. A full mug of tea sat at his elbow. Hen's open notebook was in front of him. Used crockery lay on the table, with a plate of the remaining shortbread.

'Enjoyed your walk along the shore?' he asked. Music was coming from the wireless.

Trixie wriggled out of her coat. 'It's beautiful down there but it's a lonely place.' She hung her coat on the stand with Hen's. She had almost forgotten how cold it was outside until she felt the warmth from the fire.

'Not when the fishermen are there or when the Highland cattle stand around on the sand.'

Trixie saw Hen smother a smile. With his other hand Noah brushed his blond hair off his forehead, but it promptly fell back. The faint smell of his spicy cologne wafted over to her.

'Where is everyone?' Hen asked.

'Morag, Jo and Vi are in the big barn sorting out a few things. My father had a habit of leaving stuff in there that might become damp if left in this house. Good thinking, that was. Rory McCullum has been paid for tuning the piano . . .'

Trixie gasped. Noah smiled at her. 'You've Morag to thank for that. She said you can play.'

'Play?' Hen squealed. 'She only has to hear a tune once and she can repeat it note for note.'

'I believe you played in the Yellow Duck for Donnie McKay.'

Noah laughed at Trixie's surprise. 'A relative of his owns

the post office in Bettyhill and told me all about you. You can't keep secrets up here,' he said. 'I only went in to use the telephone and then to the garage next door to have them put the spare wireless accumulator on charge and came out knowing practically all your life stories.'

'I don't know what to say.' Trixie had so missed playing the piano, pouring out her emotions as her fingers touched the keys. And for Morag to think of her and arrange to have the piano tuned . . .

'George from the post office assures me you're a damn good pianist and that Donnie thinks a lot of you. Apparently, he gives glowing accounts of you all. He said you were very popular with his customers.' Trixie looked at Hen, whose face had coloured. She was indeed very popular with the male customers – Trixie sincerely hoped that wasn't what he had meant.

'Oh, don't worry,' Noah added. 'He only told me good things.' He laughed again. A sound that came from deep inside him. A friendly, caring laugh. Trixie breathed a sigh of relief. She was stepping from one foot to the other, eager to be off to the barn and the piano.

Noah picked up Hen's notebook. 'The Forestry Commission have promised me twenty Italian prisoners of war, to be driven daily, with their own tools, from Earls

Cross House, a forestry work camp in Dornoch, to work alongside you. You will, in effect, be in charge of them, and my other men, of course. I'll be there as much as I can, but I'm sure you'll manage. The cut lumber will be stacked at each site ready to be regularly collected by road, then travel onwards by rail to Lachlan MacLeod's sawmill near Brechin, in Angus.' He paused. 'I know you've all met him. Mr MacLeod on the telephone spoke very highly of you, Jo especially . . .'

At this Trixie saw Hen smiling back at her. Jo had been offered a prestigious job at the sawmill and had refused it, preferring to be with her friends. The death of her baby and her mother-in-law in Gosport's bombing and notification that her husband was missing, believed killed in action, meant she hadn't been ready to start a new independent life in Brechin.

Hen's eyes left hers and moved to Noah MacKay's. Trixie had the most peculiar feeling that they had forgotten she was there.

Noah was talking to Hen. 'I couldn't have secured this deal without your notebook. I see now how pathetic my own efforts at business were. I'm sorry I thought so little of you when you arrived on that dreadful night. I most humbly apologize. You've put a great deal of thought and energy into planning exactly what is needed to make the MacKay Estate a viable operation. Thank you. Because of you, I can do so much for the people who have been trying to farm my land. When the government money starts trickling through . . .'

Trixie couldn't help herself. 'Don't they release it immediately?'

Noah turned to her. 'Unfortunately not, but much of the initial expense will be borne by the authorities. It will be tough going financially until the scheme is up and running. When that occurs, it might even be possible to start repairs on the place.' He waved the hand holding the notebook around the room. Then he turned back to Hen. 'Thank you,' he said.

Trixie sighed. 'Look, you two don't really need me here, do you? You're going to talk facts, figures and other things I don't want to know about. I'm just pleased we didn't come all the way here only to go back again because we haven't a job.'

It also occurred to her that she had an awful lot of news to put in a letter to Cy.

She looked imploringly at Hen, then at Noah. She wanted to be in the barn with the piano. She gave another dramatic sigh.

'Oh, buzz off, then,' said Hen, smiling at her.

Chapter Eighteen

'Alvar Lidell's news on the wireless that Stuttgart has been heavily bombed by our RAF boys is good, isn't it?' Jo pulled her flannelette nightgown over her head and wriggled her way inside the covers on the bed. Her movements made the candle on the chair by the side of the bed flicker.

'Not when ten of our aircraft are missing,' Vi said, climbing in beside her. 'I don't mind sleeping with you, Jo. You stay so warm you make the bed like an oven.'

'Glad I'm of use,' Jo replied.

Trixie doused the paraffin lamp Morag had lit earlier. She, like Hen, Jo and Vi, preferred candles to the smell of burning paraffin. She'd been writing a letter to Cy.

'Wasn't it lovely all of us singing around the piano?' Vi added.

'I was surprised at Morag's husband joining in. We don't see much of Angus, do we?' Jo said.

'We see more of him than the mysterious gillie, Duncan,' said Vi.

'Neither is around much, probably because both men's jobs are away from this house. Duncan has a small croft somewhere near the beach. His work takes him all over the estate, out in the forests, hills, and watching for illegal salmon fishermen and hunters, Morag told me. Angus has to spread himself about, fixing the outhouses and looking after the animals.'

'I agree,' said Trixie. 'Mairi from the dairy is the helper I've never yet met.' She laughed. Mairi came in very early a few mornings a week.

'Ouch!' Hen, in front of the mirror, was trying to brush out a tangle in her long hair and losing her temper.

'I'm going to cut this lot off one day!' she snapped. Earlier she'd dabbed on Guerlain's Shalimar perfume, and its exotic smell overpowered the mould and made the bedroom smell heavenly. Her silky nightdress clung to her like a second skin.

'Why on earth are you wearing a flimsy thing like that?' asked Vi. 'It can't possibly keep you warm and when the temperature drops in here which it always does, you'll likely freeze to death!' She gave Hen a look of scorn.

'It makes me feel nice! Besides, Morag won't let me wander around downstairs, where it's warmer, dressed in this, will she?'

'I should think not!' snapped Vi. 'You'd likely make Noah's eyes pop out of his head.'

'So, just because he's a man, I can't wear what I like?' Hen ran the brush down her hair and let out a sharp exclamation when it discovered another knot.

'Give me that brush,' said Trixie, trying to defuse the situation between Vi and Hen. Hen's new-found freedom from her parents' control was causing her to question discipline in all forms. 'Now sit still while I do it. And don't come out with stupid things like you'll cut your hair off. "A woman's hair is her crowning glory." That's what my mum says.'

'It's from the Bible, Corinthians, I think.' Hen said sulkily, 'Ouch! That hurt!'

'Don't be a baby. Anyway, it's out now.' Trixie gave the hairbrush back to Hen, with the offending knot hanging from it. 'Who'd have thought Noah would have such a good voice?' she added.

'And know all the words to most of the songs you played!' sang Jo.

'Yes, that was a surprise,' Hen said. 'He's not so bad, is he?'

'Well, you should know. I left you talking to him when I went to the barn to find out if the piano had been tuned properly. What did you talk about?' Trixie asked.

If she'd expected Hen to blush at the two of them having been alone together, she was disappointed. Hen answered in a monotone: 'Work, trees, how not to upset his regular workers when the Italians arrive . . .'

'Upset his regular work force?' Vi's voice was practically a shriek. 'They want sacking, the lot of them. Not Andy, though, he's all right.'

'You liked him, didn't you, Vi?' Jo said seriously.

'I did,' she answered. Then her face reddened. 'We were friendly. I can't think about men when I know that Alec could be out there somewhere ready to pounce on me.'

'He said all those horrible things to frighten you, Vi. The last time you saw him he was in the churchyard in Alverstoke, England. You're in Scotland now so I think you're pretty safe,' Trixie reminded her. But she, like Vi, would never forget the man who'd crashed into their bedroom on the one night she'd shared with Vi at her home in Gosport. He'd thought Vi was alone.

'So, Lachlan MacLeod's been asking about you.' Hen stared at Jo, who was blushing furiously. 'And not just once.'

'I was interested in what went on at his sawmill when

we visited and seriously considered his offer of a job there. However, I preferred to stay with you. I'm beginning to wonder why I bothered, though,' Jo added. 'I wish you'd stop making something out of nothing.'

'You must have made a good impression on him if he keeps asking after you,' Hen said.

'Shut up,' snapped Jo. 'I'm not ready to even think about another man. I had a family and I lost them in this bloody war, remember?'

Her icy words caused a sudden silence in the room until Trixie ended it, saying, 'Why are we arguing? We've all played a part in helping Noah MacKay keep us employed for the Women's Timber Corps. And I'm grateful and happy to be working in the forest again. Our wages are secure, the Home Timber Production Services will see to that, and that's all down to Hen. So, she deserves a vote of thanks, I'd say.'

'Yes, well done, Hen,' said Vi.

'Thank you, Hen,' said Jo. 'You know I don't mean it when I go off at the deep end, don't you?'

Hen grinned at her. 'If I don't know you now, I never will,' she said.

Trixie hadn't finished. 'I've had an idea . . .'

'Oh dear,' Hen said, climbing into the double bed she

shared with Trixie. Another waft of Shalimar filled Trixie's senses.

'Let me speak,' Trixie said. 'So far, we've been eating extremely well, better than a lot of people back home in Gosport, I should imagine. Morag is lovely to us.' She waved a hand around the room. 'We've comfortable lodgings.'

'Damp and draughty.' Vi pulled a face.

'Well, I expect some of the other lumberjills are living in much worse conditions than this,' Hen said. She pulled the blankets up around herself.

'My home in Gosport was awful,' confided Vi. 'Mushrooms growing out of the walls.'

'As I was saying,' said Trixie, 'Noah MacKay is still finding funding difficult until the government's money comes through. What if we organize a ceilidh and hand him the proceeds?'

The silence could have been cut with a knife. Then . . .

'That's the daftest idea you've ever come up with,' said Jo. 'I've agreed with every word that's come out of your mouth until now.'

'We could hold it in the big barn,' said Vi, 'charge people to come. Ceilidh and dance.' Her voice grew higher as the idea rooted and her excitement took over. 'Morag could bake cakes, sell her ginger beer . . .'

'Excuse me!' said Jo. 'I don't know if you've ever noticed but nobody lives around here, except sheep and cows.'

'We can make posters and put them up in the post office and the garage at Bettyhill.'

'Won't take long to make two posters, will it?' Jo said. There was sarcasm in her voice.

'I just happen to think we've been treated well by Noah and Morag and I'd like to do something to show my appreciation. That's all,' Trixie insisted

'Don't be a sourpuss, Jo,' Vi put in. 'Once people get to know, I'm sure they'll come. It could be a night to remember.'

Trixie hadn't seen Vi so animated since before the news of her mother's death. It was good to see her excited again, she thought. She also realized that Hen hadn't put forward her point of view. 'What do you think, Hen?'

Hen was sitting up in bed with her arms around her knees. 'I think we took a liberty taking no notice of Noah MacKay's wishes when he told us to leave his house.'

'But—'

'Please let me finish, Vi. I was determined to show that man I knew my job, when he believed I, as a woman, was ignorant about the forestry business.' She looked at Trixie. 'I went along with your idea, I might add, Trix, out of spite.

I wrongly believed he felt he was superior to us, with his accent and his public-school background. I made the same mistake people make about me! How stupid is that? It never dawned on me that he needed help. He had no idea how to ask for it, especially from us – perhaps he was afraid to. We were so lucky everything worked out the way it did.' Here she paused, then gave a long sigh.

'I believe Noah MacKay is now angry with himself for jumping to wrong conclusions. I also think he's . . . how shall I put it? . . . hurt that he had no control.'

Hen stopped talking as if to let them assimilate her thoughts. Then she began again. 'Now, I honestly believe that a ceilidh, combined with a dance, would be a good way to make some money, and for people to meet us. From what I've heard, the locals love showing others their talents, singing, telling stories, whatever. Word of mouth works wonderfully up here. I'll bet there are fiddle and accordion players just waiting to be asked to play. And we've already got our own pianist.' She gestured at Trixie. 'But . . .' she paused again '. . . I only want to do this with Noah MacKay's blessing. If he says no, we don't go ahead.'

'How on earth can we get him to agree?' Vi's eyes were wide.

'We ask Morag first. Persuade her, before him. With

her help, it'll work. What do you think?' Hen was smiling broadly. 'What do you think, Trix?'

'That you're extremely clever, Hen.' She gave her a broad smile.

'Excellent idea,' Jo said. 'All in favour, say, "Aye."'

The resounding agreement was like music to Trixie's ears.

Later, as she sat in the sagging armchair next to the window with the blackout curtains tightly closed, Trixie listened to Hen, Vi and Jo making their usual nightly sounds as they slept. She'd doused all the candles except the one on the saucer beside her. Now she reread the letter she'd earlier finished writing to Cy.

My darling Cy

You are such an important part of my life that I can't imagine living without you. I know we'll have a wonderful and happy future together when this war is over. I bless the day we met on the ferry to Portsmouth. Until then I had never believed in love at first sight, but it was Fate that brought us together. And I know Fate will keep us together even though we're miles apart.

I hope you are well and thinking a lot about me. I think of you before I go to sleep and as soon as I'm awake. I haven't had a letter from you for ages but I expect it's difficult, you being on a ship and everything and doing important work. But I will go on writing, my love. I don't give up that easily!

Sutherland is a wild and lonely place. It rains a lot and is cold. But I'm happy that, due to Ken's clever calculations and understanding of forestry work, the four of us are going to stay together and work for Noah MacKay.

He has bought us a wireless set so there is music and news now. The best thing ever is that he has had the piano tuned that I wrote to you about. I played it for the first time tonight. It made me so happy especially when I played 'Dream a Little Dream of Me', because that song reminds me of you, of when I first saw you. You looked so handsome in your American naval uniform. And when you kissed me in the café at the station, I thought I had died and gone to Heaven. I wish we were back there now, together. Remember when I said, on the platform, I will love you 'until death us do part'? I meant it then, and I mean it now.

Your Trixie xxxxxxxxx BOLTOP (Better On Lips Than On Paper)

Trixie folded the pages, slipped the letter into an envelope and addressed it. She took the photograph of Cy from beneath her pillow and studied it. He had his arm across his best friend Hobo's shoulders and from the top of Hobo's shirt pocket she could see his beloved harmonica that he had played on the ferryboat. She smiled at Cy's tight curly dark hair and studied his humorous eyes that seemed to smile back at her. She kissed the photo, put it back beneath her pillow, then blew out the candle and snuggled down in the bed next to Hen. Taking a deep breath of Shalimar, she slept.

Chapter Nineteen

Trixie put her hands over her ears but she could still hear the dreadful clanging.

'What on earth is that?' she asked Morag, who had just removed a tray of oatcakes from the oven and was sliding them carefully onto a wire rack to cool. The bowl containing porridge oats, oatmeal, butter and salt awaited her further ministrations. Trixie, luxuriating in the heavenly smell in the kitchen, was sitting at the table reading one of the books she'd discovered in the big barn.

'Someone's at the main gate,' said Morag. Her mouth disappeared into a thin line before she added, 'Botheration!' It was the first time Trixie had heard the raucous bell, apart from the night they had first arrived, when they had been the ones to set it off.

The noise had brought Vi down from upstairs. She,

like Trixie, was dressed in her dungarees with a thick shirt underneath.

'What a row!' said Vi. 'Even that racket hasn't stopped Jo making plans in our room about the cei—' Seeing Trixie's horror-stricken face, she stopped short.

Trixie put her book face down on the table and glared at Vi, then got up, moved next to her and whispered, 'You know we said we'd talk to her when we're all together, and not before.'

Morag slid the last oatcake onto the rack and wiped her hands on her apron.

The strident clanging hadn't let up.

'Do you want me to go and see who that is, Morag?' Trixie took a step towards the door.

'No! Nobody answers the main door except me. I'm the housekeeper here, remember.'

Trixie took a step back. She'd never heard such harsh words from Morag before.

Morag gave an apologetic half-smile. 'The master and I are not in favour of people seeing and knowing what a state this fine house has fallen into. Tradesmen and friends use the back gate, as well you know. This person is unexpected.' She pulled her shawl around her thin body and marched off, at last, to answer the door.

Trixie pulled a face. 'That's us told, isn't it?' Then she added crossly, 'And you nearly let the cat out of the bag about the ceilidh.'

'Sorry, I forgot. I also forgot Hen went off with Noah to the forestry work camp in Dornoch. Not sure why he wanted her to go with him, though.'

Trixie sighed. 'It'll be about finalizing details of when we can start working with the Italian prisoners of war. Hen'll be needed to check their methods are similar to ours and to answer questions on forestry Noah's not familiar with.'

'Any one of us could have asked the prisoners if they knew how to chop down a tree!' Vi reached towards the rack for a cooling oatcake. Trixie slapped her hand away.

'Ouch!'

'Morag knows how many oatcakes she's baked. Just wait a few minutes and she'll give you some.'

'Trixie! Sometimes you're worse than my mum!'

Her words were automatically spoken before Vi registered what she'd said. And when realization took hold of her, she burst into tears. Trixie's arms went round her and Vi cried into her shoulder until she wiped her face on her long-sleeved shirt and said, in a small voice, 'I keep forgetting she's gone, Trix.'

'It was my fault for treating you like a child,' Trixie

couple chatted outside. She felt silly hanging around making small-talk when it was obvious Andy had driven a long way to see Vi. 'I'll be in there,' Trixie said, pointing to the barn. She smiled at them. 'If you need me for anything . . .' What could they possibly want her for? she thought, as she pushed open the large wooden door to the airy outbuilding.

The lorry was parked just inside and it was amazing how little room it took up in such a big space, Trixie thought. She walked alongside boxes of discarded house-hold goods and broken furniture, down to where the piano stood near the wall at the far end.

She resisted the impulse to flip open the lid, sit down and play. When the music ran through her fingers, her happiness seemed to transfer itself to other people, who gathered about her joyfully humming and singing along to the music she made.

Before Cy had joined the United States Navy, he had played the saxophone in a jazz club in New Orleans. He was as gifted as Trixie and stressed that a musician didn't necessarily need to know how to read music to play well. He had told her Billie Holiday couldn't read music, and neither could Vera Lynn. She hadn't disbelieved him but it had amazed her. Thinking about Cy made her hope and pray the post bus had a letter from him on board today for her.

Trixie looked about her. To hold a ceilidh or a dance in the barn, it would need to be cleared of the rubbish that was taking up practically all of the available space. She understood why, when they were not being used, the lorry and the four-seater sports car were garaged inside. The weather in the north of Scotland could be atrocious. But both vehicles would be safe outside for one night, surely.

The barn was certainly big enough to hold festivities. It was much bigger than the large shed-like place at the back of the Yellow Duck where Donnie McKay regularly held dances. It would need a good clean. Chairs would be required. Crockery for cups of tea. Glasses for soft drinks. Blackout curtains at the windows . . .

But wait! Wasn't her mind running away with itself? Neither Morag nor Noah had agreed yet. And nothing could be done about the ceilidh until their consent was given. If it was given. Trixie determined to talk to Hen when she came home from Dornoch. The four of them could then approach Morag.

Trixie was closing the door of the barn when she heard Morag's voice.

'Trixie, Vi!' Morag was advancing on Andy, who was astride his motorbike, and Vi, who was sitting on the step leading into the barn. Both were deep in conversation. In her hands Morag was balancing an enormous tray that looked so heavy Trixie went immediately to help her.

Three mugs, a small teapot, its spout steaming, a tiny amount of sugar in a fancy bowl, milk jug and a plate piled high with freshly baked oatcakes, Morag managed a grin that swept from ear to ear as she placed the tray on top of a discarded wooden box.

'I know you'll soon be making for home, Andy,' Morag said, looking at her offering with satisfaction. 'But I couldn't be sending you home without a wee bite to eat, could I?'

Trixie watched Morag's thin back, as she walked resolutely away. She knew her generosity was another way of making sure Andy didn't outstay his welcome.

'See?' she said to Vi. 'I told you she'd give you some of those oatcakes.'

Chapter Twenty

He would discuss with equanimity changes to his forest's labour force, as long as he could refer to Hen's notebook. He would make sure her voice was heard and her ideas adopted. It was nothing to do with meeting representatives from the Forestry Commission, he thought, as he drove his car through the early-morning haze that was stealing across the heather-clad hills and black lochs. It was her presence beside him, and the subtle smell of her perfume, that was making him feel like a callow youth.

An ignoramus. He smiled remembering the jibe flung at him on the first night they had met. She was a very attractive young woman. He respected her intelligence, but he sensed her vulnerability. Someone had hurt and damaged her. He'd come across men like her in the army, men who had never been allowed to fulfil their true potential until the war. Hadn't he been one of them?

He stole a glance at her. She was staring ahead, out of the windscreen. The long road stretched snakelike into the distance. 'I like the loneliness up here.'

'You're wrong about loneliness,' she said. 'The days are ever changing, with wild animals and birds previously only seen in books, on your doorstep. There's the beauty of the mountains and the wildness of the sea. I can't believe you think that's lonely.'

Briefly, he turned to her. 'I see you've also fallen in love with Sutherland.'

She smiled. 'What's not for me to love? A couple of the girls feel isolated, though.'

He fell silent. The sun broke through the mist and the moors were suddenly bathed in magic.

'You must feel very strongly about your role as laird to want to look after the crofters,' she said.

'Morag filled you in on my family history, did she?'

'Of course,' she answered.

His thoughts churned through his brain. His words fell from his mouth as though they had been turned on by a tap. 'Dammit! I'm still trying to apologize for my behaviour when I first met you in my library . . .'

'When you thought we were feather-brained girls who didn't know what we were about?'

His face was colouring. 'Well, yes. And I'm sorry.'

'Don't be. This particular war isn't over yet. We've a long way to go before you're satisfied with the deal from the government and we prove ourselves working with the Italians in your forests.'

He slowed the engine as the single-track road narrowed still further to accommodate a stone-built bridge crossing a burn. Hoofs firmly planted, a stag stood in the fast-moving water. It lifted its magnificently antlered head from the water to stare at them, then ambled away as if certain of its superiority as the rightful heir of its surroundings.

For a moment there was silence in the car. He turned again to her and saw she was studying him. A small smile lit the corners of her mouth. He hardly knew this woman but, by God, he wanted to.

'What did you talk about?' Hen was putting the last couple of pins into her hair to anchor her plaits over her head. She frowned. Music from the wireless in the kitchen below was drifting up. Trixie could hear Bing Crosby singing soulfully. The room was tidy because the girls made sure Morag didn't have to clear up after them.

'What do you mean?'

'Well, you travelled a long way together yesterday, you and Noah.' Trixie was sitting on the bed, watching her friend get ready to go downstairs. Last night when Hen and Noah had returned from Dornoch they'd been full of the news about returning to work and of the Italian prisoners, some of whom they'd met at Earls Cross House Camp.

Hen sighed. 'We discussed work, like we told you all, how the days could be planned to best effect without wasting time, yet making sure nobody was overstretched.'

'Oh!' said Trixie.

'Well, what did you think we talked about?' Hen asked, pulling her green jumper over her head. 'We spent ages at the camp. Noah had to sign papers for the men – we're allowed twenty. They're being brought by lorry each morning and taken back to the camp at night. They'll be provided with a packed lunch each day.'

'What's their camp like, Hen?'

Hen began lacing her shoes. 'Funnily enough, it was a bit like Shandford Lodge. There's a large house and in the grounds about seven or eight Nissen huts where, I imagine, they sleep. Across the road there's another camp full of German prisoners of war. Apparently, there's no love lost between the Germans and the Italians. The Italians have been learning how to chop down trees. The Canadians have been teaching them woodcutting and forestry management so they'll be bringing their own axes, bow saws, crosscut saws and other tools.' Hen paused. 'I'm not sure if I imagined it but I thought I recognized a couple of the Italians. Perhaps in the forest when Alf was showing us how to cut trees. Or I wondered if we'd met them at Lachlan MacLeod's sawmill that day.'

'It's possible, Hen, if they move men about from camp to camp, I suppose,' said Trixie.

'Weren't you listening when, last night, we were all sitting round the table, discussing this?' Hen stared at Trixie.

'Yes, but the girls and I were fed up talking about work and were waiting for Noah to disappear so we could all ask Morag what she thought about having a ceilidh in the big barn. We'd waited for you to come back, remember? Noah didn't seem to want to leave your side. He was stuck to you like a bit of chewing gum under a table. I just wondered what else you'd been talking about . . .'

'Oh! The ceilidh!' A smile lit Hen's face as though she'd just remembered. 'Yes, we can sort out a ceilidh. Noah said it was a good idea . . .'

Trixie heard her words but wasn't sure she'd heard them

correctly. 'You asked Noah?' She took a deep breath and frowned before she let it out.

'Yes!'

Trixie jumped up from the bed where she'd been sitting and began pacing up and down. 'But didn't we decide it was best to ask Morag first, hoping to get her on our side, so she'd ask Noah for us?' She didn't give Hen time to answer before adding, 'And I believe that was your idea!'

'Well, I asked him myself.'

Trixie was astonished. 'You just opened your mouth and asked him!'

'Well, it wasn't quite like that. Sit down again and I'll explain.'

Trixie sat.

'Noah has some daft idea in his head that I've saved the estate from possible ruination by working out what needs to be done to bring in money, which is absolutely ridiculous as I was only doing the job I was taught at Shandford Lodge. You all know full well why I did it. To prove women could do anything a man could do, and sometimes better—'

Trixie cut her off in mid-flow. 'What's that got to do with asking him about the ceilidh?' Trixie was annoyed because Hen hadn't kept to their original plan.

Hen sighed. 'Look, Trix, we're driving along this

never-ending road and he's still apologizing about that first night when he sent us home without hearing us out, and then he asks if there's anything he could now do to make our stay at the estate easier, so I thank him for buying the wireless set, which you must admit was pretty damn good of him—'

'Get on with it, Hen!'

'Sorry,' Hen said. 'Well, it suddenly occurred to me that in the generous mood he was in, he was unlikely to refuse anything, within reason. So I decided to broach the subject of a ceilidh in a different way.'

'What do you mean, "different way"?'

'I said we were likely to be working for him for a long time because he had a hell of a lot of trees for us to chop down. I intimated that we felt a bit isolated in Talmine and would find it difficult to meet people because of the long hours we'd be working.' She paused. 'I was playing on his sympathy because I guessed in the time he's lived in Sutherland he's been pretty lonely. He admitted he wasn't a man for socializing. He told me he quite liked the Falls Inn at Dornoch. They were hospitable there. I said, "Us girls can't go all that way, hospitable place or not. In any case, it isn't right for women to go to pubs or hotel bars on their own." I said we'd been welcomed in the Yellow

Duck, Donnie McKay's place because you, Trixie, played the piano so well it encouraged custom. I then reminded him that Donnie McKay was a relative of the shopkeeper in Bettyhill who had spoken highly of us.'

Trixie sighed. 'Donnie McKay didn't know I played the piano when we first visited the Yellow Duck.'

'Look, I told you I was hoping to get Noah on our side. So what if I stretched the truth a teeny-tiny bit? Donnie had a farewell party for you when we left, didn't he? You were really well liked.'

Trixie nodded. 'I suppose so,'

'Then I suggested a ceilidh at the MacKay Estate!'

Trixie gasped. 'What did he say?'

'"I can't have people seeing the neglect of my place," he said. I thought he was about to blow a gasket, Trix. So, I followed that up with "Why would they need to come into the house when the big barn is more than adequate."'

'And?'

'Well, he was quiet for a long time. Then he said a ceilidh would give him a chance to get to know people as well. Maybe they'd think better of him if he told his crofters that as soon as his fortunes changed they, too, would benefit from his forests being cut down because with the money coming in he'll be able to start repairing some of the crofts.

And apparently he's got an idea about leasing parts of his land, when the trees have gone, as farmland to his tenants. Some of the crofters wanted his father, Rufus, to do that and he flat out refused.'

'Well, we all know Rufus didn't care about his tenants, don't we?' Trixie said. 'He preferred having a good time. I think Noah wants to be a good landlord.'

'I agree,' said Hen. 'I thought if I stayed quiet, he'd begin to think it was all his idea. So we drove along, me staring through the car's windscreen at the heather and gorse, and he suddenly confessed he didn't know anything about gathering people together for a ceilidh because he'd never been to one. I jumped in quickly and said don't worry, we'd take care of everything. He seemed pleased about that.'

'I should think he would,' Trixie said, 'But we know nothing about ceilidhs . . .' she added.

'Morag knows about these things.'

'She won't be happy to be the last to know the plan. She'll be hurt.'

'But she's not the last to know,' Hen said. 'Vi and Jo don't know we've got the go-ahead from Noah himself. And,' she frowned, 'Noah isn't aware we're charging entry fees so we can give him the money.'

Trixie gave another huge sigh. 'Oh, Hen, I wish you'd

stuck to our original plan about asking Morag first, and if she agreed, she'd talk to Noah.'

'But Morag wasn't in the car with me, being nice, and Noah was.'

For a moment Trixie was silent. Then she thought about her friend's words. 'What d'you mean "being nice"? Allowing men to be nice to you has already got you into trouble.'

Hen's eyes filled with tears. 'Trixie, how could you even think that? Not that kind of being nice. Noah's our boss.' Hen took a handkerchief from her jumper sleeve and dabbed at her eyes. 'That's a horrible thing to say to me.' She sat down on the bed next to Trixie and snuffled into her handkerchief, making all sorts of tearful sounds. After a little while, Trixie felt she'd been mean and tentatively slipped an arm around Hen's shoulders. 'I'm sorry,' she whispered. 'It's just that you haven't got a very good record with men, have you?'

Hen lowered the handkerchief and, dry-eyed, said, 'I happen to like Noah. I respect him. I think he respects me.'

'Well, we'll see if he respects you in a few months when you begin to show. Better to tell him as soon as possible, Hen.'

Hen stared into Trixie's eyes. 'I know. And I will. You promised me you wouldn't gossip about the baby. Does that promise still hold? To Noah? I'll tell him in my own good time.' Hen cupped her hands protectively around her stomach.

'Of course,' Trixie said. 'You're my best friend and I wouldn't hurt you, or deceive you. But there is something you have to do that I'm not helping you with.'

'What's that?'

'You've got to speak to Morag about the ceilidh. I don't like to think of her being hurt because you talked to Noah before her. We need her help to organize it. And she and Noah must agree to the charging of entrance fees. And—'

'There's more?' Hen looked shocked.

'Oh, yes,' said Trixie. 'You can tell Vi and Jo, all about sitting and chatting to Noah in the car, as well!'

Chapter Twenty-one

'What are you trying to hide, Morag?' Hen made a playful grab at the knitting that Morag had bundled out of sight as they'd entered the kitchen. Trixie could see the white wool, not quite hidden behind the cushion on the armchair in front of the fire.

Morag sat up stiffly, her many shawls falling about her thin figure. 'Dinnae you two be so nosy!'

Morag's words came too late. Hen now held in her hands the almost completed baby's bootee. 'Is that for me?' Her voice quivered.

'Won't fit you! Just because there's no sign of it yet doesnae mean it's not there. You cannae have a bairn and not prepare for it.'

Hen, Trixie noted, was, for the first time ever, stuck for a quick reply but there was the hint of a tear in her eye.

A spark crackled out from a peat turf burning steadily on the fire beneath the black pot, which was bubbling steadily, and landed on the rag rug. Morag stamped on it. Then she took the knitting from Hen and once more it disappeared behind the cushion.

'Thank you, Morag,' Hen's voice, tiny, held a great deal of emotion. Trixie saw the look that passed between her and Morag and felt suddenly like an intruder in the kitchen.

'Well, what do you two want?' Morag's voice was gruff.

Before Hen could speak, Trixie rushed in: 'What's cooking in the pot, Morag? It smells heavenly.'

'Kilmeny kail.'

'Yum,' said Trixie, though she had no idea what that was. 'What's in it?'

Morag was looking at them both irritably. 'Rabbit, bacon and cabbage,' she snapped.

Trixie felt as if they should leave Morag in peace. Instead, she said, 'I'll be looking forward to our meal tonight.'

Morag frowned at her.

Hen said quickly, 'Do you know where Vi and Jo are?'

'Gone for a walk on the beach. Vi's got the jitters again about that Alec, so Jo's calming her down. The gillie's on the mountain. My Angus is mending a dry-stone wall out the back and Noah's gone to Bettyhill to use the telephone on business. You'll be out of my hair by Monday when the prisoners of war are delivered to the clearing, and you girls start back at work chopping down trees in the forest.' She took a much-needed breath. 'Now, d'you want anything else?'

Trixie looked at Hen. Morag wanted rid of them.

It was news to her, and obviously to Hen, that Monday was the day for work to begin. She felt excited. It would be good to be out in the fresh air again, meeting different people, drinking smoky tea made in the billy-can. She wondered how many of Noah's original men would turn up to work with the Italians. Trixie was sure she was getting lazy with no proper job to do. It was all right helping Morag around the house but she hadn't joined the Timber Corps to become a domestic servant. She'd write a letter tonight to Cy and tell him how pleased she was to be returning to proper work . . .

Hen gave a small cough, then her words came tumbling out. 'When I went to Dornoch with Noah, I told him we hadn't met many people and asked him if we could have a ceilidh in the barn. He agreed, providing we sorted it out ourselves and nobody came into the house as he doesn't want anyone to see how it has deteriorated.' Hen took a gasping breath, then carried on before anyone else could

223

speak. Trixie noticed that Morag, eyes narrowed, was sitting well back in her chair, thinking and waiting.

'We have ideas,' Hen went on, 'but need you, Morag, to help us as we've never been to a gathering like that and Noah says he hasn't either. We thought we could charge people entry and the money would tide Noah over until the payments from the government start coming in. Don't say anything to Jo or Vi as they don't know yet—'

Morag put up a rough, reddened hand and Hen stopped. 'When do you propose to hold this ceilidh?'

'Not sure.'

'Does Noah agree with charging people?' Morag asked.

Hen swallowed and said, 'He doesn't know . . .'

Morag let out a deep breath. 'We dinnae charge friends who give freely of their performances and food. But . . . nobody would find fault if the hat was passed round.'

Hen frowned. 'A collection?'

'A hat going round after the men have been meeting outside for a few wee drams would usually bring in more money than daft entrance fees,' said Morag.

Trixie could tell she was warming to the idea.

'Of course, the church minister must be invited.'

'But we don't go to church!' Hen said.

Morag took a deep breath. 'Neither did Rufus but the

MacKay private pew is at the front of the church. It's always kept polished and ready. Noah is familiar with what is expected of himself as the laird. That one day the MacKays should worship regularly again. The minister is well thought of. As a mark of respect, he is invited to every family gathering and event that takes place in Talmine . . .' Morag must have noticed the shock on Hen and Trixie's faces for she added, 'Och, dinnae fash yourselves, lassies!' and when they looked even more confused, she laughed. 'Don't worry about the minister for he likes a wee dram, same as everyone else, and he'll maybe join in the dancing and then he'll want to recite the monologue, *The Lion and Albert*. It's his party piece and the only monologue he knows. He recites it at all occasions, and we clap and cheer as though it's the first time we've heard it.'

Hen shook her head. 'Isn't that the one about a little boy called Albert Ramsbottom who gets eaten at Mander's Menagerie, a Victorian Wild Beast Show at Blackpool Tower? Isn't it English?'

Trixie was even more amazed that Hen knew of it, but said nothing. Living up here in Sutherland was certainly different.

'Aye, it is. But it was written in 1932 by George Marriott Edgar, from Kirkcudbright, here in Scotland, where the minister hails from.'

'But won't the minister being present put a dampener on the dancing?'

'Och! No, Hen!' said Morag, 'He'll be enjoying himself. He's fond of saying, "Yer a long time deid," which means seize the day and live life to the fullest, you never know what might happen.'

Hen shrugged. Trixie thought it looked like the minister would attend. At least Morag wasn't against the idea of the ceilidh, but Trixie decided she ought to make sure.

'So, Morag, you'll help us?' she asked. Trixie glanced again at Hen, who seemed ready to add something else, so she shook her head to warn her friend off saying anything that might stop Morag agreeing.

'If the master has already given his consent, who am I to disagree?' she said.

'Thank you, thank you!' Trixie trilled, jumping from one foot to the other.

Hen moved towards Morag, bent down and kissed her cheek. 'Thank you,' she said. 'Not just for agreeing about the ceilidh but for everything, especially for caring about me.'

Morag had coloured. 'Get off with you both,' she said. 'Now leave me be.'

Hen turned, ready to leave the kitchen.

Morag said, 'I can understand you girls wanting to help,

with the money and everything, but when did you ask Noah, Hen?'

Hen turned again to face her. 'I told you, when we were alone together in the car,' she said.

Morag nodded sagely.

Chapter Twenty-two

'The post-bus is stopping,' cried Morag, entering the kitchen. 'I've just spotted him from an upstairs window. Trixie, you'll have to clear that table now the dinner's nearly ready. Jo, collect the letters from the postbox.' The MacKay Estate possessed a metal letterbox affixed to the wall just outside the main gate.

A Glenn Miller tune was playing on the wireless as Trixie began sorting the notes she'd made about the ceilidh and who might be asked to 'volunteer' to perform on the night from the names Morag had supplied. She'd been pleased with Jo's copious notes on what needed to be done to make the barn presentable for people to dance, eat, drink and enjoy themselves. Mostly it involved clearing out the rubbish.

Jo pushed back her chair from the table, producing a shrill, scraping noise across the floor.

'That sounds like a *ban-sith* wailing,' said Morag, putting her fingers to her ears. 'You be more careful, Jo!' she called, as Jo left the room.

'What's a *ban-sith*?' Trixie asked.

'I think you'd call her a banshee,' Morag said. 'She's a Gaelic "woman of the fairies", who foretells the death of a family member . . .'

Trixie shivered. 'Morag! It was a chair scraping, nothing more!' She gathered the pieces of paper she and Jo had compiled into a tidy bundle and put it on top of the side-board next to the wireless set.

She heard excited voices as Jo, followed by Hen and Vi, came rushing into the kitchen.

'Loads of post today!' cried Jo, as she pushed a letter into Trixie's hands.

Trixie's heart almost burst with excitement until she looked at the crossed-out writing on the envelope. It wasn't Cy's. There was a foreign stamp but she didn't recognize the writing, which was overlaid with the printed address of the MacKay Estate. She looked closer at the envelope. It was definitely an American stamp. This letter had been forwarded to her from Shandford Lodge. And just as suddenly as her excitement had escalated, it dwindled, and a sense of foreboding took its place. She put the letter down on the table and stared at it until she heard Jo speak.

'There's two for Noah,' she said, passing them to Morag, who slipped them behind the clock on the mantelpiece. 'And one for me. Gosh, I wonder who it's from?' Jo queried. She turned the letter over in her hands. It was obvious she didn't know the writing and there was no return address on the back. Trixie saw her thrust the letter unopened into the pocket of her dungarees. Trixie marvelled that so much post had come for them in one day when usually the post-van never had cause to stop.

Jo had had a great deal of sadness in her life before she'd joined the Women's Timber Corps. Becoming a lumberjill had given her a new lease on life but she often needed to take long walks alone to help her come to terms with her feelings. Slowly she was making peace with her past and moving on with the present. A letter, unexpected and handwritten, had to be considered carefully before it was opened.

A rush of cold air through the back door announced Noah's entry to the kitchen. His face and hair were wet with raindrops and his clothing was misty with damp. 'Any tea in the pot?' he called. 'It's just started raining.' There was a grin on his face and his eyes settled on the big brown enamel teapot, after he'd thrown his cold outer garments over a peg on the coat stand. He swept his blond hair off his forehead and used one of the ever-present towels lying over the fireguard to dry his face and hands.

'No,' said Morag, 'but there soon will be. There's letters behind the clock for you.' While he reached for them, she set to making tea, removing the heavy iron pot from the fire and replacing it with the huge blackened kettle.

Noah tore open the envelopes, his eyes scanning pages. 'The Italians will definitely arrive at the clearing at seven in the morning on Monday and be picked up at five in the evening,' he announced, after reading one letter. His eyes found Hen's and he smiled at her. 'I suggest we're all there ready to welcome them. Now I'll go upstairs and change.'

Morag let out a sigh and watched him leave the kitchen. 'He'll not be long. I think it's time we ate and had a cup of tea.' The kettle was boiling, and after spooning tealeaves into the pot, Morag poured on the boiling water. Then she swapped the kettle for the black cooking pot, over the fire, to reheat the dinner.

'You havenae read your letter, Trixie. It's there in front of you.' Morag said.

'I've got a funny feeling about it.' Trixie picked it up, turned it over in her fingers slowly, and put it down again. 'I'll read it after we've eaten.'

Hen rattled cutlery onto the table and set out the condiments. Jo went to the larder and brought out a fresh loaf that was waiting on the breadboard. Morag was stirring the contents of the big black pot when she smiled benignly at them. She reminded Trixie of a cat purring contentedly over her kittens.

Morag didn't serve the meal until Noah was back in the kitchen. As they ate, conversation came in fits and starts as the wind forced the rain to pound against the window. The draught through the ill-fitting frame caused the blackout curtains to dance. When they had finished, Noah disappeared, and the girls helped Morag clear away. Trixie was left with the unopened letter. As she tore open the envelope Morag's words about the *ban-sith* came to her. Suddenly she knew, without reading the letter, that it contained bad news. The *ban-sith*, the foreteller of death, had earlier made her presence known and surely this was evidence of it.

There were two pages of unfamiliar loose handwriting, and Trixie's eyes went straight to the last page.

'With much love from Rose,' were the final words. Not Trixie's mother but Cy's. How often had she and Cy written to each other saying that their mothers being blessed with similar names was yet another omen that they were destined to be together?

My dearest Trixie

I want you to know that my son loved you. I relished the plans he made for you both, when at last this dreadful war would be over.

Cy previously had sent me this address so I do hope this letter reaches you. I expect you, like me, have worried that you've not heard from him. I've been making futile excuses to myself about the reasons, and no doubt you have as well.

This morning, as his next of kin, I received a telegram from the United States Navy War Department. It says it is their sad duty to tell me my son, Cy, is missing, believed killed in action when USS Ready was sunk by the enemy. If more information becomes available I will, of course, let you know.

I feel your pain and sorrow. I believed I would know if something bad had befallen him because our religion tells us God does not interfere in lives but spirits do. I do not want to think my beautiful boy is forever gone from our lives.

Trixie, I am here for you.

With much love

Rose Davis

Trixie allowed the letter to fall from her fingers. A weariness overtook her such as she had never felt in her life before. She was too tired to cry or think. She sat on the chair, her eyes fixed on the letter lying on the table in front of her.

Then Morag's arms were about her, lifting her away from the table, pulling her into an upright position. Seconds later, as though in a dream, Trixie heard Morag say, 'Jo, take Trixie upstairs and put her to bed. I'll be up shortly with a hot-water bottle.'

Chapter Twenty-three

'Trixie, take my hand and follow me. You're going to keep Hen and Vi awake if I let you carry on like this.'

Jo's whispered words were firm. Trixie allowed herself to be guided from the bed where a sleeping Hen was snuggled up against the cold, to be led across the dark bedroom and down the rickety stairs, Jo's arms holding her safe.

At the kitchen door leading to the outside Trixie felt a thick coat, from the stand, being draped across her shoulders. 'It's raining . . .' she mumbled, remembering the wind throwing droplets against the windows earlier.

'Not now. It stopped ages ago. The moon is shining as bright as day. Let me slip these onto your feet.' Trixie felt the coolness of rubber as, crouching, Jo pushed and pulled wellington boots onto her bare feet.

The cold air sharpened Trixie's senses as Jo led her from

the house to the low dry-stone wall. 'Stay there,' Jo said, 'while I close the door. We don't want everyone else complaining of the cold . . . The ground's soaking,' she said, when she returned moments later. She too was enveloped in a thick coat and boots.

Fully awake now, Trixie asked, 'What are we doing?'

'I've taken you away from the house where you've been depriving Hen and Vi of sleep with your moans and tears . . .'

And then it all came back to Trixie. Cy's mother's letter telling her that Cy was gone. Once more, her heart plummeted, like a dropped stone. 'I didn't know I was making a noise,' Trixie said. 'I'm sorry.'

'You can't help feeling losing Cy is the end of the world. You probably didn't realize you were making a noise, any more than Noah, down the hall, is aware he keeps crying out. He's probably reliving his ordeal on Dunkirk's shores.'

'I'm sorry,' Trixie said again.

'Don't be. It's a normal part of grieving, Trix. Lying in the dark, listening to you, I remembered how, long ago, when we were at Shandford Lodge, I was having a bad night and you suggested we walk in the forest. We left everyone asleep in the hut and eventually sat on a snag, a fallen, decaying tree, and talked and talked. Do you remember?'

'Yes,' said Trixie. 'You and I shared confidences we never spoke about to the others, and we saw a badger . . .'

'Well, there isn't a forest around Noah's house but there are mountains, heather and a low wall to sit on in the moonlight, and you can cry all you want about Cy.'

'Does everyone know his ship was sunk?'

'Morag picked up the letter, so yes, we're all aware of what happened.'

'It hurts.'

'I know,' said Jo. Trixie could almost feel the tenderness in her voice.

And then Trixie remembered that Jo had not only lost her husband but her child and mother-in-law. 'Of course, you know how I feel,' she said. 'You've lost loved ones. Will the hurt go away?'

'You want the honest answer, Trix?' There was a ghost of a smile about Jo's lips.

'The answer is no. The pain never leaves you but you will learn to live with it.'

'I don't see how.'

'I promise you, Trix, one day, you'll remember this night and you'll think, My God, Jo was right. I'm not saying you'll fall in love, or as deeply, with another man, but a feeling of contentment, happiness even, will steal across you, perhaps the result of something quite simple, and you'll know, although the pain of loss is still deep inside you, you're coping with it.'

Trixie felt Jo's hand find hers and squeeze it comfortingly. It was very calming sitting on the low stone wall, she thought. The blackness of night wasn't totally enveloping because the bright moon illuminated everything. Even the ancient rowan tree, just inside the main gate and previously covered with orange berries that the birds had devoured, was bathed in moonlight. It was there to keep witches away, Morag had informed them.

'You'll need to reply to that letter,' Jo said. 'The sooner the better. Cy's mum will keep you posted with other information she receives. If you want, I can help you write . . .'

'Would you?' Trixie felt as though a huge weight had been lifted from her. 'I've been worrying about what I can say when I know her pain is so great. I keep imagining scenarios of how he died, how he felt, if he knew . . .'

'Of course,' said Jo. 'That's natural, but it won't do you any good.'

For a moment there was silence between them, interrupted by the distant sound of waves rolling against the sand on the beach.

'Do you like it here?' Trixie asked.

Jo finally answered, 'Ask me again when we've been working with the Italians. I'm looking forward to meeting people at the ceilidh, if they come. I love Morag and being with you all. But hanging about without working isn't good for me. It gives me too much time to think . . .'

Trixie decided Jo was wondering if she should divulge a secret or not. She waited, allowing her friend time to speak.

'Do you remember when I told you I wasn't sure whether I was doing the right thing in leaving Brechin, in Angus, to come here?'

Trixie did remember. 'I thought that was because you were offered a job at Lachlan MacLeod's sawmill.'

'Partly,' Jo said. Then she sighed. 'Oh, Trix, this isn't the time to tell you about the letter I had, not just when you've—'

'Had bad news? Go on, say it! You've already reminded me and I understand the world doesn't stop turning because one person is unhappy.'

Jo smiled. 'I'd like to tell you, but not the others, not yet.'

'Go on,' said Trixie. 'I'll keep your secrets for as long as you want me to. You should know that by now.'

Another sigh escaped Jo. 'Hen got in touch with Lachlan MacLeod because she hoped Noah would get a good deal for his lumber. Until then Lachlan had no idea where us four girls had been sent to work. If you remember when he showed us around his sawmill, we were amazed to discover he owned a railway track that led from the main line, right into his premises.'

'Lachlan liked you, didn't he?' Trixie couldn't help herself. That day she'd witnessed a spark between Lachlan and Jo. Later, when sitting on a fallen log in the forest, Jo hadn't exactly denied it. But she'd said she wasn't ready to think about another man.

'I'll ignore that remark,' Jo said. 'Anyway, Hen, being astute, realized the logs going by train right into the sawmill was a bonus. Slashing delivery costs is essential. The trees we'll cut down will be delivered by trailer to Lairg station then go on by rail straight into the sawmill. Lachlan and Noah have struck up a business friendship by phone and letter.'

Trixie nodded. 'I see that,' she said. But she still didn't understand why it mattered so much to Jo.

Then Jo's words came out in a rush as though a dam had been breached.. 'Lachlan has suggested he come to Talmine to see Noah and has asked if I could be here so he could spend some time with me.'

Now it made sense, Trixie thought. She couldn't help

smiling at Jo. Her arms went around her and she held her tightly. 'Go on, tell me again that you're not the least bit interested in Lachlan MacLeod!'

Jo, her voice muffled against Trixie's coat, admitted, 'Well, perhaps I am, just a little bit, but I honestly feel it's too soon for me to make decisions about another man in my life.'

'I understand. Still, I'm really pleased for you,' said Trixie. And deep down she was. Jo deserved happiness.

'You're not cross with me for sharing this with you? I wanted you to know first. I know it's bad timing . . .'

Trixie shook her head. 'Everything has a time.' She added, 'I need to tell my mum.'

'There is the possibility he's not dead,' Jo said. 'Rose said she didn't feel as if Cy had gone.'

'You think the American War Office makes mistakes?'

'It's not impossible,' said Jo. There was a pause. 'Don't raise your voice but we're being watched.'

Trixie stared around her. 'Who?'

'Not who, what,' said Jo. 'Look towards the back of us.'

Trixie twisted around and saw two red deer peering in from the other side of the wall. Silently, they had appeared, as if magicked by the moonlight. Puffs of steamy air blew from their nostrils and little snorts issued from their mouths. The animals' warm, musky scent wafted towards the two girls. Trixie saw the larger animal had impressive antlers. She counted five points.

'Male and female, I would guess,' whispered Jo. 'Red deer, probably come down from the mountains. If one makes itself known to you, it's a sign that spirit guides are watching over you.'

'How do you know all these things?' asked Trixie.

'I read a lot,' whispered Jo, 'Look how inquisitive they are and how their eyes are so soft and liquid-looking.'

There was a scraping of hoofs on gravel and peat, a showing of white hindquarters and both animals were gone.

'Well,' said Jo, standing up, 'that was a surprise. A finale to our moonlit chat.'

Trixie slipped an arm through Jo's. 'Thank you,' she said. 'I feel different about everything now. Not better, just different. And it's all down to you. But do you know what I'd love to do now?'

Jo shook her head.

'I'd like to stay awhile in the big barn and play a few tunes on the piano. I wouldn't want to wake anyone. Do you think the sound will carry to the house?'

'I wouldn't have thought so, not at all, Trix. Stone walls muffle noise, don't they? But it'll be dark in there.'

'My fingers know where the notes are.' She also knew

that seated at the piano, as soon as a tune emerged from her fingertips it would flow as it wanted, a living entity that would fill her heart with joy and carry her mind away from sadness.

'Don't stay too long.' Jo leaned forwards and kissed Trixie's forehead. 'Goodnight, love,' she said.

Trixie watched her walk towards the back door. Then she made her way towards the big barn and the comfort that music gave her.

Chapter Twenty-four

His own harsh cry woke him. Noah wiped the sweat from his forehead, a feeble effort that made not the slightest difference to the perspiration that drowned his face, his body, and soaked into the sheets. He sighed, relieved that the mangled bodies he'd screamed at as they'd advanced towards him were simply remembered images from that beach at Dunkirk, when he had dragged his commanding officer to safety. He thanked God he was in his own bed.

Moonlight streamed through the window illuminating the packet of Beechams powders next to a glass of water on his bedside table. He propped himself up on one elbow and reached towards his salvation, the unrelenting pain in his leg begging for relief.

His bedroom door opened. He swallowed the mixture, set

down the glass, and waited until the small form approached the bed.

'Are you all right?' Hen pushed tendrils of long hair away from where they had fallen across her face. Her eyes held his.

'I am now,' he said. 'Or I will be when the pain eases.' He breathed out slowly. 'Just another reminder of times past.' Her perfume, floral and musky, helped disguise the smell of the sweat caused by the nightmare.

'Did I wake you?' It was a stupid question, he thought. Why would she be here if his cries hadn't disturbed her?

'Yes. I've heard you cry out, but it's never been as bad as this time.'

'I'm sorry,' he said.

'Sleeping in a hut with other girls can give one a certain immunity from witnessing tears and cries in the night.' Hen sat down on the edge of the bed beside him. She looked at the Beechams Powders. 'Often the girls don't want inter-ference. You sounded as if you were in pain. Does that medicine help?'

'It eases my wound. Aspirin is better. The nightmares, I've been assured, will lessen as time passes,' he said.

She pulled the shapeless dressing-gown tighter round her upper body. 'Do you need anything?'

With her white-gold hair spread about her shoulders, she

reminded him of an angel from one of the many religious paintings that had hung about the walls of his boarding school. But Hen was flesh and blood, cool, beautiful and wise, and now asking if he wanted help. He closed his eyes. Images of broken men were imprinted on the lids. Noah blinked them away. 'You've already done more for me than I ever thought possible,' he said. 'I will be eternally grateful when the forests start making money . . .'

'That's my job,' Hen said. 'And when we return to the forest, you'll see how terrific our band of girls is at chopping down trees.'

'And to think, because of my own pig-headedness, I very nearly sent you all away.'

'It didn't happen, though, did it?' Hen was smiling at him. She picked up one of his hands and said, 'Why don't you snuggle down in bed and I'll hold your hand until you fall asleep? Focus on a sea of positivity not a puddle of negativity. I'm very good at this. Jo used to have terribly bad dreams at Shandford Lodge. In one night, she lost everyone she loved in an air raid.'

He did as she asked. Her hand was small and warm in his larger rough one. He had his back to her. He pondered her words. He closed his eyes. This time, imprinted on the insides of the lids, he saw Hen's face turned towards his, smiling, as she enthused about the ceilidh. She was sitting in his car as they drove towards Dornoch . . .

Trixie pulled one of Morag's shawls about her and tucked her feet into the cushioned seat of the chair near the dying fire. The rain pattered against the kitchen windows, comforting and familiar. The house, apart from the usual night-time noises, was silent. As the candle flickered, she wondered if she was the only person awake.

She finished addressing the envelope to her mother, then picked up the letter Cy's mother had sent her containing the awful news about her son. Rose would put it away with the love letters Trixie had had from him, which she had asked her to keep safe. No doubt she would also save the additional letter Trixie would enclose, baring her grief.

She began to reread the words she had penned of how Cy's death affected her. Fresh tears invaded her eyes. She used a hand to wipe them away.

She fingered the pages that explained, in depth, her misery. How she felt detached from life, helpless, bereft, and incredibly angry. She read page after page of self-absorbed drivel that had no regard to how his death would affect anyone else. Trixie stared at the tear-stained paper, reread the words saying she needed to feel her mother's arms about her, needed to be in her familiar room in Gosport for the comfort it would give her. On and on she read until she reached the end.

Trixie gave a sigh that shook her whole body.

The letter was deplorably self-centred and pathetic. How could she inflict it on her mother and make her worry? She thought then of other women who were experiencing the despair of not knowing what had happened to the men they loved. Women, with children, left to bring up a family alone and mothers who had lost beloved sons.

Cy had loved her, made her happy. Shouldn't she be thankful – no, eternally grateful – for that? Some women were unlucky enough never to experience love. She had, in abundance, even though she and Cy had known each other only a short time.

Wasn't it time to put her feelings into a proper perspective? Shouldn't she cope like the adult she was supposed to be?

She ripped the pages in half, then into quarters and fed them into the dying fire. They flared brightly, curled, shrivelled, and then they were gone.

She began again, on a fresh page of writing paper.

Dear Mum,

Today I received this letter. Please put it away with my other things that you are keeping safe for me. I must write to Cy's mum and tell her what a wonderful son she had. He made me so very happy. I will never forget him.

Love, Trixie X

Noah sat on the edge of his bed pulling on clean socks. Rain was lashing against the panes and the wind found ways to creep through the warped wooden frames to make the blackout curtains dance. That didn't matter, he thought, smiling to himself. It had been a good day, workwise. A day full of surprises. A day when he had begun to appreciate Hen even more.

His first impression of her as a vixen, who had called him an ignoramus, would never be entirely erased from his mind. Today, though, she had excelled herself in raising his profile with his new work force. And he could certainly do with the respect she had fostered for him. The result? His confidence had improved by leaps and bounds.

He'd been in the lorry, driving to work, when Hen had said, 'There can't be more than one boss in a job like this. It won't work that way.' He'd stared at her, wondering what she would say next.

'In the past, Trixie has always spoken up for Vi and Jo.' She'd looked at Trixie and received a nod of agreement. 'I, as measurer, work on the theory of the job and I'm guided, by Trixie, as to the practicalities. But I also do my share of the work with an axe . . .'

Here he had noticed a delightful blush rise from her neck and begin to cover her pretty face.

'These trees belong to you.' Here, she'd pointed her index finger at him to reinforce her point. '*You* need to show everyone, PoWs included, that you're the boss.' She had paused. 'But that's difficult if you're unsure of the work we should be doing, right?' Again she paused, probably waiting for him to speak, but he'd stayed quiet. He admired her bluntness. Not long ago he'd have been affronted to have any woman speak to him so freely. But Hen had exactly described his feelings. He'd already explained to her he wanted to be on site until the first consignment of timber was shipped to the sawmill. He wanted to understand all aspects of forestry and get to know his workers. But that would take time.

'If you'll agree,' said Hen, 'I'd like to discuss with you, after talking to Trixie, Jo and Vi each evening, what needs to be done the next day. But *you* must advise your employees of decisions we make. I want nothing to do with issuing orders. For one thing, the men wouldn't like a woman telling them what to do. For another, you're the *boss*. Do you agree?'

Agree? He could have kissed her.

He had been an army officer. He had taken orders and issued them. Now he was a sorry imitation of a man with a gammy leg and a walking-stick to hold himself upright. He might be the laird but he was as poor as a church mouse.

His trees were his only wealth.

And this beautiful girl was finding ways for him to take back his self-esteem.

At his assent, Hen produced the notebook from the pocket of her dungarees and handed it to him. 'I've folded down the page where we're to start today and listed, in order, the work to be covered. Apparently, the Italians are supposed to know how to chop down trees but perhaps it might be a good idea if we don't work them to death on their first day. You'll see I've included tea breaks and time for sandwiches . . .'

Hen had thought of everything. He was overcome with gratitude and wanted to sweep her into his arms, an impossibility because he was driving. In any case, he wasn't sure she would have appreciated his excited gesture.

'Thank you,' he'd said. And her smile told him she'd understood there was more feeling in those two spoken words than he could ever articulate.

Of course he'd had many girls. But he'd never loved any of them, until he'd met Helen.

Dark-hearted Helen, who had turned up out of the blue at the hospital where the doctors had tried to save his shattered leg and told him she was marrying a man with a title. 'He dances divinely, darling,' she'd added. An inconsiderate remark. Perhaps he might stumble around a dance floor one day in the future, but his own dancing days were definitely over. To pour salt onto the wound, he'd been included in the guest list to attend the Savoy in London for the wedding breakfast. A thoughtless gesture as he'd still be in hospital. There'd been no one since Helen, who had greatly influenced his feelings about women in general.

Sliding his feet into his worn slippers, he remembered Hen sitting in the dark, holding his hand to help him fall asleep. She'd made him feel safe.

He half wished his nightmares would return, and soon.

He enjoyed talking to her. She'd made him smile with her honesty about her life since joining the lumberjills. She was no innocent young thing, he decided. And there was definitely something she was holding back. But didn't everyone have secrets in their past? She was highly intelligent, more so than himself, he thought. Her public-school upbringing no doubt accounted for that. But, why couldn't he stop thinking about her?

He was glad Morag had decided to help with the ceilidh. She'd had a few words with the postie when his van had arrived today and by now the proposed ceilidh would be a focal point of discussion in Sutherland. She'd also handed the man some posters the girls had made, so they could be distributed to garages, shops and hotels he visited.

Noah was quite excited by the idea of a party at Hogmanay.

He'd spent time in the big barn tidying and throwing out unwanted stuff that had belonged to his father. He found it therapeutic to get rid of the past. Then he'd discovered the bag of lime. Feeling more agile than he had in ages, he mixed it with water and spent a satisfying time washing the barn walls. Afterwards he felt proud that he'd not used his stick as much as he'd thought he might need to. But he was certainly glad when the job was finished.

Hogmanay, Morag had decided, was a very good time to hold a ceilidh.

'Christmas in Scotland is for the weans,' Morag had stressed, 'but Hogmanay is a new beginning, a fresh year. A good time to start as you mean to go on, making friends.'

He looked at the Beechams Powders and decided he wouldn't take them unless it was absolutely necessary.

Chapter Twenty-five

'Drink that cocoa before it gets cold,' Morag said. The wireless was playing 'Dream a Little Dream of Me'. Trixie finished hers, passed the empty mug along the table towards Morag and hoped the music would soon end because the song reminded her of Cy. Hobo had played it on his harmonica on the ferryboat when they had first met. Now Cy was dead, it was like an arrow piercing her heart anew every time she heard it.

'So, you're saying this Alec knows where you are?' Morag directed her question at Vi, then gathered the dirty mugs and put them into the sink. 'He must be staying somewhere up here, then.'

Trixie saw fear steal over Vi's face. She'd had another bad day today, re-living her mother's Gosport funeral and Alec's threatening appearance in the churchyard.

'But I can't see it meself,' Morag added. 'I'd have heard if anyone from down south had moved up here permanently. Tongues were quick enough to wag when you four girls arrived.'

Hen scooped up the dregs of the cocoa in the bottom of her mug with her index finger. 'But what if that awful bloke has been living here or visiting long enough to melt into the background?'

'What d'you mean?' Jo asked.

Trixie frowned. Anything was possible, she thought, wasn't it?

'Well, that kind of thing happens, doesn't it?' Hen said, looking at Vi. 'What if he'd gone back to Gosport because he found out about your mum's death and guessed you'd be at the church?'

'That's a frightening thing to say,' said Trixie. Vi's face was inscrutable.

'But it's feasible,' Hen said. 'Doesn't he work for that mobster boss? What's his name – Billy Hill? It shouldn't be too difficult for him to keep tabs on Vi.'

Vi gasped. 'He did mention Andy by name,' she said.

'Well, if he's up here, he must have a job of some sort,' Hen added. Earlier she'd washed her hair and it was still damp, drying in long silver-gold strands about her face, shoulders and back. Trixie could smell the Amami shampoo.

'What's he doing? Chopping down trees?' Jo swallowed the last of her milky cocoa. 'Men like him don't do hard manual work, do they?'

'He was a bookie's runner for Billy Hill,' said Vi, 'taking in bets on sporting events, like horse racing . . .'

'Street gambling's illegal, isn't it?' said Hen.

'Yes,' Vi said. 'Alec collected and paid out money in the Gosport pubs.'

'Not many pubs up here—' began Jo.

'Billy Hill's a gangster,' interrupted Hen. 'He'd certainly be in on the black-market game as well, though, wouldn't he?' She grinned at Morag. 'You could ask your friend the spiv. He'd be in the know.'

'I never set eyes on the man,' said Morag. 'We communicate by the post-van. All I know is, he must be making a fair profit. His business has been up and running since the Americans became involved in the special commando training unit. They're based in Achnacarry House, near Loch Lochy . . . That's Spean Bridge.' Morag bent towards the peat box, picked up a turf and set it on the fire. Bright sparks spat from the fire to the rag rug but quickly died.

'See what I mean?' said Trixie. 'Morag doesn't move far

from here but she knows everything that's going on for miles.'

'Billy Hill would discover all the places where he could trade illegally, wouldn't he?' Hen said. 'He'd be in like Flynn to make money. What if Alec is running operations for him up here? Wouldn't that account for his long disappearances from Gosport?'

The colour had left Vi's face. She was about to speak but Morag stopped her. 'This is guesswork,' Morag said, 'pure guesswork – and what does "in like Flynn" mean?'

Hen grinned. 'It refers to Errol Flynn, the film star reputed to be able to get a woman into bed in the twinkling of an eye.'

Morag chuckled. 'Well I never . . . But I knew a man like that, once!'

For a moment there was silence while the girls gazed at her in amazement.

A sudden gasp from Hen made everyone turn to her. 'I felt the baby move! For the first time! A fluttering of tiny wings inside me . . .' Hen's face was a mixture of surprise and joy. Her excitement was evident in her voice. Trixie left her seat to go and put her arms around her. She saw tears in Hen's eyes.

'This is fantastic,' Hen murmured. 'There really is a baby,

isn't there?' Her hands were protectively cupped around her stomach. 'This is my child, isn't it, Trix?'

'Yes, it is,' said Morag, 'and if I have anything to do with its birth, I'll make sure you both go short of nothing.'

'Morag,' Hen said, 'thank you. I bless the day I met you.' She sighed. 'I'm sorry, I stopped you talking. You must tell us what happened next.'

Morag adjusted her shawls around herself. 'Well, I wasn't always an auld shawl-wearing biddy, you know,' she said, 'and this man got me into bed quicker than a midge bites bare skin!'

Trixie's mouth had dropped open. She closed it and went on listening to Morag's tale. From the wireless came romantic music played by Benny Goodman and His Orchestra.

'Finlay Alexander was his name. I was fifteen, pretty as a picture in those days. He came up for the day from north Lanarkshire to Edinburgh, which is where I was born. He was a salesman trying to obtain orders for the new drink his boss had produced, called Irn-Bru – 1901, it was. I was working in a newsagent's that sold not only newspapers but sweeties and groceries. He asked to see Mr Haynes, my boss, and while he was waiting for him, he got chatting to me. He was so handsome, wearing a three-piece suit, a bowler hat and two-tone spectator shoes . . .' Morag sighed and her eyes took on a faraway look. 'He had hair like golden corn. Mr Haynes gave him a small order because he said the new drink might not catch on. I thought I'd never see the man again, but when I left work, he was waiting outside for me . . .'

'He must have liked you,' said Jo.

'Well, that's what I thought,' Morag continued. 'He took me to Dolly's tea rooms in Princes Street. I thought I'd died and gone to Heaven. All highly polished tables and clean tablecloths, it was. He ordered tea. It came in a pot with cups and saucers, a silver milk jug and sugar bowl. A cake stand appeared full of tiny sandwiches and cakes, more cakes, then scones and jam.' She sighed. There was the hint of a smile on her weathered face as she continued, 'I'd never met anyone like Finlay before. Never been anywhere like Dolly's either . . .' Here Morag paused again and Trixie smiled at her. It was rare to hear the older woman talk so much about herself. Usually she was the one asking questions. 'Finlay told me he was staying at a boarding house just around the corner from Dolly's. His boss always put him in good, clean places when he was out canvassing new lines.'

Trixie could see the girls sitting around the table were spellbound with the story Morag was unfolding.

'Didn't your parents wonder why you hadn't gone straight home after work?' Hen wondered. 'You were only fifteen.'

'Och! No! My mammy had died when I was younger. I don't have a clear picture of her in my mind but I remember she always smelt of honeysuckle. Her eyes were as blue as yours, Hen.'

Trixie glanced at Hen, who was smiling affectionately at Morag.

'My daddy would be in the Oak Tree pub. He wouldn't come home until chuck-out time. And then I'd wish he was still drinking. Heavy with his fists was my daddy . . .' Morag's eyes darkened at the memory.

'Anyway, while we were drinking tea and eating the pretty little cakes, he couldn't take his eyes off me. It was like we were sharing some great secret. He'd stare at me and smile, and I was feeling like I was the bonniest lassie in the world. He said I was the prettiest girl in Edinburgh. I knew that wasn't possible but him saying it made me feel so good. He asked me if I'd ever tasted the new drink he was promoting. Of course I hadn't, had I? He had a wee bottle of it in his inside pocket and put a little in my tea. It was sharp, but not unpleasant so he gave me some more. I remember saying it made me feel all fuzzy and giggly. I also remember asking him why the drink looked different in colour from the one he'd sampled with Mr Haynes in the shop. He said he couldn't carry a large bottle around with him, could he? And it was the little glass bottles that made it look a different colour. Well, I'd had quite a lot of the drink in the wee bottle by then. I could hear myself laughing at the silliest things. I thought the icing on top of a small cake looked like a map of Scotland. I told him so. I thought it was hilarious, but Finlay said we ought to leave Dolly's as other customers were staring.

'It was raining when we left. Finlay suggested we pop into his place, just until the rain stopped. I remember we had to climb up so many stairs. By this time, I was feeling sad that soon our evening would be over. He had a Primus stove in his room and he went all the way down to the kitchen to put water in a saucepan to make tea for me even though we'd just been drinking tea in Dolly's. It wasn't a big room, just a bed, chest of drawers, wardrobe, a mirror over a fireplace with a fan-shaped newspaper in the grate where a fire should have been. Not even a chair to sit on. I took off my coat, sat on the bed and waited for him. I remember the rain pattering against the window.

'It was very dark when I woke up. We were in that big bed together and I felt so ashamed. There was blood on the sheets. I started to cry but he kissed me and told me he loved me, that I was a woman now. I knew all about love because I had read Jane Austen. My dad brought home penny dreadfuls – he bought them in the pub. They were serials that ran for about eight weeks at a penny a time. They were exciting stories but not always romantic. We hadn't drunk the tea Finlay had made, so he warmed it up on the Primus and I felt better afterwards. He kissed me some more and I liked it. It felt good to be wanted by such a handsome man. It was nice being loved.'

Morag looked across the table at Hen. 'I think you understand me, don't you, Hen?'

Hen, who had tears in her eyes, nodded knowingly.

'My clothes had been neatly folded on top of the chest of drawers. It had stopped raining so he took me home. He saw me to the end of our road. When I got indoors, there was no one in – the pub still hadn't turned out, you see.

"'I'll be waiting for you tomorrow,'" Finlay had said. 'But he wasn't. I never saw him again. Ever.

'When my monthlies stopped, I could no longer pretend even to myself that I wasn't going to have a bairn. When my dad realized I was pregnant, he called me a hoor and threw the few possessions I had out onto the road. Told me to follow them.'

'How did you manage?' Hen's voice was full of compassion. 'You were only a kid.'

Without waiting for Morag to answer Hen, Jo asked, 'Where did you go?' She looked worried.

'I don't know about you lot, but I could do with another drink,' said Morag, briskly. She didn't reply to any of the questions but got up from her chair, which was nearest the fire, and pushed the big kettle onto the flames. 'A cup of tea is what I need,' she said, sitting down again. 'Do you want me to go on?' she asked the girls sitting round the table.

'Yes!' came the chorus.

'I gathered up my things, tied them in a bundle and walked down the street. My dad stood at the door and watched me. I kept looking back, but he'd made up his mind I was a hoor and that was that.'

'Mr and Mrs Haynes took me in. They allowed me to work in the shop almost up to the day I gave birth. I never told them about Finlay. Never told anyone until now.' She gave a brief smile. 'But we all know how successful Irn-Bru became, don't we?' Not one smile emerged from the girls at the table. Morag continued speaking, but her voice had grown sharp, as if she wanted to finish the story quickly.

'My baby died at birth. It broke my heart. She had such tiny fingernails and a fluff of blonde hair the colour of Finlay's. Mr and Mrs Haynes let me work in the shop still, but I wasn't right. I couldn't think straight and spent most of my days in tears. I was hopeless at adding up money. Customers would tell me what they wanted and I'd forget immediately. Mrs Haynes had a relative living in Bettyhill and thought somewhere quieter than Edinburgh might do me good. I never told her I couldn't stop visiting Dolly's and looking through the windows, just in case Finlay was in there with another girl. I did that most nights.

'The Sands Hotel in Bettyhill took me as a live-in maid. I never thought about another man until I met Angus. He was the porter at the hotel and is one of the kindest men on this earth. We married, but there's been no children . . . We came to work for Rufus after the Sands closed down.' Morag used the corner of her apron to wipe her eyes.

'I really did care about Finlay, see? Poets talk about never forgetting your first love, and the first cut being the deepest. Well, it's all true. I never could believe Finlay didn't care for me. I prefer to think he had an accident or something, and that's why I never saw him again. I know now, of course, that it wasn't Irn-Bru in the small bottle. Even without the alcohol I'd have wanted him to love me. But I never wanted to believe he'd lied to me.'

Morag lifted herself from the chair again. 'I hope you'll excuse me,' she said. 'Jo, will you finish making the tea? The kettle's about to boil. I just need to go outside for a moment to clear my head.' She got to the back door and looked back at Trixie. 'I don't want anyone coming out after me either.' She opened the door and stepped out into the darkness.

Jo pushed back her chair and walked over to the fireplace.

Vi said, 'Why do blokes always think dosing a girl with alcohol will get them what they want?'

'Because it nearly always does,' said Jo.

Vi looked at Trixie, who remembered when Ben Tate had put whisky in her orangeade and taken her into the garden of the Yellow Duck public house. Vi had intervened then by hitting him over the head with a metal watering can. The memory, unspoken, flashed between them. And suddenly Trixie was overwhelmed by Morag's story and all that had happened to them recently. She wondered if she dared ask if anyone minded whether she disappeared for a while into the big barn to play the piano. So many things were running helter-skelter through her mind that she needed the tranquillity of her music to settle her perception.

'It makes perfect sense now why Morag cares so much about Hen.' Jo scooped tealeaves into the big pot and poured boiling water over them.

Hen nodded. 'Morag went through hell, didn't she, the poor—'

She was cut short by the back door opening again and

Morag stepping inside, her face screwed up like a used paper bag.

'Can't even have a quiet think outside,' she grumbled. 'It's damn well raining again!'

Chapter Twenty-six

'It's a bitterly cold morning.' Hen rubbed her hands together to warm them. Then she tucked them beneath her overcoat and into the pockets of her dungarees. 'I've got gloves somewhere but I can't think where I've put them,' she added. She had to raise her voice above the noise of the engine.

Trixie was sitting next to her in the lorry and Noah was driving. 'You look the part of a gentleman in your brown corduroy workwear,' she said, to him. His stick was lodged at the back of the seating.

He moved his eyes briefly from the road and smiled at her. 'I've practically memorized your notebook, so I hope I'll sound more like a boss who knows what he's talking about when I'm checking work.'

'You will,' Trixie said. 'And we'll all soon get warm in the forest, once we've swung those axes a few times.' Earlier, she'd made sure all the necessary felling equipment was in the back of the lorry. Now she gazed through the wind-screen at the early-morning mist clinging wetly to gorse bushes and other plants lining the sides of the single-track road. Sheep with damp-looking fleeces cropped the grass unconcernedly. The hills and lochs in the distance were mauve-tinged where a weak sun was trying to shine through the clouds.

'Well, I hope Andy's got a fire going,' came Jo's voice from the back of the vehicle.

'Not only a fire but the billy-can on its flames,' said Vi. There wasn't room in the cab for five people so the girls took it in turns to sit in the back on cushions that slid across the floor when the vehicle went round corners.

'What did Morag say was for tea tonight?' Jo asked.

'You're always thinking of food!' Vi said.

'My favourite, Pigs in Clover.' Noah sounded pleased.

'That's because you're Morag's favourite,' said Jo, and laughed. 'Anyway, what on earth are Pigs in Clover'?

'I know,' said Hen. 'Big potatoes with the middles cut out and sausages stuffed in, baked in the oven and served on a bed of chopped cabbage. Yum!'

'Sounds good,' said Trixie. 'It always amazes me the stuff you know.'

'It's because she went to a posh school,' said Vi.

Trixie saw Hen raise her eyes heavenwards. Her friend was used to the jibes about her going to public school.

'Pudding is apple crumble and custard,' supplied Noah.

'Yum again,' said Vi. 'Though, no doubt, by the time we get back after a day in the forest I won't care what I'll be eating. I'll just be ready for my bed. Eeow!'

Vi yelled as the lorry swerved around a bend and she careered across the floor into Jo.

'Sorry!' Noah said, as the lorry slowed, then halted. 'But we're here now.'

He turned off the engine and began the laborious job of climbing out of the cab and down to the ground, using his stick. Trixie and Hen followed from the passenger side, just as Vi and Jo scrambled out of the back. Noah had parked near the huge truck used to transport the Italians to and from their camp. Andy's Norton motorcycle was in its usual place nearby.

As the freshness of the pine-scented air enveloped Trixie she sighed with happiness at being back in an environment she loved.

The huge clearing within the tall conifers was a hive of activity, with men hard at work. Such was the amount of timber already cut that fresh sawdust was littering the pine needles on the forest floor. Trixie was pleased to see an enormous pile of logs assembled near to the road. They were ready to be removed by lorry to the station at Lairg and onwards by rail, straight into Lachlan MacLeod's sawmill in Brechin.

Trixie watched Hen walk over to the stack and move around it checking the logs were in good condition. She had taken off her coat and was wearing her dungarees with her green jumper underneath for warmth. Trixie noted her usually slim figure now showed definition of her baby's growth. The secret would soon be a secret no longer, she thought.

Another stack was being prepared next to the first and was growing by the minute. She watched four Italians in their serge uniforms – the huge red circles on the backs of their jackets denoted their status as prisoners of war – carrying and setting down safely the huge trunks. She knew when that stack was built to the required height another would be started. She especially liked the way the men called to each other in their native language, laughing and smiling as they toiled. They were content, working with each other and for Noah in his forest, she thought.

Trixie went to the rear of Noah's lorry and removed some of the tools she knew the girls would need to begin work.

The wind blew the smell of the fire in her direction and

she looked to where red-haired Andy was frantically waving at Vi. Her face was almost the same colour as Andy's hair and a couple of the Italians were laughing at them good-naturedly. Trixie smiled to herself. Vi obviously liked the lad. She deserved a little happiness in her life after what she'd experienced in Gosport.

'What you waiting for, Vi?' Hen shouted. 'Go and help Andy get the billy- cans going. No doubt everyone's parched for a cuppa! And, thank God, with the light wind there's no sign of a midge today.'

More ribbing came from a couple of the Italians who were busily sawing off lower twigs from a tree as Vi walked, head high in the air, carrying her axe, towards Andy. Trixie allowed herself to look around the site for the men who had worked for Noah before. 'Where's Duncan, Lachie, Callum and the others?' she asked.

'Not here,' answered Hen. 'There was a great deal of fiddling going on between the men and the manager of the sawmill Noah was using. It all came to light while you were down in Gosport. Noah was being paid by the load, receiving next to nothing for overweight shipments while the men and manager profited.'

'Is Noah going to prosecute?' Trixie asked.

'This is a sparsely populated community where the Scottish

people stick together. He's an outsider, an Englishman, trying to right the wrongs of his father. Noah decided to take his business elsewhere, to Lachlan MacLeod's sawmill, of course. And the perpetrators have decided not to work for him. They came up with that excuse of not wanting to work with Italian prisoners.'

'So, it's all worked out fine?' Trixie didn't think it was a fair outcome for Noah.

'It's as fair as it gets,' said Hen. 'Noah doesn't want court cases. He just wants to sell his trees and help win this damned war.'

'You've been brilliant in helping him achieve those goals,' said Trixie.

'It's not definite until the money starts arriving,' Hen reminded her.

'With more prisoners on the job, won't we be redundant?' Trixie glanced around. 'They're damn good workers here,' she said. 'And what about Andy?'

'He wasn't involved in anything underhand. He's actually been a big help.' Hen smiled at her, then added, 'I'm just going to see Noah.' And she was gone.

It was then Trixie caught sight of a familiar face among men sawing the brash from the bases of the conifers to gain access to the forest. The handsome Italian paused, the saw in his hand, and curved his sulky lips in a knowing smile. It sent shivers down Trixie's spine as he watched Vi's obvious joy at meeting Andy. Then he turned back to Trixie. His eyes met hers, lingered, before he looked away. Trixie shuddered.

That first time she had spotted him, months ago, in Lachlan MacLeod's yard, her reaction had been of immediate dislike and fear, even though she had no idea why the good-looking Italian engendered such feelings in her.

'I said, "Are you going to do any work today?"'

Jo was holding a brashing saw, waiting for Trixie to take it. At her feet were two fourteen-pound axes.

'Sorry,' Trixie said. Mentally, she shook herself. 'Don't look now but there's an Italian working with that group of men over there I saw working at Lachlan MacLeod's sawmill. Surely, it's not possible for him to have been transferred up here?'

'Don't see why not.' Jo took a sneaky peek. 'You mean God's gift to women?'

Trixie nodded.

Jo faced her again. 'I remember him,' she said, and shrugged her shoulders, 'Maybe the powers that be, move prisoners around all the time. Who knows?' Jo pressed the brashing saw into Trixie's arms. 'We've still got to work, though, Trix.'

'Must we work, here? Can't we move further away?' Trixie didn't want to stay within sight of the man who seemed to scare her.

Then she began talking, the words pouring from her lips. 'I'd rather go a little further into the forest. We can keep to the skidding row where other logs have been hauled through the trees. Actually, Jo, I feel a bit surplus to requirements now. Look around you, at the prisoners working hard. Look back to the piles of lumber they've already cut. If Noah had more men, and these seem to be working willingly enough, he wouldn't need us at all. These men know what they're doing – they've been taught well. I'm not talking about Hen – she's a measurer, Noah's brains of the outfit. But these aren't aggressive prisoners wanting to escape, and they're obviously fed well, by the look of them.' Here she took a deep breath and motioned towards the two guards sharing fags and conversation, while sitting on tree trunks. 'And they're trusted. They must be.'

Jo was staring at her. So, she added, 'Just two guards with all these Italians who have axes, saws and knives in their hands. If that's not trusting prisoners, I don't know what is.'

Trixie walked away leaving Jo to follow her through the maze of men working.

She was listening to the chopping and sawing sounds

echoing through the forest, the noise of various conversations interspersed by laughter. She moved as quickly as she could carrying her axe and saw, keeping an eye on which way all the cut trees were falling, and had fallen, but keeping close to the skid line, the trail made by dragging and carrying the trunks through the forest to the stacking area.

Then Trixie stopped. Before they began brashing lower branches, a large enough landing area for a tree had to be identified, taking into account not only its height but its width, so it could fall without becoming tangled with other trees.

Trixie took off her heavy coat, folded it and laid it on a patch of moss. Bending down, she began clearing the dead twigs and stones from the base of a tree on the edge of the skidding trail. It wouldn't do to slip on any unseen object while wielding an axe.

'What's going on, Trixie?' Jo's question hung in the air.

Trixie sighed before answering. She thought carefully before she said, 'If we could have come straight up to Scotland and had started work immediately, I might not feel like this. But we didn't. We've all had a hand in sorting out Noah MacKay's livelihood and now everything is practically settled for him. But it's taken right up until now before I can get on with the job I've come to love.'

'But there've been compensations for that.'

Trixie looked up at her. 'Have there?'

'God, yes. Morag's lovely. She's like a mother to us.'

'But Morag isn't my mum. I have a mother back home in Gosport. It takes for ever for the train to get there and I didn't get to spend much time with her the last time Vi and I were there, due to bloody Hitler's air raids. I've had to write a letter to her about Cy.' She'd also written to Cy's mum, Rose, in New Orleans and cried all the time she'd been composing the letter.

Trixie heard how unreasonable she sounded. Hadn't Jo lost not only her mother-in-law in an air raid but her child as well? 'I'm sorry, Jo,' she said. 'I'm only thinking about myself and that's selfish.'

'I'm sorry, too,' said Jo. 'We were all concerned for you when you received the letter from Cy's mum telling you he was missing in action, but you really needed your own mum then, didn't you?'

Trixie didn't answer, at least not straight away. Then she nodded. 'As soon as the money starts coming in for Noah, and his business is well and truly established, I'm going to suggest I move back to England. I'm not like Hen, who loves the peace and solitude up here. I prefer towns with a bit of dirt and noise.'

'Have you spoken to anyone else about this? About how you feel? To Hen? The girls, I mean?'

Trixie shook her head. 'And, please, I'd rather this was just between you and me. I don't want the others worrying.'

'Of course,' Jo said. 'I know you love the work.' Trixie had already begun using her saw on the lower branches of the pine tree.

Was homesickness making her feel like this? Was it because she'd lost Cy? Perhaps it was fear of the unknown at seeing the Italian who somehow managed to make her flesh crawl.

'If I get stuck into work, I'll feel better . . .' Trixie began, her voice tailing off. It also crossed her mind that playing the piano when she got back to the MacKay Estate might also raise her spirits.

Jo began working alongside her. After brashing, they knew stance was crucial when hitting the tree with the axe to provide the hinge that decided which way the tree should fall.

'Always be aware of your surroundings,' said Jo to Trixie, repeating a sentence favoured by Alf, the elderly man at Shandford Lodge who had taught them all he knew about the forests. 'It's important, isn't it, that the hinge is cut on the same side we want the tree to topple?'

Trixie smiled at her. She moved her feet in their heavy

boots to offset her stance when using the axe. It was, Trixie thought, rather like looking past the tree and not at it. That allowed her to follow through on her swing. It also reduced the chance of injury if the axe head ricocheted off the tree's bark.

There'd been a terrible accident in the woodland at Shandford Lodge when a Birmingham girl, not paying attention, had had the axe rebound onto her leg. Vi had saved the girl's life with her quick thinking: she had tied a scarf above her knee as a tourniquet. The girl had disregarded the advice Alf had drummed into them all.

Trixie would never forget the girl's screams. Equally she'd never forget the roaring, whistling sound of birds' wings as, disturbed by the first shriek, they'd flown straight upwards from the trees to the heavens.

Trixie and Vi had been congratulated on the immediacy of their life-saving actions. Despite that, though, the girl's leg had had to be amputated.

It wasn't long before Trixie and Jo were well into their normal work rhythm when Jo, as the morning warmed up, paused to take off her outer clothing.

'I actually like the kind of glow I get when swinging the axe,' she said.

'You're being polite, aren't you?' shouted Trixie. 'Why not

just say hard work like this makes us sweat?' She was down to her dungarees and shirt. Her green jumper had joined the clothing pile.

A shout made Trixie pause. Vi was waving from a fair distance away. Once she had Trixie's attention she mimed eating. 'They must be stopping for sandwiches,' said Trixie. She'd never get used to calling them 'pieces'. 'We worked through the tea break. You coming?'

Downing tools and leaving their discarded clothing, Trixie and Jo walked down the skidding trail to the clearing around the fire where some of the Italians, Hen and Vi were drinking tea and opening packets of food. Trixie guessed the prisoners split up into small groups to eat, and for necessary tea breaks. A couple of the men were singing in their native language. They were harmonizing. Trixie had no idea what the song was about but the melancholic tune was quite beautiful and she hoped she'd be able to remember enough to repeat it on the piano keys.

'Issa love song. Very nice.' The words came from a young man with dark curly hair and enormously long eyelashes.

He looked hardly more than a boy, Trixie thought. She smiled at him. 'Very, very nice.'

'Eat your piece!' said Hen. 'Vi's sorting your tea.' She thrust a tin from a carrier bag into Trixie's hands.

'What have you got?' asked Jo, lowering herself onto the huge log next to Trixie near the crackling fire. Trixie opened her biscuit-tin lunchbox and discovered Morag's home-made bread cut into sandwiches. Some were filled with pickled beetroot and cheese, which she loved, and others with grated carrot and Spam, which she wasn't so keen on. Tucked in beside the sandwiches were three buttered rock buns.

'Oh, we've got the same.' Jo sounded disappointed.

The two Italians who had finished their love-song and probably their own sandwiches, prepared earlier in their camp kitchen, looked longingly at Trixie's. They were fed better than some families trying to exist on ration-book allowances, back home in war-torn Gosport, Trixie thought.. Nevertheless, she offered them the grated carrot and Spam sandwiches. '*Grazie mille*' and 'Fank you' came back to her.

'Teas up,' said Vi, appearing in front of Trixie with a steaming mug.

'Thanks,' said Trixie, relieving her of it. 'You look happy. Had a good morning then?' Vi's face was flushed.

'I have, actually. While Hen and Noah have been wandering about, making notes and talking to the guards, I've been working with Andy. We got into a good rhythm, felling trees together.'

'Did you now?' said Jo, who made it sound like they'd not been working at all but having fun. Trixie laughed and Vi blushed even more. Trixie was glad to see her happy.

'He's also offered to take me on the back of his motorbike to see *Gone With the Wind* at the picture-house in Inverness.' Trixie grinned at Jo.

'Well, now, fancy that!' said Jo, grinning back.

Just then Noah appeared. He was walking heavily, using his stick. Trixie guessed his injured leg was hurting.

Hen looked up, a sandwich part way to her mouth, and asked, 'Where have you been? You must be hungry.' By her side, on the grass, another biscuit tin contained Noah's lunch.

'I've been talking to the guards and got us more help in transforming the big barn for the ceilidh.' Noah looked pleased with himself. 'Looks like we have a few men who can sing as well.'

'You mean the Italian prisoners . . .' Hen's voice wavered.

'Some,' he said. 'The guards have been saying a few of the men working here are trusted to come and go, within reason, at the camp. Of course they have curfew times. They aren't a threat to the community and some have been "adopted" by families.' He took the Crawford's tin Hen handed him. Morag must have saved every tin she'd ever bought, thought

Trixie. She leaned across to see if his food was any different from theirs. She counted four rock buns.

'Morag might have something to say about that,' Vi said. 'Even if she agrees she won't let them over the doorstep of your house,' she added.

Noah eased himself down on a tree stump. A shadow seemed to pass across his face. 'No one needs to enter our pathetic living accommodation at present. I agree with Morag on that. The place requires too much restoration, which it'll have when the money rolls in,' he said. 'But only after the crofters have had their share for renovating their homes.' He moved around some of the food in his biscuit tin and seemed content with his findings. 'Of course I can't take the guard's word as gospel. I'll need to find out at source if we can borrow a few men to give a hand on the day with the last-minute collection of wooden chairs from the chapel, which the minister has kindly allowed us to borrow, as long as he's allowed a stage slot.'

'Oh, no! That means he'll recite *The Lion and Albert*,' said Hen.

'Actually, he did mention that.' Noah treated Hen to a lingering smile that seemed only to include her.

The smile didn't go unnoticed by either Jo or Trixie. Jo surreptitiously dug Trixie in the ribs. 'Hurry up and finish eating,' she said to Trixie. 'We've got to end what we started this morning. Those trees want limbing.' She meant that the conifers they'd cut down now needed to have their top branches removed before they could be hauled to the site entrance to be stacked ready to go by road to the railway station.

'You carry on back to where we were working,' said Trixie, setting her empty mug on the earth. She snapped on the lid of her tin, which still contained her rock buns. She'd eat them later. She handed the tin to Jo. 'Take this with you.' She stood up and dusted herself down. 'I'll go over to the lorry and bring up the pruning saws, loppers and any other tools we might need.'

After limbing, the logs had to be bucked, brought to a uniform length, before they were removed from the site. They could use axes to do that, Trixie decided. 'See you all later,' she called to the others sitting around the fire, still eating and chatting.

'Hurry up, then.' Jo was already walking away.

Trixie knew she was as eager as herself to get back to where they'd been working, so they could gossip about 'that look' between Noah and Hen.

Chapter Twenty-seven

'No one needs to enter the house to see the state—'

Morag wouldn't let him finish. She banged the wire tray of ginger biscuits fresh from the oven down so hard on the table that some jumped onto the scrubbed wood. Noah loved ginger biscuits and the heavenly smell of spices in the kitchen whenever Morag baked them. It was early morning and winter dark outside. Noah hoped the aroma would linger to greet the girls when they came down, ready for breakfast and another day of work.

'It's your reputation I think about,' she said, glaring at him. 'You're the laird. Let them think you're fine, living well, and have everything under control.'

'Hopefully, soon, that will be fact, Morag. But in the meantime, I've made arrangements for a few Italian prisoners to be collected from the camp and they'll help ready the barn on the day of the ceilidh, which they will afterwards attend. Then I'll return them. All I'm asking is that you feed them while they work for us. They're also going to bring up the chairs from the church.' Her face looked as if it was set in stone. 'Two have volunteered to sing . . . That reminds me. Our Mairi has a good voice – I've heard her singing in the dairy. Will you ask if she'll do a turn at the ceilidh? I know it will be a busy day for you – and you've been marvellous at spreading the word. Will you do as I ask?'

There was a long pause. 'Aye, I suppose so,' she grumbled.

'Sometimes I wonder why I ask you to do things when I'm the boss or, as you remind me, the laird here,' he said. 'I should simply command you.'

He picked up a ginger biscuit, which burned his fingers, and let it fall back onto the wire tray. 'Ouch!'

He heard her reply: 'Aye, you can try commanding me!'

Noah decided for the sake of peace and quiet to ignore her remark.

Morag was smiling because he'd put his burned finger into his mouth. 'Stick it under the tap. The cold water will ease the pain,' she said, as he removed his finger.

'It's all right, it doesn't hurt now. I wanted to talk about Henrietta,' he said.

'Why? What's she done?' Her eyes narrowed.

'Look, I know she's in the family way . . .' He thought he'd state the obvious instead of asking Morag if his speculation was correct.

'Yes, it's noticeable now,' she agreed. She'd accepted his conjecture without batting an eyelid.

Did that truth make a difference to his thinking? Not at all.

He'd thought there was a possibility she was pregnant after he'd been woken several times, some time ago, by the sound of her early-morning retching outside. Worried, he'd left his bed and looked out of his window. He was glad she'd had Trixie with her. Trixie was a reliable friend. He'd wondered, at the time, if he should mention anything, but decided against it. He'd never heard any of the girls talk about her condition so Hen obviously wanted to keep her secret as long as she could.

'I'd like to know . . . to talk . . . I don't want to make a fool of myself.' He saw another smile creep across Morag's weathered face.

Suddenly he could no longer talk intimately about Hen. He decided to work towards it from a different angle. 'Hen was talking about the possibility of a charcoal kiln being built.'

'Aye?'

'I asked why we'd need to go to all that trouble when in Ardeer, down the road in Ayrshire, there's one of the largest dynamite plants in the world. She said we'd be doing a bit more for the war effort, and as it wouldn't be on the same scale as Ardeer . . .'

'Naturally,' said Morag.

'. . . we might sell the charcoal commercially and locally.'

'Whatever for?'

'We'd be burning offcuts of timber and branches that are useless to us, and the charcoal, because it absorbs poisons, can be used in the manufacture of gas masks.'

'It's a dirty job, making charcoal.'

'Quite so,' Noah said, 'but its uses in art for drawing materials and increasing utilization in medicines make it a viable operation.'

'So, you've thought about building a few kilns . . .'

'Apparently it's not difficult. They can be made from sheets of tin. The girls learned about it at Shandford Lodge.'

'Did they now? Well, it sounds to me as if your mind's made up,' Morag said.

He stared at her. Why had he prattled on about kilns when that wasn't what he wanted to talk about? He'd been awake most of the night after eavesdropping on gossip mixed with grains of truth in the forest. He tried again.

'There's every possibility I'll be able to hire more Italian prisoners, quite a few, actually. The ones I've got, I don't mind telling you, certainly know what they're doing, Morag. However, I've heard rumours on the grapevine that once my forests are being managed properly and the money's coming in, the girls will probably move on to pastures new . . .'

Morag put her hands on her skinny hips and faced him. 'You're telling me you don't want to lose Hen?'

He took a deep breath. 'I don't.' Morag was a witch, he thought. She knew exactly what he meant.

'Sit down while I make tea and begin breakfast,' Morag said.

The wireless was playing Artie Shaw's 'Begin The Beguine' and the soft tones of the clarinet made Noah feel he wanted to unburden himself. He hooked his stick over the back of a kitchen chair and sat down.

The blackened kettle was already steaming, sharing the peat fire's flames with a large pan of porridge. Morag poured boiling water into the metal teapot, and then gave a stir to the oats. She faced him. 'The girls will go where they're needed. That's the job they signed up for, Noah,' she said. 'And being in the wilds up here isn't a young girl's idea of living life to the full, is it? The weather's changing day by day. It's dark in the morning when you all leave for work and dark when you get back. Soon the snow'll come. Those girls should be dancing and going out with young men, having a fine time as well as working.'

'Vi seems to be getting on well with Andy,' Noah protested.

'Aye, but what about Trixie and Jo?'

'I see your point, but it's Hen I'm worried about.'

'You think I don't care about her? I've told her she can have a home with me for as long as she wants. Whether you like it or not.'

That was no surprise to him. Of course Morag cared about Hen. He'd spotted it from the first time she had met the girl. Perhaps she saw something of herself in her or just understood Hen. It was as plain as the nose on his face that Morag loved her.

'I know you care,' he said. The music on the wireless had changed. Gertrude Niesen was singing 'Smoke Gets in Your Eyes'. He heard the words and wished he could say as much and so eloquently.

'What are you trying to say?' Morag asked.

'That . . . that I've come to care for her.' Why, oh, why, he wondered did his mouth seem so full of his tongue it was difficult to speak?

'Does she know that?' Morag wiped her hands down her apron.

'I – I don't know. I haven't said anything.'

'Not surprising. And you're not making much sense now! But she'd hardly be talking about charcoal kilns if she was thinking of leaving any time soon, would she?'

He couldn't answer that. He didn't want to think about it. Instead . . . 'What would she want with me?' he blurted. 'She's a beautiful woman and I'm a cripple.' He looked down at the table.

Morag rounded on him: 'Aye, and you're full of self-pity!'

His head shot up and he stared at her.

'You think you've got problems, Noah? That poor girl's parents have left her with such mind-tangles it's a wonder she's had the time or patience to sort out your life for you. But she has. By God she has. Because she cares about you and me. And she's done all that while knowing she's a bairn growing inside her that she's bloody determined no one will take away. Now tell me this. Why do you think she's so set on doing the best for that bairn?' Morag didn't give him a chance to answer. She spat: 'She needs to love and be loved! That's why!'

His own voice rose above hers: 'I could love her and the child.'

For a moment there was near silence while the clock on the mantelpiece ticked and the porridge in the big pan bubbled.

Her shawl had slipped down and Morag shrugged it over her shoulders, 'Even though the first time you two met, the lassie called you an ignoramus?'

'I might have known you were listening outside the door that night,' he said. 'You nosy old woman.'

She grinned at him. 'Nosy I may well be. But I'll tell you something for nothing. All this talking to me is getting you nowhere. The only way to find out what Hen is planning is to ask her!'

'Post-van's late tonight,' said Hen, throwing letters onto the kitchen table.

'Anything for me?' asked Trixie. She wasn't expecting anything.

'It looks like bills in brown envelopes for Noah.' Hen laughed. 'But there is one for Vi.'

Vi set the toasting fork, a hunk of golden-brown bread speared on its tines, on the fire's fender to cool so she could toast the other side.

'Hand it over, then. You can see I'm busy,' she said to Trixie.

'I don't know how you can still be hungry after the meal you've not long eaten.' Nevertheless, Trixie put down the dog-eared *Woman's Weekly* she was reading, rose from her chair and handed Vi the letter. 'And say, "Thank you, Trixie," because you never said "please".'

'Thank you,' muttered Vi. She reached for the envelope, tearing it open and scanning the single sheet.

Trixie loved the smell of freshly made toast. A short while ago she was fully sated by Morag's delicious evening meal but now she was sure she could fit in a hot buttered slice of—

'Oh, no!' Vi's voice was a strangled cry.

The page dropped into the fireplace. Trixie moved speedily to retrieve it before it fell into the burning peats. 'Read it,' commanded Vi. Trixie saw she was close to tears, her face ashen.

Trixie read aloud the single line: '"Vi, I'm keeping an eye on you."'

'Who would write that?' exclaimed Hen.

'Surely you can guess,' said Trixie. 'It's Alec's idea of a joke.'

'It's not a joke, it's a threat,' Vi said, through her tears.

Hen removed the paper from Trixie's fingers. She scanned the words, then bent down and picked up the envelope from where it had fallen to the rag rug. She turned it over in her fingers. 'Is it Alec's writing?' she asked.

'Who else would write something as awful as that?' Vi

used the sleeve of her jumper to wipe away her tears. 'He's here in Scotland, isn't he?'

'Don't upset yourself, Vi,' Hen said.. She held up the envelope. 'The letter has a stamp on it and it was found in our outside letterbox. It's been posted to you. If Alec is here in Sutherland, wouldn't he simply drive to the MacKay Estate, pop the letter in the box and leave? Why would he bother with a stamp?' Then, in one fluid movement, she snatched the letter, crumpled the envelope and chucked them into the fire.

'Vi,' she said, 'that's the best place for rubbish like that. Now you go on upstairs and get ready for bed. Trixie will finish making the toast. She'll put extra butter on it and bring it up to you. In fact, she'll make some for all of us. Won't you, Trix?'

Trixie had no heart to refuse.

When Vi had left the kitchen and the sound of her footsteps had faded from the stairs, Trixie looked at the scant ashes of the burned letter and said, 'That was very astute of you, noticing Alec must be far enough away to warrant posting—'

'Not at all,' Hen interrupted, staring hard at her. 'There was a stamp on the envelope. He definitely wants to scare her. He wants her to believe he's not close by.' Hen took a deep breath. 'But the stamp wasn't franked. He could be anywhere and my guess is he's nearer than we think.'

'Don't you think Vi should know the truth?' Sharp as a tack, as usual, was Hen, she thought.

'Not at present. She's too fragile,' Hen said. 'We'll keep close to her. Make sure she's never alone. Promise me you won't say anything?'

This wasn't a secret Trixie wanted to keep but Hen was her best friend. 'I promise,' she said.

Chapter Twenty-eight

'Well, that's the last load. Goodbye and good luck,' said Hen, wiping the perspiration from her forehead with the back of her hand. She waved to the last driver towing the conifer tree trunks, then smiled at Trixie, who was also watching the trailers disappear down the road to Lairg station.

Trixie's muscles ached. The girls had been working alongside the men, hauling the timber from the stacks to the vehicles so they could begin the journey down to Lachlan MacLeod's sawmill at Brechin.

'And now we start again,' said Trixie. Despite the cold, her work shirt clung with sweat to her skin. 'Hopefully Noah will be paid soon. How do you feel?' she asked, her eyes dropping to Hen's baby bump.

'Fine,' she said. 'I hurt all over, but it's a good hurt because we've worked hard. I'm hungry. I could eat a horse! No one ever told me carrying a child would make me want to eat all the time.'

Trixie glanced around the glade where the men had started work again. 'Where's Noah?'

'Why are you asking me?' Hen sounded annoyed. 'We're not joined at the hip.'

'Sorry!' said Trixie. 'Just wondering.'

Hen was looking towards the stream where Andy and Vi were rinsing mugs in the fast-flowing water. Vi hadn't mentioned the mysterious letter again. Trixie hoped she was trying to come to terms with it, just as she was reconciling herself to her mother's death. Noah was standing, leaning on his stick, talking to Andy. 'Oh, I see him,' she added. 'It's just that you spend a lot of time together. I can tell by the way he is when he's around you that he cares about you.'

'He's a good man,' Hen said. She'd started walking towards the parked lorry. 'I'm going to get something to eat,' she said. 'Coming?'

Trixie followed. She watched Hen searching beneath the canvas for the tins with their food in. Morag had marked them with their names. Hen shoved the appropriate container into Trixie's hands and, carrying her own, began walking towards the fire where misshapen logs were balanced on the pine needles for them to sit on. Hen prised open the tin's lid.

Trixie watching her poke about inside the metal container, finally producing a cheese scone.

'Morag's a superb cook,' Hen said. Crumbs fell as she began to eat.

'You suit each other,' Trixie said. Hen would know what she meant, she thought.

'I'd been falling apart before we came to work up here,' Hen flicked a cheesy crumb from the side of her mouth. 'Messing with blokes I didn't care about. I think I went off the rails. But when Noah tried to dismiss us as if we counted for nothing, it made me angry. We're making a difference in this war, working as hard as, if not harder than, some blokes. I knew I could do the job I'd been taught at Shandford Lodge, and I wanted to show the arrogant man we were a force to be reckoned with. But . . .'

Hen tried to blink them away but Trixie saw the glitter of tears in her eyes.

'Go on,' Trixie said. 'You can talk to me, you know you can.' She waited.

Hen sniffed. 'The more I got to know about Noah's past, his father, what happened to Noah during Dunkirk . . .' she took a breath '. . . not that he told me but Morag talked and I listened, well, I put two and two together from him and her.' Hen gave a small smile. 'I began to admire the man for what he was trying to do. Not only to do his bit for the war but to help redress the balance his father had upset when he was the laird here. My thinking changed, Trix. I wanted to help him achieve the goals he'd set himself because he's a good man. Does that make sense to you?' As if she had suddenly remembered the scone in her hand, Hen bit into the softness and began to chew.

'Of course it makes sense. I think you've fallen for him.' Trixie stared at her.

'All I know, Trix, is that I was falling apart and I came up here and Noah fixed me together. If that's falling in love with him, I suppose I have.' She sighed again. 'But I'm going to have a child. My child. Things are different now. I'm different. Do you know what I mean?'

Trixie understood. Her friend, the flirtatious girl, had become a woman. 'Yes,' she said.

The fire in the bar of the Falls Inn at Dornoch spat out a knot of burning wood that sizzled and hissed on the cast-iron fender.

Noah MacKay sipped his ale. 'Good thing that didn't

land on the parquet flooring. One of us would have had to stamp it out.'

Lachlan MacLeod, for once dressed in a suit instead of dirty overalls, pushed his horn-rimmed spectacles further up the bridge of his nose. 'It wouldnae be me. I'm too comfortable after that fine meal.'

Noah laughed. 'It was good,' he said, smiling at the slim young man, who was around his own age. 'I usually find venison a trifle dry but that was cooked just right.' He was agreeing with Lachlan because his conscience pricked him that he couldn't give him perfect hospitality at his home on the MacKay Estate. He'd preferred instead to treat his new friend to a meal and a bed for the night at his favourite watering-hole. Noah felt the guilt gnaw at him. The meal he'd eaten wasn't a patch on Morag's cooking.

He watched as Lachlan picked up a log and positioned it among the flames in the fireplace. The bar wasn't busy tonight, just a few locals playing dominoes. No one was at the dartboard. The rain, as usual, lashed against the windows.

On his way in to book rooms for the night, James at the desk had asked him how the wireless was performing. He'd told him it was fine, because it was. 'A damned good purchase. Only changed the battery once, so far,' he'd said.

The bar was warm and smelt of lavender polish. The

two men were sitting in easy chairs at either side of the fire with their pints.

'I'm away to my bed when that one burns down,' Lachlan said, after he'd dusted off his fingers. 'I'd like to set your mind at ease, though, Noah. I never knew your father, but I'm aware Rufus left his property in a bad state and was practically a pauper when he died. Except for the forests, of course.' He paused. 'Those forests are going to make you and me rich men.' He paused again. 'I'm happy doing business with you and look forward to a prosperous future together. If – no, when we win this blessed war, I hope we'll continue as friends.'

'I hope so, too,' agreed Noah.

'You may not feel the same when I tell you that coming up on the train today wasn't just to meet you after all the phone calls and messages we've shared.' Noah stared at him. 'A while back I met one of your four Timber Corps lasses . . .'

Noah's heart dropped like a stone. Did he mean Hen? Surely he didn't mean Hen. Did he?

'Aye,' said Lachlan. 'I was fair taken with Jo . . .'

Noah breathed a huge sigh of relief. 'Jo's a fine worker.' Did he say that too excitedly?

'Aye,' said Lachlan, again. 'A while back I asked her to come and work for me.' His gaze faltered and he looked down into the fire. 'I asked her if she wanted a job long before she came to you. She was on a tour of my sawmill. I offered her work because I was panic-stricken she'd turn me down if I asked her out. Anyway, to cut a long story short, even though she's working for you, I'm determined to win her over. If you losing her causes us to be enemies, then so be it.' He pushed his spectacles back up the bridge of his nose. 'When I want something, I usually get it.' He picked up his glass and took a deep swallow.

Noah smiled at him. 'I have no argument about that, Lachlan,' he said. 'No argument at all.'

Hadn't he already known change was on its way?

Chapter Twenty-nine

'Morag says Christmas is just for the children but I'd really like to give her a present for all she's done to make living here in Sutherland happier for me, after everything that's occurred.' Trixie was sitting on the edge of the bed towelling dry her hair. She was taking her time because she loved the fresh smell of Amami shampoo. Outside the rain, as usual, was lashing against the window panes.

'So, what are you going to do, Trix? Pop up to the shops and buy her a present? Catch a bus to Woolworths? This isn't Gosport, you know.' Jo picked up the mug of tea she'd brought upstairs with her and swallowed a mouthful.

Trixie ignored her sarcasm. 'No. I have an idea for a gift for her and Noah. I've even made a few sketches, but it means putting in some hours of hard work.'

'As if we don't do enough hard work already,' said Vi.

She was rubbing arnica cream into the tops of her arms. Morag had given it to her because she'd complained of her muscles hurting.

'I'm up for it,' Hen said, through the cloud of her silver-gold hair, which she was brushing with her head bent down, almost touching the floor. 'If you tell us what it is.' She parted her hair and looked at Trixie.

'It's something we have to make out of wood.'

'And where are *we* supposed to find any wood?' said Jo.

'Very funny, Miss Sarky,' said Hen.

Jo finished her tea and put the mug on top of the chest of drawers. 'I shall ignore your remark, Henrietta, because actually I find the suggestion of a gift, made by us all, an excellent idea.' She faced the girls in the bedroom. 'It will be, whatever it is, something for Morag and Noah to help them remember me when I leave.'

'What do you mean?' asked Hen, standing up. Her baby bump was quite pronounced now.

Trixie glanced first at Vi, who obviously knew nothing about Jo leaving. At her enquiring look, she'd shrugged her shoulders.

Jo sighed. 'I've been wondering how to say something. I'm glad this talk about a gift has come up because it makes it easier for me to tell you.' She took in a deep breath and let it out slowly. 'When Lachlan MacLeod visited Noah recently on business, it wasn't only him he'd come to see . . .'

'We gathered that,' said Hen. 'Possibly from the way you wandered off into the forest together . . .'

Jo smiled. 'Well, yes . . . Look, you all know Lachlan offered me a job in his sawmill before we came to Sutherland, but I preferred to come to Scotland with you lot.'

Heads nodded. A blush crept up from Jo's neck and spread across her face. 'The job was a cover for him wanting to see me again . . .'

'Oh!' said Vi. 'That's really sweet.'

Jo smiled at her. 'Back then I wasn't in the right frame of mind to think about the future. All I knew was I needed you girls around me to keep me sane after losing my home and my loved ones.'

'Well, I think it's marvellous if you now feel able to strike out on your own – or maybe not on your own. I think you should give the man a chance,' Hen said.

'My own words,' said Trixie, remembering her and Jo's long, night-time conversations in the forest, of how insecure they felt about life, work, the war.

Trixie remembered asking Jo to find out if the good-looking Italian she'd spotted working for Noah was the same prisoner she'd encountered at Lachlan MacLeod's

sawmill. Jo said Lachlan had refused to have Lorenzo
Pace around, as he'd been involved in some black-market
business. Lachlan had no intention of becoming mixed
up in anything unsavoury, so he'd had the man transferred
elsewhere. When Trixie heard this it sent shivers down
her spine. She'd feared all along there was something
not quite right about the man. Vi must also have noticed
Lorenzo, who, at the sawmill, had been unable to keep
his eyes off her. Not that Trixie intended to ask her as
drawing attention to him might upset Vi. At present Vi
seemed besotted with Andy, spending time with him and
chatting whenever she could. Of course, she had talked
about the picture-house and seeing *Gone With the Wind*,
until the girls were sick of hearing about Clark Gable and
Vivien Leigh, and how marvellous it had been riding on
the back of Andy's blinkin' motorbike.

Trixie would miss Jo very much. She wouldn't like to lose
her as a friend – but perhaps she never would. The four of
them, Hen, Jo, Vi and herself, had been through too many
hard times together to lose touch. But life couldn't stay the
same. Things moved on.

'So, you're going to leave Sutherland and find happiness
with Lachlan?'

'Not necessarily!' Jo exclaimed. 'What I'm trying to say is

I'm going back to Brechin where I was happy. I don't want to leave the Timber Corps, so perhaps they could find me a job locally. I'm going to refuse Lachlan's offer of work. But I feel I'm able to stand on my own feet now without you lot bolstering my confidence. I'll take things easy with Lachlan and allow matters to go on from there . . .'

Trixie, who had wrapped her towel like a turban around her damp hair, went over to Jo and put her arms around her. 'That's what I love about you,' she said. 'You always do the right thing. I'm really happy for you.'

'When will you leave?' Hen had asked the question.

'I'm not sure, Hen. You know I'll not let you down. But I can feel a change coming. Things here are moving faster now, engineered by you, thank goodness, and Noah's fortunes are on the upward swing.' Trixie saw the smile of complete understanding that passed between her two friends. She decided to lighten the atmosphere.

'Well, if no one's interested in my idea of a gift for Morag and Noah . . .' She pulled a face.

Vi groaned. 'Of course we are. What is it?'

Trixie smiled broadly. 'It's not an it, it's a them.'

'Get on with it!' Hen said.

'We could make a couple of wooden seats for them to sit outside in the summer when the sun comes out.'

Silence filled the bedroom. More rain hurled itself against the window panes.

Tentatively Hen said, 'How and what with?'

'After we chop down the conifers for the actual logs, there's branches we pile up ready for your kilns.'

'Yes,' Hen agreed.

Trixie continued. 'But there's still plenty of strong limbs and boughs left that are thick enough to withstand heavy weight. Some might need reinforcing. We could make decorative outside furniture.' She waited a while as more rain spattered on the glass, 'And twiggy frames for photographs, decorative mirrors, shelving from knotted wood.' She stilled her excitement. 'I've a simply marvellous idea about covering metal lampshades with twigs . . .'

Vi laughed. 'You want to make a couple of chairs out of branch offcuts?'

Trixie nodded.

Vi had finished massaging the muscles on her arms with arnica and had started on her calves. She shook her head. 'Let me get this right. You want us to fashion a couple of chairs for Morag and Noah to sit on, outside in the rain, to watch Hitler's planes go over?'

Trixie felt exasperation rising. 'The war's not going to last for ever, you daft twerp! And it doesn't always rain!'

Jo spoke up, silencing them both: 'The fresh new wood may not be suitable to make anything that will need to last.'

'What do you mean?' asked Trixie.

'Remember when Lachlan led us around the sawmill? He showed us the piles of wood that had been standing to dry out before it could be used.'

Trixie's heart plummeted. Yes, she did remember. Lachlan had explained that the wood needed to air-dry for at least a year until all the moisture had gone. He'd called it 'maturing'. Damn! She'd thought they could work on something immediately to show Morag and Noah their appreciation of all they'd done for them. She'd even made sketches of quirky little tables, shelves, stools, frames, as well as the chairs.

'Another of my ideas bites the dust.' Trixie didn't want to elaborate but she was more than a little disappointed.

She shook the towel from her head, picked up her hairbrush and began to tug ferociously at the tangles that had materialized in her hair. She knew a line of mouse showed at her blonde roots. Thank God her mum had sent up some peroxide and ammonia in the post, well wrapped so it wouldn't leak. It was so difficult, she thought, to buy items locally in Sutherland that could be found easily in chemists in Gosport. Back home Trixie had taken great care of her bleached-blonde locks and was proud of the way her hair fell across one side of her face in waves, like film star Veronica Lake's. Now it seemed to spend most of its time shoved beneath a headscarf. Never mind, she consoled herself. She intended to bleach it before the ceilidh, when all the girls had decided to dress up and look their best.

'Goodnight,' called Vi. Trixie glanced at her, she was already in bed, the covers pulled up to her chin. On the bedside table was the finished letter she'd been writing to Irene in Gosport, the neighbour who had been so good to her and had organized her mother's funeral. They wrote frequently to each other.

As did Trixie and Rose, Cy's mother, in New Orleans. Well, as often as they could during wartime when nothing was working as smoothly as it used to, including the post.

Rose had told her all about the small flower shop she owned in town. She'd also said she still hadn't been able to reach Cy's spirit. Rose maintained her belief that Cy was not dead but 'waiting', as she called it. The letters gave Trixie hope and comfort even though she didn't always understand them. She loved reading the ones describing Cy's childhood, the antics and scrapes he'd got into with his best friend, Hobo. Cy's photograph remained beneath Trixie's pillow. It was her belief that you couldn't turn love on and off, like a tap.

Jo was now in bed. 'Goodnight,' she called, then blew out the candle perched in a saucer, next to Vi's letter, on the bedside table.

'You going to read?' Trixie asked Hen, who slept nearest the wall in the double bed.

'Not tonight,' Hen said.

Earlier, Trixie had witnessed Hen sighing over her cream silk marabou-trimmed nightie and dressing-gown while searching in her suitcase beneath the bed. She'd been looking for something to wear to the ceilidh at Hogmanay.

'It's too tight,' she'd said, of the nightie.

'But it won't be too tight for ever. You'll be all slim and lovely again, afterwards.' She'd thought she'd seen the glint of tears in Hen's blue eyes as she'd answered.

'And perhaps one day I'll even have someone to wear it for.'

Trixie was about to blow out the candle on the chair next to the bed when Hen said, 'That idea you had, about using the offcuts from larger tree branches to make decorative garden seating and novelties, was damned good! It could make a great deal of money.'

'Oh, yes, and pigs might fly,' Trixie answered.

Hen ignored that remark. 'Will you show me the sketches you made of all the furniture, and the bits and bobs?'

'Now?' The last thing Trixie wanted was to disturb everyone by scrabbling about in her suitcase on top of the wardrobe for her drawings. She thought of the twig-decorated wall mirrors, shelving, clocks and picture frames she had sketched when she was alone in the big barn. She had taken breaks from playing the beloved piano and allowed her mind to run free of work, the war, tragedies that had befallen her friends, and her loss of Cy.

'No, you big daftie! Tomorrow.' Hen raised her eyes heavenwards.

'Yes,' muttered Trixie. 'If you really want to look at them. I'm no artist, mind.' Then she asked, 'What do you mean, could make money?'

Hen lowered her voice so she wouldn't disturb Jo and Vi. 'Blow out the candle. We can talk quietly for a moment or two. I'm not going to get any sleep while the baby's kicking.'

Once again, Trixie marvelled that the new grown-up Henrietta could deal with everything and anything.

In the darkness she listened.

'You're thinking about the twigs and thick branches that at present we can't use for pit props, telegraph poles, aircraft- and shipbuilding, aren't you?'

'Yes, the heavy brash we clear and sometimes burn,' Trixie whispered.

'I think I understand,' said Hen. 'I believe that when the war ends finances may begin an upward swing. We all hope so. When rationing finishes, people will want more than the vital survival-for-life things. They'll perhaps want to make their homes pretty again. If they can't afford it, people in England might do what the Americans did in the 1920s and buy on credit. There's a saying, isn't there, that "What America does today, we do tomorrow"? Your stuff will sell like hot cakes.'

Trixie hadn't heard that about America but Hen's education had, of course, been better than hers. And Hen was looking ahead, taking Trixie's little idea and making it grow.

'We'd need to know how to prepare and cut the wood properly. Lachlan MacLeod's the man for that. You'd need premises to store materials. Noah could be persuaded to help. He'd provide the timber . . .'

'Wait a minute, Hen! All I wanted to do was make a gift.' Trixie felt she was being swept up in something much bigger than she could control. Hen stopped talking but she propped herself on one elbow. In the room's dull light Trixie could see the concern on her face.

'I'm sorry – I got swept away with your idea, didn't I? I didn't mean to take over, but it really is a good idea. What if I shut up now and go to sleep? We've another hard day in the forest tomorrow. But if you decide you want to take this further and you'd like it if we went into business together . . .'

'It's a big step to take, Hen.'

'Sleep on it, Trixie. I won't say another word about it, except it's a terrific idea.'

Chapter Thirty

The wireless was playing 'Dream a Little Dream of Me'. Trixie wanted to get up from her chair, go over and switch it off. But that would be pathetic, wouldn't it? It was simply a catchy song that was played over and over on the wireless. It made her think of Cy, who had died fighting for her in a dreadful war. It was about time she started to put her heartache behind her and grow up. The song faded, and Jimmy Dorsey and His Orchestra came on playing 'Amapola'. Trixie breathed a sigh of relief and began to hum along with the music.

She was tired after today's work and nicely full of Morag's evening meal of baked cod and mashed turnips. Morag had waited on the pier, down at the beach, with some of Talmine's crofters, for Ewan McKay's fishing boat to come in. Her reward had been a fish huge enough to last for a couple of days' meals. Trixie licked her lips, remembering the steamed pudding with jam and custard that had followed it.

'What did you think of the extra men today?' Morag asked.

Twenty more Italians had turned up in two canvas-covered lorries, trained by the forestry unit and sent from the PoW camp. What surprised Trixie was that Lorenzo Pace had driven one lorry, a guard sitting alongside him in the cab. He could speak very good English unlike some of the Italians. No doubt he'd wormed his way into somebody's good books, she thought, even though Lachlan MacLeod had wanted him gone from his sawmill in Brechin because he considered him a bad lot. Seeing Pace, she'd immediately looked around for Vi, wanting to keep her and the Italian apart. She couldn't forget the way his eyes had raked lasciviously over Vi at the sawmill. But she needn't have worried: Vi had been down at the stream, with Andy, collecting water in the billy-cans. Trixie shivered. The Italian always seemed to be watching Vi.

'They know their stuff, Morag. What's more they seemed not only to respect the forest but to enjoy being away from the camp. It was different listening to the resounding cracks of axes on wood and good-natured banter in their own language as they worked. When we first set foot in that particular clearing, all we could hear was the running stream and the birds singing. Now it's a hive of activity. I guess there'll be a few aching backs, though. Training is a lot easier than putting in a full day's work. And they all had their sandwiches.'

She waited for Morag to correct her with the Scottish word for sandwiches, 'pieces', but she didn't. What she did say was 'You girls have turned Noah's life around.'

Trixie didn't know how to reply to that. She asked, 'Where is he?'

'Outside talking to the gillie and Angus. The post-van's due and he wants to remind the driver about the ceilidh and discover how many people he'll be bringing to the barn at Hogmanay.'

Trixie nodded. She'd found it difficult to sleep lately, thinking about Hen's suggestion of working together. She'd shown her the sketches she'd made of decorative wood furniture and the smaller 'fun' items, as she thought of them: the photo frames, mirror surrounds, clock casings. Hen had been ecstatic as she'd looked at the drawings.

Hen had left the table after the meal saying she needed to lie down for a while. 'Leave the drying-up, girls. I'll do it when I come down again,' she'd said. 'This little one's been so active today. I think I've a footballer in here, scoring goals!' She'd put her hands tenderly across her baby bump before she'd left the kitchen.

Trixie knew she ought to let Hen into her own thoughts of moving away from Sutherland. Otherwise, before Trixie realized what was happening, Hen, in her own ambitious way, would start activating proceedings for a cottage industry. She had no doubt Hen was already turning over in her mind how many people she might employ in their own homes, working on Trixie's ideas.

'Back in a minute,' she said to Morag. 'I need to talk to Hen.'

Morag handed her the oil-lamp sitting by the wireless on the sideboard. 'You'll need this to light the way upstairs,' she said. 'Shut the door after you. The draughts whistle through this house.'

Hen wasn't asleep: she was still fully dressed, lying on the bed, reading an Agatha Christie.

'Good book?' asked Trixie. She put the oil lamp next to the candle Hen was using to read by. She didn't blow out the candle because she didn't intend to stay in the bedroom for long.

'Yes,' said Hen. 'Noah gave it to me. You can have it when I've finished it.'

'Thank you,' mumbled Trixie. She took a deep breath before she sat on the edge of the bed next to her friend. She suddenly realized that what she had to say wasn't going to be as easy as she had thought.

Hen turned down the corner of the page, closed the novel and looked at Trixie. 'What?'

Why did she feel like a naughty schoolgirl having to explain a misdemeanour to a teacher? 'Noah has a good workforce now, doesn't he?' Her voice shook.

'Have you come upstairs to talk to me about work? About Noah?'

Trixie looked into Hen's blue eyes, and then she couldn't stop herself. words suddenly flowed from her. About her mum's and Des's postponed wedding, about how she'd miss being with them for Christmas, how she hated the rain that seemed never to stop falling, how she missed going to the Criterion picture-house. 'I even miss swimming in the sea!' she added.

'The sea is just outside this estate,' said Hen, in a remarkably calm voice.

'But the water's too cold. Even on a warm day it's freezing. Everyone in Gosport learns how to swim at Stokes Bay because the water's lovely.'

Trixie heard how pathetic she sounded. She hadn't

mentioned losing Cy but he was part of her anguish as well.

'I suppose if you want to put things in a nutshell, Hen, I'm homesick. I know you love the solitude but I miss Gosport. Like Jo, I'm not ready to give up working in the Timber Corps but I want to be nearer my home.'

Trixie could see Hen was upset. She was making a good job of hiding her feelings, though, as she said softly, 'I understand, I really do.' Then came the surprising part when, instead of talking about any of the things Trixie had mentioned, she added, 'I don't want an answer now about the possibility of us going into business together, you with the ideas, me the administration side of things. It could still work, Trix, even if we're at opposite ends of the country.'

'What about the money? A scheme like that needs cash behind it.'

Hen's voice was still quiet. 'I'm sure Noah would finance everything. It'll be his wood we'll be using, won't it? And once the government payments start arriving, he'd see the importance of speculating to accumulate. Actually, I think P. G. Wodehouse said something about that.'

Trixie had read a couple of Wodehouse's Bertie Wooster comic novels but wasn't familiar with the saying. She was glad she'd told her friend how she felt. Hen slid a hand across and Trixie felt its satisfying warmth on her skin. It would be all right, she thought. Everything would work out for the best. In the end it always did. It was fate. What was meant to be would be.

Hen spoke again: 'How about I don't mention anything about the possibility of a new venture until after the baby is born and you've had time to decide whether you want to pursue the idea or not?'

Trixie stared at her. By then, she and Hen might be at different ends of the country but they would always remain best friends. 'Going to them posh schools certainly made you bloody clever, didn't it?'

Hen laughed. She eased herself off the bed. 'C'mon, let's go downstairs,' she said, blowing out her candle.

When they entered the kitchen, Trixie set the lighted lamp back on the sideboard, where it usually resided. Glenn Miller's 'In the Mood' finished playing on the wireless and the news was announced with Alvar Lidell reading it. Trixie, Hen, Vi, Jo and Morag listened while they sat around the table.

Afterwards, Morag said, 'That man William Beveridge is a saint, and that Eleanor Rathbone, who's campaigned since the 1920s for a separate family allowance to be paid to women, is an angel.'

'I'm not sure what it all means,' said Vi.

'The Beveridge Report has just been published,' said Hen. 'Workers and bosses pay contributions, a sort of insurance so that if employees are unable to work because of old age, illness or unemployment they will be able to claim money to live. Proposed also is free school milk for children. And a free health service. Just think of the people who haven't been able to afford a doctor's fees.'

'That's really good, isn't it?' said Vi. 'Thank you. You explain it and I understand.'

'I should say so,' said Morag. 'I know there's this dreadful war going on and on. But I'll say one thing about the government. It does its best to look after us.'

The back door opened with a flourish and a cold draught. Noah eased himself into the kitchen with his cane. He was hampered by an opened letter held tightly in one hand. He had a smile a mile wide across his face. He was just about to speak when Morag beat him to it.

'Well, is the postie picking people up and bringing them to the ceilidh?'

Noah nudged the door closed with his arm and a slam. 'He says Jock McKay will play his bagpipes wearing his full tartan dress, and the MacGillivray triplets will give an exhibition of Highland dances.'

'Och! Those wee lassies are wonderful,' Morag gushed.

With a contented smile, she bent down, picked up a peat and wedged it onto the fire.

Noah waved the letter he held. 'I have some of the best news ever,' he said, rattling the letter again. 'This is all thanks to you, girls.' He looked straight at Hen. 'And, most importantly, thank you, Henrietta, without whom this would never have been possible.' Trixie saw how his face and eyes lit up even more just looking at her. 'This is the detail of the first amount, plus a cheque, for the conifers.'

Chapter Thirty-one

'So, we have Christmas Day off?' Trixie clutched the back of the lorry's driving seat, which held Noah, and pulled herself up so she could peer out though the windscreen. Icy patches clung to the single-track road where the weak sun behind clouds hadn't melted them. Snow had been forecast but, as yet, it hadn't arrived. It was Trixie and Vi's turn to sit on cushions in the back while Jo and Hen occupied the front bench seat.

'All I'll want to do is sleep that day! Why can't we have a longer break?' Vi moaned.

'Because the country needs as much wood as we can possibly cut down. Coal is wanted for industry, which the miners can't dig out unless they have pit props. Or had you forgotten there's a war on?' Hen replied.

'I ache all over, and I don't get a chance to forget about

the war when all I see when I get into bed is bleedin' chop-pers and logs!' Vi muttered, under her breath.

'What was that you just said?' asked Noah. 'We went over a patch of ice and I wasn't listening properly.'

Vi dug Trixie in the ribs with her elbow. 'I said, "'I've often wondered why, living so far out in the country, you don't own dogs."'

In the front of the lorry, Hen smothered a laugh. Trixie tried to keep a straight face. It helped to look at the dark lochs beside the road. The grey water was deep, forbidding: did anything manage to stay alive in there during the winter? She supposed it must. The mountains were white-tipped where snow had fallen. They were beautiful, she decided, but, oh, so cold. Even the pine trees appeared black against the dull landscape. She noticed Noah was now driving more slowly and carefully on the narrow, slippery road

'It's cold in here.' Vi complained, her breath white as it left her mouth.

'It's cold everywhere,' Noah said. 'I had to scrape the windscreen this morning, now the big barn's been painted up for the ceilidh.' Trixie knew he'd found a home for his Morgan in another ramshackle barn but the lorry had to stand outside in the yard.

'We'll soon get warm chopping down trees,' said Hen.

The girls were now well wrapped up but would soon be throwing off layers of clothing when they began working.

Eventually, Noah drove into the forest's clearing and parked near the lorries that ferried in his workforce of Italian prisoners of war. Andy's Norton motorbike was propped against a tree.

The girls alighted from their vehicle. Jo, carrying axes, walked ahead to where she and Trixie had finished work yesterday.

'Doesn't that fire smell good?' Trixie couldn't help saying. Burning pine wood snatched at the air. A billy-can was already bubbling. She watched Vi walk through a crowd of Italian lads, who goaded her good-naturedly. She was on her way to speak to Andy, Trixie guessed. Trixie grabbed the tins containing her and Jo's sandwiches. She liked working with Jo: she was used to the way she operated and how Jo synchronized her cutting movements with Trixie's axe swings. Noah was out of the lorry, had made his way to a guard and was leaning on his cane while showing him something in his notebook. Hen was close by.

The scream caused Trixie to drop her and Jo's food tins. She had recognized Vi's voice. She saw Vi being pushed inside the front cab of one of the camp's smaller Bedford lorries by one of the PoWs. She had flung herself against its closed door and her arms were flailing madly as she shrieked. Trixie caught a glimpse of Vi's terrified face. She watched dumbly as Lorenzo Pace struck her with a fist. Vi crumpled.

The vehicle started with a roar and speedily swung out from the forest clearing onto the road. Trixie watched, horror-struck and appalled.

It was Andy's voice that pulled Trixie's confused brain into motion as he shouted her name, then, 'Come on!'

Fully aware now and shoving male onlookers out of the way, Trixie followed in his wake as he ran towards his bike. He was already astride the purring vehicle when Trixie grabbed his shoulders and slid onto the leather seat behind him. And then he was moving, the wheels not properly gripping the frozen earth until he could right the machine and follow the lorry.

Trixie clung to his slim frame.

What was happening to Vi was incomprehensible to her. The punch the girl had received from Pace must surely have stunned her. Fear for her friend consumed Trixie.

Andy was driving so fast her face and hands ached with the freezing wind rushing past. She hugged him tightly, eyes streaming, unable to look ahead over his shoulder to recognize the road they were travelling.

She thought she heard him shout, asking if she was all

right, but his words were blown away. The noise from the Norton's engine destroyed the sounds before she could properly understand them. She pressed her face against the back of Andy's jacket, near his shoulder-blades, and tried to see where they were. It was the road back to Talmine. Fear grabbed her anew as she remembered Noah's hesitancy at encountering icy patches on the single track.

Where could Pace be taking Vi? Not Talmine, Surely, he would drive onwards towards Bettyhill. From there to Thurso? Possibly Wick? The further north he drove to densely populated townships, the more possibility he had of escaping Andy.

She thought of Vi. If she was conscious, she'd be too scared to open the cab door to escape. In any case, Pace had probably locked it. If not, Vi would surely know that tumbling out onto the road could kill her.

Inclining her head, she caught sight of Andy's face reflected in his shiny chrome-framed wing mirror. His skin was hard and grey, much like a stone statue. Trixie had no idea how fast they were going, only that they were now keeping pace well behind the lorry. Her heart was hammering in her chest as, with terrific speed, they were passing sheep, cattle, conifers, broken fences, and coming up to the lochs at either side of the road.

The lorry launched itself into a skid on the icy road and was suddenly airborne. As if shot from a catapult, it hit a tree, driver's side on, with a metallic screech as the front of the cab collapsed. The lorry hung over the greyness of the loch, momentarily suspended, then fell into the icy water. It seemed to Trixie an eternity before the motorbike caught up to the scene of the crash.

Andy halted the bike, its wheels kicking up gravel and ice. His feet firmly planted either side of the upright machine he used his hands and sleeves to wipe his face and eyes, all the while muttering, 'My God! My God!' He allowed Trixie to get off the back of the bike, before he kicked the rear stand down and was running after her to the loch-side trees and the black waters.

Shattered glass twinkled among the short grass. Pieces of metal lay about, like strange flowering plants. The tree looked as if a madman had attempted to hack it down.

The twisted Bedford lorry was not totally submerged. Water lapped against metal rim tips bereft of complete rubber tyres. The cold air now smelt of petrol and exhaust fumes. Trixie ran to the verge and was about to wade straight into the freezing water but Andy pulled her back. 'Leave it,' he said. 'The cold'll kill you!'

As she swivelled to face him, she heard a sound.

Like a newly born kitten mewing.

Trixie turned back. In the long grass, near the gorse and a rusted barbed-wire fence, lay Vi.

Andy was at her side before Trixie made it. His jacket was off and he was kneeling, tucking it carefully around her shivering body. But not before Trixie had thrown herself onto the wet grass beside Vi, her eyes raking the younger girl's body for torn clothing, blood and misshapen bones before Andy's coat covered and warmed her. She was lying on her back, wet through. Her hair hung about her head and face in rat's tails.

'I hurt,' whispered Vi. Her breathing was erratic. Trixie pulled the sleeve of her flannelette shirt down past her wrist and used it to wipe away blood that was trickling from Vi's head down the side of her face. Trixie, aware head wounds bled profusely, peered intently through Vi's hair, without success, to see where it was coming from. Small scratches covered her face. A large red mark ran from her chin to her cheek.

'You swam out?' Andy asked.

Vi tried to nod, but it was a mere movement of her head.

'You'll be fine,' Andy said. The smile he gave Vi warmed Trixie's heart.

He stood up and went to the edge of the loch. A rutting

stag bellowed from the hills. A large black and white bird flew out from a nearby conifer, its wings rustling, like crackling paper, as it shot high into the air.

'I'm here,' said Trixie, finding Vi's hand and slipping her fingers inside her cold palm.

'He . . . was taking me to Alec. In Thurso.'

'Sssh, don't try to talk,' Trixie said. Vi was becoming agitated, moving her head from side to side.

'Screen shattered . . . got away . . .'

'You swam out through the broken windscreen?'

Vi stared at her. She tried to smile but instead shivered. 'It's Alec . . . runs . . . black-market business . . . Spean Bridge . . .'

'Well, Alec won't get you now, will he?' She smiled at Vi, looking deep into her troubled eyes. 'I've got you instead.'

'Told Lorenzo . . . Passport . . . Norway . . .' Vi's eyes closed. She was weak, cold, dazed, but her breathing was steady. Trixie gave a sigh of relief.

She looked to where Andy had walked towards the wreck, the loch. He was already chest high in the freezing water and naked from the waist up, searching for the Italian, no doubt.

But Vi needed help. Trixie went on smoothing the skin on her friend's hand and wondering what her next move should be. Should she insist Andy cease hunting for the Italian, who, had he escaped the lorry, might possibly been swept away by underwater currents? Should she ask him to find the nearest telephone to summon help? Or should she leave Vi and walk out to the roadside to try to flag down a passing vehicle? Motorists on these isolated roads were as improbable as hen's teeth.

Her dilemma was solved by Noah's lorry pulling onto the verge.

He was alone.

'Noah!' Trixie called.

Then he was by her side, leaning on his cane and gazing down on Vi. He was clearly worried sick.

'She's frightened, soaked,' said Trixie. Vi's eyes were still closed.

'Hurt?'

Trixie shrugged.

'We must get her to safety,' he said. 'I was on the road when I heard the smash. Thank God you're not hurt . . .'

He looked around, presumably for Andy, adding, 'We need to get her warm . . . hypothermia.'

Andy was walking towards them. He, too, was shivering.

'The lorry's empty, as far as I can see.' He was struggling to put on his shirt over his wet body. He'd also shed his trousers before going into the loch. The material now clung damply to his knees, his legs. On his feet were dry boots.

'Take this,' said Noah, shrugging himself out of his jacket and handing it to the younger man. 'Take it!' His voice rose when Andy demurred. Trixie saw Andy kept glancing at Vi's inert body lying on the grass.

'Andy,' Noah said, 'I need you to help me to lift Vi carefully into the cab of my lorry. There's not much room, but it's warmer there. Trixie, you climb inside with her. Andy, ride your bike into Bettyhill. Ask the doctor to call as soon as possible to the estate. Then go into the police house and tell them what's happened, will you? The police will search the loch. If Pace is there, they'll find him.'

'Of course, sir.' Andy's forehead creased as he agreed.

'When that's all done, come along to my house, understand? I know you're worried about Vi.'

Andy's forehead creases disappeared, and he grinned gratefully at Noah.

Chapter Thirty-two

'Get the camp bed from upstairs, Noah.' Morag was in charge, her words clipped, direct. While he was out of the kitchen, she carefully stripped off Vi's soaking clothes, looked her over for visible injuries and wrapped her in her own warm shawls, which she unwound from her shoulders. Trixie was sent to bring blankets and a thick nightdress from the bedroom. She was amazed by Morag's ability to hear Noah's explanation of what had happened to Vi, then act calmly and quickly.

When Vi was in bed, near the fire, with stone hot-water bottles about her, Vi said shakily, 'I'm all right! I don't need the doctor.'

'You don't know what you need, so be quiet,' Morag said. Trixie saw her examining the huge discoloured bruise on Vi's face, where the Italian had punched her. In the cab of the lorry, Vi had slept, but in lucid moments she'd spoken of what the Italian had told her of her abductor.

Morag tucked the blankets in so tightly that Vi was practically unable to move. 'Where's Jo and Hen?' Morag asked.

Noah turned from the fireplace where he'd put fresh peats on the flames, ready to boil the big kettle again. He'd already moved the black pot containing an aromatic stew.

'Down at the forest with the men. Keeping everyone working, I hope.' He smoothed his fingers through his dirty-blond hair, easing it away from his forehead – a useless gesture, for it fell straight back. 'I'll go and pick them up. No doubt they're worried. If the police call or the doctor appears, you can deal with them—'

Morag's glare stopped his flow of words.

Trixie knew exactly what she was thinking. Of course Morag could deal with them! But Trixie could no longer deal with the secret she'd been keeping of Vi's hand-delivered unfranked letter. She should never have dismissed its relevance. It had proved Alec had been and still was a very real danger to Vi.

Noah was still speaking. 'I've also instructed young Andy to call in, on his way back from Bettyhill. Look after him. He'll be worried about Vi.'

'But—'

Trixie guessed what Morag was about to say. She was against people coming into their dilapidated home. Gossip was rife and malicious. She didn't want visitors to see to what extent his father's gambling and drinking had practically destroyed the entire estate.

'I know you want to preserve my reputation, Morag, but soon I'll be able to put things right. Most decent people will realize that, won't they?'

After a very short while, she nodded. Of course he was right.

'Drive safely,' she said to him, as he left, immediately tackling the job of much-needed tea. After a while, she spoke to Trixie who was at the sink, rinsing out Vi's wet clothes. 'So, it looks like that Italian was in league with Alec, the spiv at Spean Bridge?'

'I believe so,' said Trixie.

'He accosted her at her mother's funeral, didn't he?' Morag's voice was tearful. 'Poor girl.'

'He frightened her,' Trixie answered. 'He bribed Pace, with the promise of a false passport, to abduct her. Pace wanted to escape to Norway. I wonder why.'

Morag said quietly, 'I suppose he had his reasons. The spiv won't hang around, though, will he? No more black-market goods for us.'

Trixie shrugged, 'When Alec's boss finds out what he's been up to, he'll not be happy. Billy Hill might want to improve the black-market outlet, if it's profitable.'

'I've heard about the London gangster, Billy Hill,' said Morag, quietly so she didn't wake Vi. She was setting out mugs on the table. 'Aye, protection rackets, extreme violence,' she whispered.

'I guess if the police can't pin anything on this Alec for kidnapping Vi, Billy Hill will soon sort him out.'

'Well, until I hear that some locking-up of felons has occurred, I'm going to suggest that Vi stays in the house.'

'She won't like that,' Trixie said. 'And what if no one's brought to book for abducting her?' Her thoughts were whirling. Vi was about to become a virtual prisoner on the MacKay Estate. Surely this could have been avoided if only she and Hen hadn't kept quiet about the unfranked stamp.

Morag didn't answer. The outside bell was clanging, making a raucous noise, and Morag put her hands over her ears. 'That'll be young Andy. Tell him in future to come round the back and not use that damned bell,' she said.

Andy was waiting outside with his bike. His face broke into a smile when he saw Trixie. She told him to leave the Norton next to the big barn, then walked with him round to the rear gate.

'This way leads to the kitchen, so don't forget,' Trixie said.

'Does that mean I'm invited to call on Vi again?'

'The master seems to think so,' Trixie said, as she pushed open the back door.

He coloured, seeing Vi in bed. He must have glanced into every corner of the room until he allowed his eyes to rest on the girl in a flannelette nightie buttoned to her chin.

The bell had woken Vi. Seeing Andy, her face broke into a smile. She tried to sit up but the struggle was too much. Trixie moved forward and eased another cushion behind her.

'Hello,' Vi said, looking straight at him so he could see her lips move. She was mindful of his hearing defect.

Trixie also saw the shy look on his face as he answered her. She picked up her and Morag's mugs of tea and handed them to Morag, 'Come outside with me while I hang these on the line.' She picked up the tin bowl from the wooden draining-board, containing the wrung-out clothes, and nudged Morag into the yard.

'Are ye daft?' Morag said, waving at the grey clouds. 'It'll rain within the hour!'

'Just give them five minutes, Morag. He's obviously been worried sick about her.'

Morag glowered. 'Five minutes and not one second more!' But Trixie noticed the smile on the housekeeper's face.

The clanging anew of the gate's bell dictated when Andy should leave.

With the promise he could return, Andy was shown out when Dr Gillespie in his red 1928 Model A Ford arrived. Wearing his usual attire of a deerstalker hat and cape, over plus-fours, he was treated to his usual nip of whisky before he examined Vi. As he put down the empty glass on the table, he said, '*Uisge beatha*, water of life,' and licked his lips. By the smell of him, Trixie assessed he had already partaken of more than a few nips.

The doctor licked the remaining drops of whisky from his long moustache. 'You'd nae need to call me out, Morag. Surely you saw for yourself the lassie has nae broken bones. I cannae do any more than you've done yourself.' He stared at Vi. ''Tis a guid job you can swim. But in future dinnae hop into any mair strange lorries.'

After he'd gone, Vi burst into tears. Trixie turned on the wireless to cheer her up. Benny Goodman was playing swing music.

'The doctor made me feel as if it was my fault!' She wept. Trixie put her arms around her.

Morag said, 'Aye, he's a bit sharp but he's a good doctor. If it had been left to me I wouldnae have bothered him, but Noah was worried for you.' Morag suddenly smiled at

Vi. 'I worry too. The shock of what's happened has nae hit you yet. I meant what I said. You'll not return to the forest. Noah has enough labour—'

'What about the ceilidh?' Vi interrupted, frowning.

'You'll sit beside me and I'll watch your every movement!' Vi seemed to shrivel in on herself. 'Aye, you can look like that all you want. The ceilidh's still some days off and young Andy'll be coming here when he's not working.' Morag paused. 'Did he say anything about the way we live?' Her eyes flew to the large patch of blackened damp above the window, then to the wooden floor beneath where another patch seemed determined to reach it.

'He said he grew up in a place that was worse! You shouldn't worry so much about what other people might think, especially people like Andy who know all about Rufus MacKay.'

'Hmmph.'. Morag picked up the empty bucket used to carry in peats from the outside stack and the kitchen door slammed behind her.

Trixie looked at Vi's woeful expression and knew she could no longer hold herself back. 'Vi, I've got to explain.' Trixie's heart was beating fast. Her words came out in a rush. 'When that horrible letter came for you—'

'Stop right there,' admonished Vi. 'I know exactly what

you're going to say. I might be the youngest of the four of us but I'm not stupid. The first thing I did was look at the envelope to see where it'd come from. My upbringing in Gosport taught me well, Trix, even though Hen tried to soften the blow by trying to persuade me the letter-writer had posted it.' She took a breath. 'She did this to stop me worrying. The three of you have shown me nothing but friendship when I needed it most. I played along because I know you all care about me.'

Vi's eyes filled with tears. She used a hand to wipe them away. 'Morag's right,' she said. 'It's best I stay close to home, for now,' she added.

Chapter Thirty-three

'It was a pity the police had no evidence that the spiv tried to abduct Vi,' said Trixie.

'He was too clever for that. Even the unsigned letter I burned wouldn't have been proof,' Hen said. 'I would imagine when Lorenzo Pace didn't arrive with Vi at the specified time and place in Thurso, he left pretty damn quick. He could be anywhere now.'

Hen was searching her suitcase for something suitable to wear to the ceilidh. On the chair at her side of the bed was a pile of discarded clothing that, due to her pregnancy, no longer fitted. She looked the picture of health with her newly washed hair cascading about her shoulders and back. Rain threw itself so hard against the window panes that it sounded like hailstones,

'Don't let Vi hear you say that. It'll make her even more

upset,' scolded Trixie, then more thoughtfully, 'She's definitely lost her glow since she was bundled into the lorry.'

'What d'you expect? Now the spiv's disappeared, she's frightened he could turn up anywhere, anytime to harm her.' Hen frowned, then threw onto the chair a pencil skirt. 'Never going to fit into that again and didn't like it anyway.'

Trixie said, 'She's safe enough with Morag.'

'Oh, come on.' Hen stared at her. 'She can't stay locked up here for ever. That won't do her any good . . . even though Andy comes to see her as often as he can and he really enjoyed spending Christmas evening with us.'

Trixie thought back to the Christmas that had come and gone. No one had bothered with gifts because all their energy had been spent on making the big barn welcoming. It now gleamed with cleanliness and was decorated with crêpe-paper garlands running across the walls and ceiling.

'Bright decorations bring good luck,' said Morag.

The girls had brought home from the forest mistletoe for romance, fertility and vitality, holly for happiness and good luck, and ivy for eternal life. They had placed the greenery among the garlands, where it looked pretty and reminded them all of the freshness of the forest.

On Christmas morning Trixie had woken to an empty room. She could hear voices from downstairs and music from the wireless so realized the girls had risen quietly and left her sleeping. She didn't bother to dress but had slipped her dressing-gown over her pyjamas. The chatter ceased the moment she opened the kitchen door, when Hen, Jo and Vi, all similarly attired in nightwear, turned to her. The peat fire was burning brightly, smelling of the summer past, and the room was warm.

'Morning,' Trixie said.

Morag, dressed for the day, said, 'Hello, lassie. I suppose you'd like a cup of tea?' Without waiting for an answer, she busied herself with the big teapot. 'Hark The Herald Angels Sing' played on the wireless.

Vi giggled and put a hand over her mouth as though to stifle laughter. Trixie could feel tension in the room. Hen, her long hair in a single plait hanging almost to her waist said, 'We thought you were never going to wake up.'

'It's lovely not to have to get up early for work,' Trixie said, making her way to her usual place at the table. She stifled a big yawn.

Vi smiled at her. 'We wouldn't know about that,' she said. Hen and Vi began laughing. Morag slid a mug of tea along the table towards her. Trixie frowned at Hen, then pulled out the chair she usually sat on.

It was then she noticed the newspaper-wrapped parcel placed in the space where her plate usually rested.

'Go on, open it,' cried Vi.

Trixie looked at Hen, who was grinning insanely. She nodded.

Jo said, 'Don't keep us in suspense.'

Trixie stared at Morag, who shook her head. ''Tis nothing to do with me.'

'We three wanted to do something special for you because you're a lovely friend and you've been there for us when bad things have happened,' Hen announced.

Trixie felt a lump in her throat as she fumbled with the paper. What she saw inside brought tears to her eyes.

Her photograph of Cy looked up at her from a driftwood frame that had tiny shells and sea-glass stuck to it. It glittered in the firelight.

'Oh!' was all she could manage, before she dissolved into floods of tears.

'Stop your greetin', lassie,' admonished Morag. 'These girlies thought you'd like it.'

'Oh, I do, I do,' said Trixie. 'I just never expected this . . .' She turned the gift in her hands, her heart full to bursting with love for her friends. 'But . . .' her voice wavered, '. . . how did I not know you'd taken it from beneath my pillow?'

Hen waved a hand airily. 'I just waited last night until you'd begun tossing and turning in your sleep, like you usually do, then brought Cy's photograph down and we fitted it into the frame. It's taken a while to collect the sea-glass from the beach.'

'I found the driftwood,' claimed Vi, 'and Jo discovered the piece of unbroken glass in the barn.'

'And I'll be happy to have my kitchen to myself again without the three of them under my feet, stealing moments to make the wee gift when you weren't around,' said Morag. 'And, if you all don't mind, I'd like to make a start on breakfast!'

Now Trixie looked at the picture frame containing Cy's photograph, which sat proudly on the chair next to her side of the bed. She had loved and lost him but she had three friends who really cared about her.

She was brought back to the present when Hen asked, 'I know the police searched the loch but they found no trace of Pace. D'you think he got away?'

'Either that or he didn't survive the crash. The undercurrents could have taken the body anywhere.' A flash of light blue material caught Trixie's eye. 'Is that the frock you wore once to the Yellow Duck?'

'This?' Hen pulled a dress from the discarded pile and

threw it towards her. 'Yes, fancy you remembering that. Take it. It'll fit you better than it does me.'

Trixie held the garment in front of her. All of Hen's clothes were of a quality Trixie could never hope to afford. This dress was of the palest blue silk, buttoned to its tight waist, then flaring at the front in box pleats. The three-quarter sleeves had cuffs of white to match the Peter Pan collar and white belt.

'I'll try it on when I've washed this stuff out of my hair,' said Trixie. Her head was swathed in one of Morag's oldest towels because she had brushed peroxide and ammonia into her roots to bleach her hair the same colour all over.

'That dress'll fit you beautifully,' Hen said. 'It used to be one of my favourites.'

'I'll make sure I don't spill anything on it,' Trixie assured her. She smiled as Hen lifted out the marabou-trimmed nightdress and matching dressing-gown, looked at them longingly, then tucked them back into her suitcase along with the high-heeled cream satin slippers. Hen sighed and Trixie saw resignation steal over her pretty face.

'Keep the dress,' Hen insisted. 'These clothes,' she waved an arm towards the chair, 'I'll never wear again, not even after I've had the baby. I'll keep some for "make do and mend" and all that war malarkey, but I'm not that same

346

person any more. I need maternity smocks to hide the bits of elastic and safety-pins holding up my skirts. Thank goodness my dungarees are really baggy.' She smiled at Trixie, 'Morag's promised to take me into Thurso where there's proper shops, like Jenners. I've been saving my coupons. She says we can buy material to make maternity clothes. She's got a sewing machine.' She looked at the abandoned clothing. 'If there's anything else you'd like, help yourself.' Hen dug into the pile. 'Not this one, though.'

She pulled out a dark red button-through cotton dress with big patch pockets. 'This dress would suit Vi, don't you think?'

'She'd love it,' said Trixie.

And suddenly, watching Hen sorting through clothes she was relegating to her past, filled her with sadness that after the ceilidh she'd be making arrangements to leave Talmine.

Silence filled the bedroom until Hen said, as if reading her mind, 'We'll keep in touch with letters, won't we? You'll let me know if you want to go ahead with us, you and me, starting a business using your sketches, won't you?'

'Of course,' said Trixie. 'I do think Noah half expected me to tell him I wanted to leave, though. Especially when Jo said she intended to go back to Brechin.'

Hen nodded, as though agreeing with her. 'Whether she

eventually ends up with Lachlan MacLeod is anybody's guess,' she said, 'but living up here in the wilds isn't everyone's cup of tea, is it?'

'You seem to thrive on it,' said Trixie.

'I'm very fond of Morag and I understand Noah,' she replied. 'It feels like home, up here, to me. I'll stay as long as they'll let me.'

'I don't think somehow that Noah will throw you out.' Trixie paused. 'You must realize he cares for you.'

'I don't really want to talk about it, if you don't mind, Trix,' Hen said, pushing a swathe of her long hair away from her face. Trixie wasn't surprised to see tears in her eyes. 'It's bad enough thinking about you and Jo leaving, even though she's assured me Brechin is close enough for her to come and visit me often.'

'Nothing stays the same,' said Trixie, placing her arms about Hen's shoulders and pulling her into a warm hug. They stood like that for a while, Trixie thinking of all the good and bad times they'd shared. All the laughter, and the tears that had been shed, since they'd first met that day on the train, coming to Scotland and Shandford Lodge. 'The one disadvantage in going home to Gosport is that I won't be here when you have your baby. But I promise that wherever I am I'll come to see you both as soon as I can. We'll always stay friends,' said Trixie, stepping away. 'And I'm thinking very seriously about going into business with you.'

'Are those promises?' Hen asked.

'Yes.'

Hen smiled at her.

'And we've achieved what we set out to do when Noah told us women weren't who he needed to sort out his business,' added Trixie.

'He was very arrogant, then, wasn't he?' said Hen.

'You called him an ignoramus, remember?'

'Yes, I did,' Hen smiled. 'But the future looks good for him now. He has nothing to complain about, with money coming in regularly, and a good workforce.' She laughed. 'We certainly showed him what lumberjills can achieve, didn't we?'

'You have to take the credit for that, Hen.' Trixie was serious.

'I couldn't and didn't do it alone,' she protested.

Trixie remembered she was bleaching her roots. 'I'd better wash this stuff off before my hair falls out,' she said. 'I'd like to look decent in that blue dress, not bald!'

Noah stood beneath the stars, leaning against the dry-stone wall. Moonlight bathed the yard in brightness. The rain had stopped, leaving sparkling drops of water clinging to the pegs on the washing-line and the branches of the rowan tree. Birds had long ago eaten the bright-orange, juicy berries. Not all, for he knew Morag had picked some and made rowan jelly. He'd spotted the jars in the larder. He could hear the waves rolling on the beach and the air smelt, as always, fresh and clean, with just a hint of ozone.

The constant chatter in the kitchen of the forthcoming ceilidh wouldn't allow him to think. He'd deserted the warm room, the wireless and the Christmas cards lining the mantelpiece to reflect on the difference the arrival of the girls had made not only to his life but to his finances. In the new year he hoped he'd be able to start maintaining and preserving some of the crofters' homes on his land. It was giving him pleasure that he could, at last, begin to reverse the damage his father had done. He smiled, thinking of Morag's plans for the estate. He'd tried telling her that their own comfort came last in the long line of desirable refurbishments, especially as there was a war on and building materials were at a premium if, indeed, they could be found at all. He wasn't stupid, though: everything she planned was with his happiness and comfort in mind.

'I saw you leave and thought I'd join you. Do you mind?' The soft voice startled him.

He turned his head to Hen. 'Of course I don't mind.' She

had one of Morag's voluminous shawls wrapped about her, covering her glorious hair. She barely reached his shoulder. 'So,' he said, 'we're losing Jo and Trixie.'

'It's what they want,' she said. 'And if you were to ask Vi if she'd like to leave, I think she'd jump at the chance.'

He didn't answer. He was digesting her words. 'Where would she go? She has no home in Gosport now,' he said eventually.

'She'd be all right with Trixie.'

This time the silence was longer. He supposed Vi would indeed be happier with Trixie, who would work for the Forestry Commission in Hampshire.

Noah thought he felt a spot of rain hit his face. He waited. A second spot failed to materialize. He took a deep breath. It was time to ask Hen, even though he might not like her answer.

'I suppose you'll be wanting to move on, too?'

'And why would I want to do that? It'll not be long before I'm unable to work in the forest at all. I'm carrying a child, or had it escaped your notice?'

He moved his body now and gazed down at her. He caught the faint aroma of her expensive perfume and smiled. She was an enigma. A contradiction. A woman he'd never fully understand. And he'd give anything to present her with a gift of more of that perfume so she'd never be, or smell, any different.

'That fact hadn't passed me by,' he said, pulling his thoughts into order. 'I don't want to lose you. I'd like you to stay. I'd like to marry you,' he said. He didn't have long to wait for her answer. She'd obviously thought there was the possibility he might ask.

'I'm not ready to think about marrying anyone,' she said, staring him full in the face. 'Not just yet. And if I stay, I'll be bringing a bastard into your home.'

'What am I, if not a bastard?'

'But people will think you're the father.' The shawl had slipped from her head, showing the wondrous colour of her hair.

'Then they'll remember Rufus and say the apple doesn't fall far from the tree.'

'Won't that upset you? Your good name?'

'It's Morag who worries about that, not me. Hopefully I'll be remembered as the laird that righted his father's wrongs.'

She looked up at him. He could see her past sorrows, like a picture, shining from her eyes.

He lowered his head, his lips in her hair, that small contact giving him comfort in the moonlight. Slowly, she raised herself on tiptoe until, their cheeks meeting, he felt the coldness of her tears. For a moment they stood, that simple contact enough, warming, giving him hope. For the first time ever, he felt he wasn't alone, that he was one of two people desperately clinging to each other because they had discovered that wonderful oneness.

'When I said I wasn't thinking about marrying anyone, I really do mean not now. But I'd like to consider marrying you in the not-too-distant future.'

His heart leaped. He picked up her warm hand and kissed each finger in turn, then pressed her palm to his mouth and allowed his lips to linger there before releasing her.

'Don't stop,' she whispered. He felt his blood surge through his veins. He pulled her close. Her lips were wet where her tears had fallen, and as he kissed them, he tasted the salt in those tears. Their kiss was soft, hesitant, an exploration of two people wanting to discover if their lips could offer a salve to ease the pain each had known.

Another raindrop hit Noah's cheek. A few more fell. Then more.

He didn't want to go indoors. He wanted to stay outside, with her, for ever. But instead, he said, 'C'mon, beautiful girl,' and pulled away from her.

Her eyes lingered on his for a long, long, moment, then Hen said, with a smile, 'Yes, let's go in.'

Chapter Thirty-four

'Where did these glasses come from?' Trixie picked up a tumbler from a large box at the side of the sheet-covered table. It was dusty and a piece of straw clung to its side.

Morag, swathed in a wraparound pinafore, threw a clean rag at her. 'Catch! You can polish each one and set them out. The SWRI kindly offered them and they want them back.'

'What's the SWRI?' Vi frowned.

'Scottish Women's Rural Institute. A wonderful group who meet up and do good things for women who live in outlying places,' said Hen.

'Like the WI in Gosport who provide tea and blankets to people who've been bombed out?'

'Exactly,' said Hen. She stood back from the table. Trixie tore the piece of rag in half and handed a piece to her. 'You're pregnant, not dead! You can help me with this lot,' she said. Hen tutted, but pulled up one of the chairs placed round the sides of the hall, sat down and began polishing. 'Looks good in here, doesn't it?' Trixie said. 'I hope people come.'

'They will,' Hen replied confidently, wiping a glass and setting it down. 'They'll come. It's Hogmanay, remember? It's the start of a new year at midnight, so the festivities will go on into the early hours.'

'They'd better turn up,' said Morag, patting out a crease on the folding table's sheet. 'I've cooked and baked until I'm sick to death of shortbread, scones, black bun and oatmeal cakes. My store-cupboard once kept full by the Spiv is quite depleted now.'

'Shall I put a cloth on this last table?' Vi asked.

'No, leave it uncovered so people think we didn't have enough cloths.'

'Don't be mean, Trixie. Vi's only asking.' Morag glared at her. 'Everyone will bring something to eat, no matter how humble, so we'll need space to put it all.' She turned to Vi. 'Yes, love, it needs covering.'

Trixie, duly chastised, regarded the hall. Chairs were set out along all four sides and a large space had been cleared near the piano for the acts to take place.

The floor gleamed with cleanliness in readiness for

dancing, and the decorations gave the place a welcoming feel. It wasn't very warm, but that couldn't be helped. Trixie remembered Donnie's big shed at the rear of the Yellow Duck hadn't been heated but the dancing and excitement had soon warmed the atmosphere. Morag had supervised the hanging of oil lamps, and blankets doubled as blackout curtains across the wide doors.

'Sorry,' said Trixie to Vi. 'I didn't mean to be sarcastic. I'm on edge because the ceilidh is a big event and I just want everything to go well.'

'I understand,' Vi said. 'And I'm not myself because I keep thinking Alec will turn up.'

'Which he won't,' Trixie assured her. 'Noah's thought it best to leave the main gate open for guests – can't have that blessed bell clanging every few minutes, but . . .' She put her arm through Vi's and turned her towards the doorway where Morag's husband, Angus, dressed in his Sunday suit, sat on a chair watching who came in and went out. A glass with a tot of whisky could just be seen, not quite hidden behind the chair-leg, to keep him company, hidden because the minister might frown at alcohol drunk at the ceilidh before the new year was celebrated. 'Angus has everything under control and . . .' Trixie cleared her throat '. . . I don't want any arguments from you, but when I leave here, you're coming back to Gosport with me. Alec won't dare show his face there. Billy Hill will have too many of his informants keeping an eye open for him. We'll stay with my mum and Des, just until after their wedding. You know how much she likes you. By then, the Forestry Commission should have found us jobs together—' She had no chance to finish because Vi had thrown herself at Trixie and was practically squeezing the life out of her. 'Get off, you daft mare!' a choking Trixie managed. 'It's a good job I didn't have a tumbler in my hand or there'd be broken glass on the floor!'

'I don't know what to say! Thank you, thank you, thank you!' Tears sprang from Vi's eyes.

'Don't you dare cry! You'll spoil that lovely red dress,' warned Trixie, 'which, by the way, looks sensational on you.'

'Thank you,' sniffed Vi. 'I've never owned anything as lovely or expensive.' She wiped her eyes, careful of her mascara. 'I thought I might have to stay in this house for ever,' she said. 'I mean, I love Morag but I keep remembering all the happy times we had in the Yellow Duck . . . I'd never been to a dance until you took me.'

'And look how that turned out!' Then Trixie said, 'We'll be all right together, Vi.'

'You two going to stand there all night, gassing? Is it only Angus welcoming guests?' Jo had walked in with Lachlan

MacLeod. Her green button-through woollen dress, with its straight skirt, complemented her red hair and she wore a broad smile. Lachlan looked as if he might burst with pride standing beside her.

Trixie answered, 'Morag's brought her ginger beer out now. I should get some before everyone else discovers it.' She went to hand Jo a couple of clean glasses.

'Morag said nobody eats or drinks until the interval,' Vi warned. Trixie frowned and set the glasses back on the table. As she did so she noticed the bottles of whisky and sherry in boxes on the floor, supplied by Noah, to be opened at midnight to toast the traditional first-footer when he arrived.

There were quite a few people in the barn, now. Some had claimed chairs, others were standing, talking. The musicians were alongside the piano readying their instruments.

As Lachlan and Jo walked away, Trixie thought what a nice-looking couple they made. Assorted dishes of food, not made by Morag, were taking up space on the tables, and Trixie's spirits lifted. The Scots were warm-hearted people, she thought. People, in their Sunday-best finery were chatting, laughing. Already the barn felt warmer and the scents of food, perfume and expectation wafted in the air. Everything was going to be fine, she thought.

Then Trixie gasped. Morag had taken off her pinafore

and sat primly watching the proceedings. There wasn't a shawl in sight! She was wearing a neat brown woollen suit and heeled court shoes! Trixie wondered where she'd been hiding them. Her hair in its bun was sleek. A dash of red lipstick made her look younger, and Trixie could now see the beauty Morag had possessed as a young girl.

'You look nice, Trixie.'

The words had come from Andy.

'Thank you,' Trixie said, careful to face him so he could see her lips move. The beautiful blue silk dress skimmed her body and she'd spent ages with the curling tongs, heating them in the fire, then coaxing her hair into her favourite Veronica Lake style. 'You look pretty good yourself.' He wore a dark suit that probably only saw the light of day at weddings and funerals. It was a little tight across his broad shoulders and he'd tamed his red hair with a good dollop of Brylcreem. His eyes left her face to glance around the hall.

'Vi's over there.' Trixie smiled at him and pointed him towards Morag, who'd lured Vi into sitting next to her. Vi lit up as soon as she saw him. She would miss Andy when she left Talmine, thought Trixie. She'd write to him, of course she would. No doubt Andy would be unhappy to see her leave Scotland but it was necessary for her own peace of mind, and Andy would never argue with that. They'd meet again, if it was meant to be. Sutherland wasn't at the end of the world, was it? Perhaps a little too far away for Andy to drive down on his Norton, but who knew? Fate was fickle, thought Trixie. And hadn't she promised to return to Talmine when Hen gave birth? Vi and Andy would be reunited then.

Hen loved Sutherland. Her baby would be born on the MacKay Estate. Noah wanted her to marry him. They were ideally suited, Trixie thought, especially when earlier she'd asked her friend, 'Do you love him?'

'I'm not sure what love is,' Hen had answered. 'I trust him. I admire him. He's not like anyone I've ever known before. He's tough, but he's fragile, if that makes sense, Trix. I like it that he talks to me and listens to what I have to say. The other men liked my looks, my body, but Noah likes my intelligence.'

Trixie thought if all that wasn't love, she didn't know what love was either. And she did know. She'd fallen in love with Cy, the curly-haired man with dark brown gold-flecked eyes, whose photograph she would always keep beneath her pillow.

Trixie had kissed Hen's cheek and said, 'I think you will wed him, eventually.'

'Oh, why's that?' asked Hen.

'On your wedding night you could wear your satin night-dress with the marabou feathers. It's a shame to let such a beautiful outfit go to waste.'

Hen had laughed and vanished into the crowd.

Trixie was suddenly aware she was standing alone, while couples were dancing about her to the fiddles and the accordion of the small band. Suddenly Vi was tucking her arm through hers. 'God knows where you are, Trix, but it's not in this barn. I've saved you a chair next to me,' she said, leading her away from the dancers. 'Jock McKay, in full tartan dress, is just about to be announced by the minister to do a turn with his bagpipes.'

And, sure enough, the minister, in his black cassock, walked onto the area set aside for the 'acts' and waved his hands, advising the band to cease their music. 'We'll be needing you to accompany the piper in a wee while so the MacGillivray triplets can give an exhibition of Highland dancing,' he said to them. He encouraged everyone to clap for the accordionist and violinists and to welcome Jock.

Trixie sat down next to Morag and Vi, watched and listened as the bagpipes were played. A new experience for her. She gazed in awe at the brawny, kilted, red-haired and -bearded man as he played 'Scotland the Brave', followed by 'Flower of Scotland'. Everyone cheered and shouted after his turn. Then he stood with the musicians and they made music together as an introduction to three small, angelic girls who came dancing through the crowd dressed in MacKay tartan skirts, white blouses, black bodices and knee-high tartan socks, and accompanied by their mother.

The minister again hushed the crowd, welcomed the girls, and named some of the competitions they had won.

'What do they call those soft shoes they're wearing?' asked Vi. She looked as though she was enjoying the show.

'They're "gillies", Morag said, 'not to be confused with our gillie, Duncan, who's enjoying the show over there.' She pointed across the room to where, at the door, Angus now had a companion. A second glass of whisky sat on the floor beneath the chairs.

In perfect symmetry, heels springing, toes pointed, arms held high, the three identical girls danced to the music. Trixie was amazed at their self-assurance as they pirouetted and leaped, clearly loving every moment of displaying their prowess. When the dances ended, the room erupted with applause.

Trixie stole a glance at Noah sitting with Hen. She had never seen him look so proud and happy. Hen caught her eye and winked broadly. Trixie grinned back at her.

Up popped the minister again: 'And now we have two

visitors to Scotland, who have to stay awhile, but who have assisted today in bringing chairs from the church and doing sundry jobs to help make this event possible. They are going to sing, unaccompanied, a love song in Italian, called "The Sun". Please put your hands together for Tommaso and Riccardo.'

As the minister sat down, the guests broke out with claps and cheers. The Italian boys were from Noah's workforce. Trixie recognized the one with the wavy dark hair and long eyelashes. Nervously, he and his friend stood close together and began singing. Trixie understood not one word, but the harmony and the sadness of the melody touched her heart. As she looked across the sea of people, she could see they, too, were spellbound. When the lads finished, people whistled and clapped.

'They're going to help clear up when everyone's gone,' said Morag. 'Nice lads. A guard accompanied them and will drive them back to camp.'

'Does the minister always preside at ceilidhs?' Vi asked Morag.

Morag grinned at her. 'Och, aye. He fancies himself as a raconteur, a spinner of tales. Well, it's his job, you ken? But we all know he comes along for the *uisge beatha*, the water of life, even though he professes to condemn alcohol.'

Trixie began to laugh. 'And will he speak his monologue, *The Lion and Albert*?'

'Och! Without a doubt!' said Morag. 'That's what he's here for, that and wee drams. He'll be coy about it. He'll make everyone persuade him to begin. But there's no way he won't spout it!' She paused. 'Having said that, if anyone's in trouble, the minister is the finest man to approach to help them out of it.'

Mairi was introduced next and she sang two songs in Gaelic. Again, Trixie understood not one word. She'd heard her, many times, singing in the dairy. Each time, the sweetness of the girl's voice had brought her close to tears. And this time was no exception. Trixie used her fingers to dab at her eyes.

Dancing for everyone came next. Trixie found herself pulled from the chair onto the floor and whirled away to the music by Lachlan. She caught Jo's eye and laughed at her for she guessed the dance had been Jo's suggestion.

Dancing near the doorway, Trixie asked Morag's husband, Angus, 'Would you like me to take your place while you dance with Morag?'

'Aye,' he said. She sat in his chair so she could watch if any undesirables entered the barn. Lachlan left her, with a smile, to dance with Jo. Trixie then watched a succession of men slip through the blackout curtain, after patting their pockets to make sure their half-bottles of whisky were safe. After a while, the same men would return, walking a little unsteadily. Later, she watched Angus and Morag waltz by, Morag stately as a galleon in full sail. Smiles were exchanged as they passed.

Trixie had no idea what the time was only that it must be very late, when Noah stood up with the aid of his cane. This time there was no need for the minister to introduce him, though he stood patiently at Noah's side. Everyone clapped and a stamping of feet began.

The noise abated as Noah calmed the people to silence.

'I hope you're all enjoying yourselves. I am.' He waved his hand to encompass the people about him. 'We are. I'd like to ask you to help yourselves to food. There's plenty, so don't be shy. This is also a chance for me to tell you that in the new year changes will be made in Talmine. I intend to make a start on renewing and rebuilding your homes. I'm responsible for them.'

At this, great cheers shook the barn. He waited until the noise died down. 'I know there's a war on and materials are scarce but I promise to do as much as I can, when I can. This means there'll be jobs going on the estate, as well.' More clapping ensued. 'I'd like to tell you none of this would have been possible had it not been for my four lumberjills. They've been a tower of strength to me. Sadly, I'm about to lose them, all except Henrietta who is staying on in an official advisory capacity . . . which means if you have any grievances, you write a letter to her, not me.' He laughed at his joke. At first nervously, then, as if remembering he was, after all, the laird, his laugh became bolder. 'When it was decided to hold this ceilidh, we thought a small donation from each of you might be in order . . . No, might be needed to help finance it. I'm happy to say this won't be necessary. There will be no passing around of any hat, not tonight or in the future as I intend to make this a yearly event.'

'Three cheers for Noah MacKay!' shouted a male voice, and the cheers were duly echoing around the hall.

Noah smiled, and when the noise dwindled, he carried on: 'Thank you, dear friends. I'll be sorry to lose my lumberjills but I'm sure you, like me, wish Jo, Vi and Trixie all they'd wish themselves in 1943.' He paused. 'There's also a wee dram there,' he pointed towards the laden tables, 'so we can all welcome our first-footer when he arrives . . .' The rest of his words were lost in cheers.

Noah cut short the noise, saying, 'I propose we have one last act before we eat and drink. I have heard our minister can tell a decent story. I'd like to hear from him, wouldn't you? Perhaps a monologue? How about *The Lion and Albert?*'

The minister rose to his feet from the chair he'd been sitting on and, before the audience could make any noise at all, said, 'Och! No! You don't want to hear my feeble efforts. Surely you hear enough from me in church.'

'Please, please, please!' Morag had started to bang the side of her chair. 'C'mon,' she said to Trixie. 'Show your appreciation, it's expected!'

The minister was shaking his head, a woeful expression on his plump face.

'Och! No, I cannae!'

'Yes! Yes! Yes!' echoed everyone. Trixie realized this was indeed a regular performance.

The minister stood up, almost as though he was commanding silence from his pulpit, and began, "'There's a famous seaside town called Blackpool . . . "'

The rest of the evening passed in a blur of eating, drinking, dancing and people displaying their talents, until a loud knocking, comprising three hard bangs on the wooden door of the barn could be heard.

'It's the first-footer!' came the cry.

'It's the new year!' came excited whoops.

The curtain was drawn back to allow the tall, dark-haired man to enter.

In his arms he carried a small basket. Trixie, who was close to him, saw the basket contained a lump of coal, for warmth, a coin, for prosperity, salt, for flavouring, bread, for food, and a bottle of whisky for good cheer.

In the barn, near silence took over as the man spoke the traditional words: 'A happy new year and good tidings to you and yours!'

Clapping began, and Trixie was swept up, her hands held by those standing either side of her, singing 'Auld Lang Syne' to bid farewell to the old year and welcome in the new.

Chapter Thirty-Five

Trixie sat at the piano. She was alone in the barn, which had magically been restored to its former state. Even Noah's Morgan and the work lorry were parked in their usual places instead of in the yard. Not before time, she thought. When she'd last ventured outside, soft white flakes of snow were falling. Sutherland's weather changed capriciously. She had no idea what hour it was, not that it mattered, for the first of January had been proclaimed by Noah as a holiday, so the day was hers to do whatever she wanted.

Earlier, when the crowd had dwindled, she had presented him with the sealed letter of recommendation from the Forestry Commission. 'A little late,' she'd said.

He'd taken it from her, turned it over in his hands. 'Nothing written in there could ever explain how you were about to change my life for the better,' he said, passing it back to her, unopened.

And now Trixie had stopped playing to take stock of would happen within the next few days.

She was going home. She would be able to talk to her mother about Cy. Letters were fine, but she needed her mother's arms about her. There wasn't a day, an hour, when she didn't think about him. Trixie believed Fate was partly related to one's actions, and could, to a certain extent, be controlled. Hadn't she, all her life so far, lived by the maxim that she could do as she wished as long as she hurt no one? Fate was also decided for you. Cy said that Fate had decreed they should be together.

Cy wasn't dead to her: he lived suspended in her mind.

And soon she'd be back in Gosport where they had first met, on that ferryboat.

Her fingers touched the piano keys once more, 'Dream a Little Dream of Me' came to life beneath her touch. Trixie said softly, 'Gosport, I'm coming home. So, c'mon, Fate, let me see the next hand you're about to deal me.'

Cy Davis took a deep breath of the honeyed smell from the blooming shrubs growing in his buddy Hobo's garden, in a deserted part of the compound beneath palm trees. His shirt hung in rags about his thin body and his rubber-soled shoes were shredded. He was hungry. He was weary after working in the heat all day every day and being in this hell-hole in the Pacific, Pearlien Island, dominated by his Japanese captors.

Cy automatically patted his top pocket where he kept his tattered and folded photograph of his girl, Trixie.

The thought that she was close to him, albeit in paper form, kept him alive.

There'd been no letters: writing and receiving mail was forbidden. Every day and night he wrestled with the thoughts that she might presume him dead. It was only the memory of her soft lips on his own that gave him the strength to carry on. That, and his belief that they were meant to share their lives. He smiled, remembering their first kiss in that dingy Portsmouth station café. He had known then they were destined to fall in love. He swallowed the lump in his throat that threatened to bring tears to his eyes and forced out the words, 'That pikake vine smells swell. The white flowers sure are pretty.'

Hobo picked off a petal and began chewing it. 'Tastes fine, too,' he said.

Cy wondered how his pal could find the energy to work until the evening gave way to darkness and the camp's order for lights-out. All Cy wanted to do was sleep. 'One of these days you'll poison yourself,' he said. He studied the long scar that ran from beneath Hobo's eye to his chin. A relic from an angry Japanese guard's bayonet upon their arrival at the camp. Slightly mauve in colour, amazingly the skin had healed well and no longer made his face appear split in two. Hobo was a shadow of the man Cy had known since he was a kid.

Hobo had saved Cy's life, pushing him into the sea shortly before USS *Ready* had been sunk by enemy aircraft. He and Hobo had later been plucked from the waves by a Japanese sailor, to end up in the hold of *Havana Maru*, one of the Japanese hell ships.

'Not me,' said Hobo, chewing. 'This is jasmine. They flavour tea with it and make perfume from the petals by placing them on wax, turning them by hand until the scent has fully leached out. The wax is then cleaned to separate the perfume from it.' He bent down to sniff the red hibiscus, then fingered the plumeria. 'Now this little beauty, she's toxic.' He grinned.

'I wonder sometimes how your head can hold so much information,' Cy said. 'Or how you got the stamina to work on this flower patch after we've been killing ourselves toiling all day on the restoration of the airport road.'

'I like to spend free time wisely,' Hobo said.

Reconstruction of the road, bombed by the Japanese, meant clearing jungle foliage, digging out palm roots, bringing in stones from the quarry, in panniers carried by the prisoners, putting on a layer of gravel, also from the quarry, and stamping down its surface. Guards with bayonets willingly urged them on when they were flagging in their efforts.

Hobo had already soaked his plants. Cy was happy that water was the one thing they had in abundance.

When the Japanese bombed Pearl Harbor they took control of Pearlien, once used as Pan Am Airways' refuelling base.

'Why you want to grow more stuff when this place is already a gardeners' damned paradise beats me.' Cy waved his arm towards the perimeter fence. It wasn't particularly high or threatening but it didn't need to be: the tiny island, surrounded by coral reefs, with a lagoon in the middle and inhabited by birds, small mammals, insects and a profusion of palms and plants, was a fortress.

'My daddy taught me all he knew about the soil and plants,' said Hobo. He grinned at Cy. 'Spent his whole life working for the gentry in the antebellum houses in Natchez. There wasn't nothin' he didn't know about growing stuff.'

A sudden horrific scream caused the birds to take flight,

skywards, with the terrifying sound of fast-fluttering wings. Hobo looked at Cy and asked, 'You think it's that poor bastard they brought back? The one who tried to escape?'

'You got it,' Cy said. 'When we were taken to work on the road this morning, he was still tied down.'

Another scream cut through air. Hobo bowed his head and pressed a hand across his eyes. A huge sigh escaped him.

'Don't think about it,' warned Cy. Hobo had spent a lot of time lately worrying about what was happening to other prisoners. Mainly because when the guards discovered something they didn't like the camp commandant ordered punishment for all. The men were already down to one bowl of soup per prisoner per day. 'Why plant so many flowers?' asked Cy, trying to take Hobo's mind away from yet another strangled scream.

'Who says there are only blooms growing?' Hobo asked, picking up a hoe he'd made out of a piece of wood and rusted nails. He bent down and pinched a couple of leaves off a small green plant and passed them to Cy. 'Go on, eat!'

Cy put them in his mouth. A chew and a swallow later, he said, smiling, 'Tastes like arugula!'

'Because it is! I pinched a few stems of leaves from the crown of the plant last time we were served up rocket, stuck 'em in my pocket, looked after, prayed over and watered 'em well. In a few weeks, hopefully, it'll be ready for us to eat.' He looked pleased with himself. Then he gently touched a couple more plants almost hidden in a profusion of orange campsis. 'Rutabaga,' he said. 'Grown from the sprouting tops. I think the English call 'em turnips or swedes. We ain't got no chefs here so when we get veg it's practically raw and cut in chunks. You'd be surprised at the food that'll grow from scraps.' His face broke into a smile. 'I got beans, peppers and squash coming on.'

'If the guards find out . . .' Cy couldn't bear it if anything happened to Hobo, who looked after him like he was his daddy. The screams from the tortured prisoner were still ringing in his ears.

'I trust you. You trust me. Who's gonna find out? They all just think I love flowers. Maybe I'll take a few pikake blossoms back for the camp commandant to wish him *akemashite omedeto*!'

'What the hell is that?' asked Cy.

'Happy new year in Japanese. You ain't forgotten it's 1943 tomorrow, have you, pal?'

Acknowledgements

Thank you to my editor, Florence Hare for making this into a better book. Thank you to Hazel Orme for sorting me out. Thank you to all at Quercus who work so tirelessly for me. Thank you to my loyal readers who must love Gosport as much as I do.